CHASING
TERROR

CHASING TERROR

A FEDERAL AGENT
SAM CAVIELLO CRIME MYSTERY

BOOK 2

STAN COMFORTI

Chasing Terror

Copyright © 2022 by Stan Comforti

This book is a work of fiction. Names, characters, places, events, or incidents are created by the author's imagination and used fictitiously. Any similarity to actual persons, living or dead, events or locales is coincidental and not intended by the author.

Production & Publishing Consultant: AuthorPreneur Publishing Inc.—geoffaffleck.com

Editors: Annie Bemke, Laura Apgar
Proofreader: James Osborne
Cover Designer: pagatana.com
Interior Designer: Amit Dey—amitdey2528@gmail.com

ISBN
979-8-9861641-4-4 (paperback)
979-8-9861641-5-1 (hard cover)
979-8-9861641-6-8 (ebook)

FIC022020   FICTION / Mystery & Detective / Police Procedural
FIC031010   FICTION / Thrillers / Crime
FIC030000   FICTION / Thrillers / Suspense

DEDICATION

In memory of my friend and ATF colleague
Richard Coccaro, who passed some years ago.
Rich is remembered for his strong ethics, team
work and close friendship, emulated by the
character Rick 'Ziggy' Ziglar in this series.
Rest in peace, my friend. You are not forgotten.

CHAPTER

1

ATF Special Agent Sam Caviello took vacation leave to help his son, Drew, move into his new apartment in East Boston. Drew had successfully completed training as a Diplomatic Security Special Agent with the U.S. State Department at the Federal Law Enforcement Training Facility in Glynco, GA. As a result, the agency assigned him to his first field office in Boston. Sam could not be happier that his son had followed in his footsteps in federal law enforcement. He was proud of him.

It was late in the afternoon on a Saturday. Sam suggested they take a break for dinner after moving and emptying dozens of large U-Haul boxes into the apartment. While on their way to a restaurant, Sam noticed his Acura SUV was low on gas, so he pulled into the first gas station he saw driving north on Route 1A toward a seaside restaurant in Revere. When Sam stopped at the gas pump, Drew exited the SUV to buy a six-pack of beer and some snacks from the convenience store.

After Sam reached for the gas pump and started pumping gas into his vehicle, an older tan van pulled up along the gas pumps on the opposite side. Sam watched as the van's side door slid open, giving him a quick look inside the back of the van. It was only seconds, but he observed someone bound at the arms and ankles with a black hood over their head, sitting between two men. A third man exited the van, glanced at Sam, and entered the convenience store. A moment later, a dark-bearded companion left the van's front passenger seat and strolled to the gas pump across from Sam. He reached into his pocket and pulled out a credit card. A slip of paper, and something Sam couldn't make out, fell from his pocket. The bearded man who wore a black skull cap over his long black hair took his time removing the gas cap before he began filling his tank. He didn't notice what fell from his pocket. While pumping gas, the guy deviously stared at Sam. He wore a light gold-colored jacket over a white t-shirt and tan baggy pants.

Sam realized an abduction was in the works, and he needed to report it to the state police. He turned away from the guy staring at him and adjusted the gas pump lever to a slower speed. Sam didn't want to finish filling the tank before the other guy did. He then took out his cell phone and clicked on the camera icon. When the guy across from him finished filling the tank, he helped his associate returning from the store load bags of goods into the van. While doing so, the bearded guy turned several times to keep an eye on Sam while purposely obstructing Sam's view of their captive. Finally, as the van's side door slammed shut, Sam finished filling his tank and drifted to the van's rear, ensuring the gas dispenser tank gave him cover. When Sam heard the van start its engine, he peeked around the gas pump and took photos of the van's New York license plate as it began driving out. Sam wanted to ensure he had the correct plate number to report to the state police. The van stopped at the gas station's exit and waited for the traffic to clear before turning north on Route 1A.

Seeing his son exit the store, Sam yelled to him, "Drew, hurry, get back in the car! I'll explain on the way!" Sam picked up the slip of paper and a silver necklace with a pendant dropped by the suspect, shoved them into his pocket, and slid into the driver's seat.

"Jesus, Dad, what's going on?" asked Drew as he climbed into the passenger seat.

"I don't know if you saw that van that pulled up opposite me. They had someone in the back tied up with a hood over their head. Bad shit. I got the plate number, and I'm calling the state police."

Sam floored the gas pedal, throwing Drew back in his seat as he raced out from the gas pumps and onto Route 1A. Sam had already located the emergency phone number for the state police, selected the number, and waited for the police to answer his call. While speeding north on 1A, Sam's call finally got answered.

"State police. You are being recorded. What's your emergency?"

"This is ATF Special Agent Sam Caviello. My son and I are following a tan van carrying five or more male occupants holding a bound hostage in the back of the van. We are off-duty federal agents and not armed. The van is traveling on Route 1A north in East Boston."

Sam dictated the license plate number and heard the officer dispatch troopers to the area. "Agent Caviello, could you stay on the line to provide updates on the van's location?"

"Will do. I recommend that any responding officer consider them armed, proceed with caution, and have adequate backup before pulling the van over. I'm driving a dark blue SUV with Connecticut registration. We're about a mile north of the Suffolk Downs racetrack, coming up on a traffic circle. The van stopped at the traffic light. There's a strip mall on the right. Okay, the light turned green, and the van continued toward the circle."

Sam followed two cars behind the van as they approached the traffic circle.

"Dad, there's a state cruiser on the merging street on your right," said Drew.

As Sam entered the circle, he viewed the trooper move in behind him through the rearview mirror. Up the road, they approached another traffic light that had just turned green and continued north past the intersection at Ocean Street, onto a long, straight stretch of road. Sam glanced at his review mirror and noticed the trooper had turned on its blue flashing emergency lights.

Sam gave caution to the desk officer. "I see a lone state police cruiser approaching from behind me. I do not see any backup. So, again, I recommend adequate backup before pulling over the van."

As Sam relayed his message, the state police cruiser passed him and pulled in behind the van. A short distance up the road, the van pulled off into a turnaround loop and stopped, with the cruiser stopping a few yards behind it.

"The trooper pulled over the van. He should wait for backup," warned Sam.

Sam pulled into the loop and stopped about fifteen yards behind the cruiser, expecting the trooper to wait for support. Seconds later, Sam heard a police siren. He saw the hue of blue-emitting lights heading toward them in his rearview mirror, but it seemed a minute or two out. It then troubled Sam when he saw a female trooper step out of the cruiser that pulled over the van. The cruiser's headlights and spotlight lit up the van. The trooper's hand was on her holstered firearm as she walked cautiously toward the van.

"What the hell is she doing? She should wait for the backup," questioned Sam.

Drew suddenly called out, "There's a guy with a gun at the rear passenger side." Sam saw a muzzle blast as the guy shot at the trooper twice, causing her to drop to the ground. The guy then fired a volley of bullets, hitting the state cruiser's headlights and spotlight. The van quickly sped off as Sam screamed on his phone, "Officer down! Request medical help ASAP! Drew, grab the medical kit on the floor in the back."

Sam rushed out of the vehicle to help the downed trooper, with Drew quickly behind him, carrying the first aid emergency response bag. The second cruiser arrived at the scene. Sam and Drew quickly inspected where the female trooper was injured.

"She's wearing a vest, but she's hit on the left arm and hip area. Hand me a pressure bandage from the QuikClot Kit. I'll use this on her arm. Get another one and hold it tight to her hip." While Sam was giving aid, he yelled to the approaching trooper to call for an ambulance. Sam worked feverishly to stop the trooper's bleeding. He kept speaking to her. "Stay with us. Don't close your eyes. The ambulance is on the way. Stay with us. You're going to be okay."

Not long after, additional police cruisers and an ambulance arrived. Sam gave way for the EMTs as they rushed to the downed trooper. As he stepped back, Sam stepped on a bullet casing. Then, with a pen, he inserted it into the casing, checked the caliber, showed it to Drew, and then placed it on the pavement where he found it.

"That's a 7.62 bullet casing. It looks like the shooter had a Russian AK-47 with a folding stock." Drew followed Sam toward their vehicle while Sam whispered to him. "For your information, AK stands for Avtomat Kalishanov or something like that. I'm sure I didn't pronounce his name right. However, I can identify the shooter. He's the same guy who pumped the gas at the station. I'm going to find that bastard, and he will pay."

CHAPTER

2

The shooting scene on Route 1A was in chaos afterward. Several State and Revere police vehicles and personnel surrounded the location, some holding up the northbound traffic while others assisted the ambulance EMTs with the injured officer. Not long later, plain-clothes detectives arrived and gathered around the uniformed officers. Occasionally, a female detective looked toward Sam and Drew while waiting near their vehicle. When the police finally began opening the closed lane to traffic, the female detective approached Sam and Drew.

"I'm Detective Juliana Ospino. Are you agent Sam Cavello, who called this into us?"

"It's Caviello, C-a-v-i-e-l-l-o," answered Sam.

"Got it. You two called in the report on the van, right?"

"Yes."

"And you both are ATF agents and were unarmed?"

"No. I'm an ATF agent, and Drew is an agent with the Diplomatic Security Service."

At that point, Detective Ospino saw an unmarked cruiser arrive. A guy dressed in a suit exited the sedan and walked toward the five other officers huddled together several yards away. Sam guessed the guy was about six feet, three inches tall, and in his forties.

"Stay put. I'll be back in a few minutes," Detective Ospino said. She joined the other officers standing tall as the guy in the suit approached them.

"Wow. The detective is a doll. I wouldn't mind getting to know her. That guy who just arrived must be the boss. Maybe there'll be some direction now," remarked Sam.

There was a discussion among the officers, followed by Detective Ospino pointing in Sam's direction. Shortly after that, the guy in charge and Detective Ospino walked in unison toward Sam and Drew.

"Agent Caviello, I'm Major Jack Burke. You already met Detective Ospino. I understand you called the state police for help after witnessing someone held inside the van at a gas station."

Sam gave him the whole story.

"I'll need to take statements from both of you," advised Detective Ospino.

"I feel partially responsible for the trooper. I hope she's going to be alright. My son and I will cooperate fully and provide any help you need to find these creeps. I can identify the shooter."

"I want to thank both of you for calling it in and aiding Trooper Phillips. Detective Ospino will take it from here. Juli, I'm heading to the hospital," said Major Burke.

The detective turned back to face Sam and Drew. "Follow me to the state police barracks on Revere Beach Boulevard. I'll take your statements."

At the state police facility, Detective Ospino interviewed Sam and Drew separately for nearly two hours. During their time there, Sam overheard officers talk about the incident, mentioning that Officer Kristyn Phillips was a rookie with only a year and a few months on the job. Once the detective finished the interviews, Sam requested copies of their statements to take with them. Ospino hesitated for a moment before agreeing to make copies. Sam was very much attracted to her. When Ospino handed Sam the copies, he gave her the slip of paper the suspect dropped from his pocket at the gas station.

"What's this?" asked Ospino.

"In all the excitement, I forgot to give you that at the crime scene. The guy who pumped the gas and later shot the trooper dropped it from his pocket. It could be a phone number of an associate they might call for help, knowing the police will be searching for them."

"I'll check it out," she said without thanking him.

"Again, detective, we are sorry about what happened to the trooper. Drew and I are heading a short distance up the road for dinner. You are welcome to join us if you haven't had dinner yet."

"I need to get to the hospital to check on my colleague."

"What hospital did they take her to? I would like to stop by to get an update on her condition."

"That won't be necessary," said Ospino.

"It's necessary from my perspective, detective," responded Sam.

"I have your cell number. I'll call you with an update."

"Do you have a business card with your direct number in case I need to reach you? I'd like to assist in the investigation to get the guy who shot your colleague."

"I have all the help I need," responded Ospino.

"One more investigator can't hurt. The more working to find the perp, the better."

"If I need outside help, I have your number." Ospino handed him her card and walked away.

Sam and Drew left the facility and drove a short distance to an Italian restaurant overlooking Revere Beach. Before entering the restaurant, Sam called his supervisor, Steve Roberts, the Boston Assistant Special Agent in Charge (ASAC), to report the incident.

Once settled in the busy restaurant, they ordered draft beers, two side salads with ranch dressing, and two penne and meatball dinners with marinara sauce. While enjoying the cold beer with dinner, Sam asked, "What do you think of Detective Ospino? She is one hot-looking woman but very stand-offish and all business."

"She was hot and cold to me, but she's investigating the shooting of a colleague, so her mind is on doing her job, not joining us for dinner," said Drew.

"I know. It was stupid, but I hoped I could convince her to let me help in the investigation. I feel some responsibility for putting the officer in that predicament, especially since we were not armed and unable to back her up."

"Dad, it all happened in seconds. You wouldn't have had time to exit the car and respond before the van drove off. You warned them about pulling over the van without sufficient backup. There is nothing else we could have done. It's a state police case now. Let's finish eating and get back to the apartment to finish setting up the beds, so we have something to sleep on tonight."

"I hear you, but I want to help get that guy who shot the trooper. I'll call the detective later to get the status of the trooper and offer my help again. Then, if she has the same attitude about my support, I'll do some digging on my own."

Drew shook his head. "That van has to be miles from here by now. You don't think they'll stick around when the state has an army of troopers looking for them, do you?"

"I don't think they'll stick around in plain sight after shooting a cop. The state police will have an all-points bulletin out with the description of the van and the license plate number. My guess is they'll get rid of the van as soon as possible. I have a couple of ideas where they might dump it. Once they do, they'll need wheels. They could have an associate nearby to pick them up. But, hey, I'm not going out tonight. I'll head out in the morning after breakfast for a couple of hours and see what I can find."

"Dad, you finished the Harrington investigation in Hartford not long ago. That investigation also was outside your jurisdiction, by the way. Now you want to get involved with another investigation outside your jurisdiction when the lead detective doesn't want your help. Let her handle it. Remember, you're on vacation. There is no need for you on your own to chase four or five guys with guns. You can get shot, too. So relax now and enjoy your vacation helping me move."

"I'm not stupid enough to think I will find these guys on my own. That's the job for the state police. I'll play out my hunch and see where it takes me. If it takes me nowhere, I'll be back at your place before you know it.

Since you brought up the case in Hartford, don't forget that Forster Harrington made threats to get even with me by getting at you. I put his kid in jail, where he hung himself, and his father blames me for his death and wants revenge. So, be aware of your surroundings and suspicious of anyone or anything you see that doesn't seem right. I don't want anything happening to you either. I'm proud of you and love you. Anyway, I'm done eating. I'm on vacation to help you get settled, so let's get back to it."

Later, back at Drew's apartment, the first thing Sam did was call Detective Ospino. It took several rings before Ospino answered.

"I'm in the middle of a strategy meeting and can't talk. I'll call you back later," said Ospino, hanging up.

Although disappointed, Sam put it aside and helped Drew put the two beds together and set up the television. Afterward, they relaxed and watched television while drinking beer and munching on snacks before heading for bed. Although tired, Sam found it difficult to sleep. In all his years on the job, he had never witnessed anyone shoot at a police officer, especially a female officer. Shooting incidents may frequently occur in the movies or TV police dramas, but it's rare in real life. Sam thought back to the number of times a criminal with a gun confronted him. He could only remember two incidents in his entire career. He realized, however, that the job was becoming more dangerous.

Since he was a teenager, Sam wanted to be a federal agent and work high-profile cases against bad guys. As an ATF agent involved in several notable criminal cases, none involved shooting at ATF agents, the local police, or the abduction of a hostage. Shooting at police was new territory for Sam, but he became determined to help find the shooter. Not to mention, he was captivated by the detective's looks and determined to uncover something critical in the investigation. Hopefully, that would convince her to ask him to join her in the investigation.

Sam knew he could help find the perps. After all, he had something other officers didn't: he experienced unexplained mysterious internal senses that guided him in finding hidden clues and suspects. As a youngster, Sam first experienced bizarre feelings that freaked him out. But the more he experienced these unique sensations, he realized they were not a curse but a gift. These cryptic auras were especially effective as an investigator. However, this gift had limitations. He wasn't psychic or clairvoyant and certainly couldn't tell the future or know what others were thinking. No one knew of his sensory ability, and he intended to keep it that way, especially since he couldn't explain how or why it began. With this phenomenon, he intended to prove to Detective Ospino that he could help her and hopefully gain her trust.

CHAPTER
3

The following morning, Sam was out of bed by six o'clock. He left a note for Drew that he was having breakfast out and would return later in the day. Detective Ospino never called back, so Sam shrugged off calling her again. Instead, he grabbed his tactical bag, slid his gun holster through his belt, and took two extra magazines loaded with sixteen rounds each. He took the elevator to the garage, locked the bag in the secured trunk, and left in his SUV. He drove north on Route 1A and stopped at a Dunkin Donuts takeout window, ordering an egg and cheese English muffin and a medium coffee with cream only. He took the time to finish his breakfast before driving north towards Revere.

Now forty-six years old and a twenty-year veteran as a federal agent, Sam was the Hartford, Connecticut ATF field office supervisor. ATF is the acronym for the Bureau of Alcohol, Tobacco, Firearms, and Explosives. The agency's primary law enforcement responsibility is enforcing the federal criminal and regulatory laws regarding firearms, arson, and explosives. In addition, the agency still plays a part in dismantling the interstate trafficking of illicit liquor and contraband tobacco.

Congress first established the agency during Prohibition as the Alcohol Tax Unit. Its most famous agent was Eliot Ness and his team of just thirty-four agents whose job was to eradicate illegal alcohol operations by violent organized criminals, the most notorious being Al Capone. In addition, the agency works closely with local and state authorities to prevent and prosecute criminals and felons who illegally possess or use firearms in the commission of a violent crime and the distribution of illegal drugs. ATF agents also assist local and state authorities in investigating major arsons and preventing the unlawful manufacture, sale, purchase, and use of explosives and destructive devices.

Sam's first stop was the gas station, where he'd stopped the night before and observed the hostage in the van. Inside the convenience store, he asked to speak to the manager on duty. The woman behind the counter with the name Roberta embroidered on her pull-over polo shirt asked how she could help. Sam showed her his federal badge and asked to see the security video recording from the evening before. Roberta asked if he had a subpoena. Sam thought Roberta had watched too many TV lawyer shows before answering.

"With your permission, I don't need a subpoena to view the recording. However, I can have you subpoenaed before a federal grand jury in the Boston federal court. The subpoena will require you to bring the recording and testify why you refused to cooperate in a state and federal investigation."

He concocted the grand jury line, hoping to convince her to cooperate. "Roberta, I'm only requesting to view the video. It's evidence in an attempted murder case I'm investigating."

The woman thought it through before she asked him to follow her. She guided him into a back office where a desk contained three monitors and keyboards attached to computers on a table. She inquired what specific time she should search for on the video.

"Start at five-thirty in the afternoon facing pumps one and two, and I'll let you know when to stop. I also want to view the video inside the store during the same timeframe."

Roberta stopped the fast forward at five-thirty-five and pressed the symbol for play to view the action in real-time. Sam watched for several minutes until his SUV entered the scene at five-forty-seven. The van pulled in on the opposite side of the gas pumps a minute later. Sam watched the monitor screens covering the external gas pumps and the inside of the convenience store.

He watched as the first suspect exited the van's side door and entered the store. The second suspect left the passenger side door and strolled to the gas pump across from Sam. He inserted a credit card and took his time before pumping gas into the van. Sam noticed the time on the monitor as being five-fifty-two. From that point, he focused on the suspect in the store. He watched him grab a twelve-pack of beer, a six-pack of water, pre-packed sandwiches, and bags of chips. While the clerk rang up his bill, the suspect reached for a colorful container on display near the register. He placed it on the counter to purchase it but returned it after the clerk said something inaudible to him. He then paid for his purchases in cash.

"What did the clerk say to that guy that caused him to put that item back on the shelf?" asked Sam.

"I can only guess she told him it was a display item, and he would have to get one from the shelf in aisle three," advised Roberta.

"What is that item? Is that same item on the shelf today?"

"It's a thermos to keep coffee hot. Most likely, it's the same one that was there yesterday."

Sam watched the suspect exit the store carrying several bags. He returned to the van, where his associate, who had finished fueling, helped load the bags inside the vehicle. They then drove off.

Roberta recognized Sam taking photos of the van as it drove away. "Are these the guys you're investigating?" she asked.

Before answering, Sam noticed the time of eight past six on the monitor as the van left before responding.

"I'm sorry, Roberta. I'm not at liberty to discuss an ongoing investigation, but it's a top priority for the Mass State Police. I'm sure the state police will be grateful for your help in solving this case." Sam wanted to give her recognition for her help. "I kept track of the times of the video section we're interested in, so you will know exactly where to start and end the recording. A state police detective will return here before the end of the day requesting a copy of what we just reviewed. If you can make two copies now, it will save you time later when you might be busy."

"We don't have many flash drives left," declared Roberta.

"I'm sure the detective will be happy to reimburse you for any cost you incur," countered Caviello.

"What time could I expect the detective to arrive?" she asked.

"Detective Ospino is coordinating every aspect of this investigation, so it's difficult for me to predict. As soon as I leave, I'll contact her and ask her to get here as quickly as possible. I would appreciate it if you could have the copies ready for her. If you give me your number, I'll have the detective call you with the time she expects to be here."

Roberta agreed and gave Sam her cell number. He gave her his business card, thanked her immensely, and said he would mention her cooperation to the detective commander. As he left the store, Sam smiled while thinking, *Maybe Ospino will be impressed with what I'm doing. Although, on second thought, maybe not.*

Back in his car, Sam took another look at the necklace dropped by the suspect. He never gave it to the detective, thinking it might help lead him to the suspect. Sam studied the pendant and realized it was a locket that opened to a photo. The heart-shaped locket was an antique. The image inside was that of a teenage girl. He cupped it in his hand, hoping it would bring him luck. He then drove north, pondering where he should look first. Sam suspected the perps would need to dump the van since every cop in the state would be looking for it. He didn't see much in the way of car dealerships in Revere on his side of the road, so he drove further north to Lynn, figuring he would later circle back through Revere and the arteries off Route 1A. As he crossed into Lynn, he saw a line-up of several new and used car dealerships on both sides of the road. Slowly passing a couple of new dealerships, Sam scanned the lots for an old tan van but didn't notice any. Then, when he slowly passed a used car lot, he experienced a familiar eerie feeling throughout his body. Sam felt a strange quiver down his spine and an annoying ringing in his right ear. He pulled over to the side of the road as he passed the lot's entrance.

Sam waited for the traffic behind him to pass, then quickly backed up several yards and entered the used car lot. The dealership didn't have a large showroom, but had up to forty used luxury cars and SUVs on the spacious lot. He drove down the first row looking for a tan van but found none. After going down two more rows without any luck, he advanced to the last row of cars. He turned right and slowly drove past each vehicle until he stopped halfway down the aisle. There on his right, Sam grinned and slapped the steering wheel. He just sat there for a moment while his body stirred with excitement.

"Son of a bitch. I found it," he screamed.

* * *

It was Sunday morning at the Allenwood Federal Prison, a medium-security correctional facility. Rachel Peterson visited her father, Forster Harrington, imprisoned for obstructing a federal investigation and conspiracy to commit murder. Under the circumstances, it surprised Rachel to see her father looking well, in good spirits, and in better shape. She asked how he was surviving prison life.

"It's different from what I had imagined it would be. Most of the inmates here are professional people and not considered violent, so I don't have to worry about being shanked. I have my own television, the library's adequate, and I get to walk and exercise more than I have in years. I actually feel better physically, but I can't stop thinking of that bastard who put me here."

Forster had made sizeable donations to the political campaigns of both the governor and several high-ranking legislators. He used his political influence to get Rachel and his son, Richard, jobs at the statehouse. However, Richard's arrest for kidnapping and murder and his subsequent suicide in jail, followed by Forster's arrest and imprisonment, caused financial damage to his successful business. As a result, Rachel resigned from her job at the statehouse and temporarily took over as president of her dad's company with the help and guidance of her father's second in command, Gus Walker. Rachel periodically visited her dad to get tutored on all aspects of the Harrington Construction Company business.

During Forster's tutelage of Rachel, he always brought up his disdain for Agent Sam Caviello, the nemesis he blamed for his arrest and his son's subsequent suicide.

"I blame Caviello for Dickie's suicide and me being in jail, not to mention the heartbreak it caused your mom. I want him to feel the same agony I'm going through every day I spend in this hellhole. I normally would've had Tony handle what I had planned for the guy, but he can't, so I'm going to need you, sweetheart, to help me."

"Dad, I understand why you want revenge, but you've got to let this go. You also have to understand my position. I don't want to put myself in jeopardy of being arrested and imprisoned. I have to consider what a burden it would place on my family. I have a husband and daughter to think about, not to mention dad; I'm pregnant."

Surprised, Forster sat back in his chair, pleased by Rachel's announcement. "I didn't know. I'm so happy for you and Ron, and I'm sure your mom is too."

"She's thrilled. She's already picking out things to buy for the baby."

Forster was content that things were going so well for his daughter. He was proud of her running the family business and respected her reasons for not getting involved with anything illegal. However, he felt disappointed that his plan for revenge was evaporating since the only person he trusted on the outside was Rachel.

"I know I'm letting you down, but I'm working hard to keep the company afloat. With a baby on the way, I can't risk being involved in a scheme to get back at a federal agent for doing his job. We have to accept the fact that what Richard did was horrible. I have to move on and live my life."

"I understand, Rachel. I shouldn't put you or your family at risk. With Tony in jail, I'll have to find someone on the outside who can do the job, but it'll cost me, and you're the only one who has access to my money. You won't have to meet anyone. You can use Gus. Once I know what it will cost me, I'll just need you to put the money in an envelope, seal it, and give it to Gus, who will meet with a guy. I'll have them meet, maybe by the lunch wagon out front of the company. I'll think of a code and use fake names for when Gus meets and pays the guy."

Although she did not want to be part of her father's plan, Rachel felt she owed him some help. "I guess I can do that much, Dad. But right now, let's talk about the business. I'm catching an earlier flight back home, so I've got to go shortly."

"Okay, sweetheart, I'll make sure my plan doesn't come back on you. Tell your mother it would be nice if she came with you to visit sometime. I know she is still angry, but I miss her."

"I know, Dad, but what Richard did devastated her, and then having you get arrested for planning to kill the agent was enough to put her over the edge. She was depressed and stayed in her room for days other than to eat. I'll do my best to get her to visit the next time I come, but don't count on it. Now, let's focus on why I came here."

CHAPTER
4

Sam found the van. After staring at it for several minutes, he finally exited his SUV and walked closer to examine it. It was the same van. It had a small dent just behind the right rear tire. Sam never considered the damage significant when he noticed it at the gas station until now. He saw the license plate was missing and figured the suspects disposed of it since the police had the plate number. Surveying the area in the back of the used vehicles, Sam noticed a dumpster within twenty yards. *That could be where they buried the plate*, he thought.

He looked at his watch, seeing it was only ten o'clock. He strolled over to the dumpster and lifted the lid. It was nearly full, and he saw nothing of value as he scanned the top layer of debris. He walked back to his SUV to fetch a pair of latex gloves. As he pulled on the gloves, he studied the roof of the office building.

Sam was ecstatic that the building contained security cameras on the front corner, with one camera facing the van's direction. He hoped it was operational. Sam returned to the dumpster and pushed aside the top layer of debris, mainly paper bags, towels, cups, and newspapers. He dug deeper, shoving more garbage away, becoming anxious that he may find nothing. Finally, he had to stop his search because he couldn't reach deeper into the dumpster. Sam combed the outside of the dumpster and spotted an old five-gallon paint container leaning up against the far side. Using the can to stand on, he reached further down in the dumpster and swiped more trash aside. While he did, he spotted a corner section of an orange-colored piece of metal. Sam pulled at it and was not surprised to find the discarded New York license plate formerly attached to the van. He brushed aside additional debris and spotted a key ring with two keys still attached. He snapped photos of the plate and keyring with his cell phone and closed the dumpster lid. While doing so, Sam heard a car approaching from behind. He turned to see a man exiting a black Mercedes and walking toward him. Sam stepped off the paint can and moved toward him.

"What can I do for you? I assume you're not looking for a car in the dumpster?" the guy asked.

Sam estimated the guy was in his forties, maybe six feet, two inches tall, and weighing around two hundred and ten pounds. His scruffy reddish-brown hair and stubble facial beard gave him a rugged, unkempt appearance. Sam took out his badge and introduced himself as a federal agent. The guy changed his cocky demeanor by offering his hand to shake.

"I'm Ray Mitchell, the owner of the dealership. How can I be of service?"

"Are you the owner of the tan van parked there in the rear aisle?" asked Caviello while pointing at the van.

Mitchell took a quick look at the van. "I never saw that van before. I don't know why that piece of junk is in my lot. I only sell newer premium used vehicles here."

"I'm investigating a kidnapping and assault of a police officer that occurred last night, and the crew responsible for the assault drove that van. They apparently hid the van here and discarded its license plate in your dumpster."

Mitchell looked surprised. "I closed early at six o'clock last night, and that van was not in the lot at closing time."

"I'm sure they arrived later than six. Please tell me the security cameras you have affixed to your building are in working order," pleaded Sam.

"Yeah, they should work."

"Let's go see what the recording captured."

Sam followed Mitchell into the office building and a back office where the security monitors sat on a desk. Mitchell sat at the desk and asked where he should start. Sam asked him to fast-forward the digital recording to six-fifteen the previous night. They watched the monitor screen for several minutes before the van appeared in the video and entered the back row of the parking lot. It turned into a vacant space. There was no movement for approximately ten minutes, with Sam wondering what's taking them so long to exit the van. He doubted they parked there to spend the night. They would be in a precarious position if a patrol car circled the lot to check on the business. Finally, the front passenger door opened, but the passenger remained inside. Sam pondered if they were waiting for an accomplice to pick them up. He impatiently waited in anticipation of the suspects' next move.

The front passenger exited the van a moment later while holding a phone to his ear. He then slid open the van's side door. Sam recognized him immediately as the shooter of the police officer. Next, another guy exited from the back, followed by two others who assisted the bound and hooded person out of the vehicle. Then, a fifth suspect, presumably the driver, appeared from around the other side of the van and kneeled to remove the license plate. The suspect wore a dark colored jacket with its hood up preventing any identification. After removing the plate, the suspect walked to the dumpster, lifted the lid, and buried the evidence under the trash. Sam figured the suspect didn't want to take the chance of getting stopped by the police and having evidence linking the group to the van.

While the van's side door was still open, two men went back inside and exited again a few minutes later. Both were carrying what appeared to be small towels. Sam figured they were probably wiping down the inside to avoid leaving fingerprints behind.

Moments later, a silver-colored Toyota SUV entered the picture, drove down the last aisle, and stopped close to where the van's occupants were waiting. As the rear lid of the SUV opened, the van's occupants placed four long black canvass bags, grocery bags, and cases of beer and water into the trunk. The hooded hostage wore khaki shorts, white sneakers with a pinkish stripe, and had long, straight, light brown hair. Sam was sure it was a female. They placed her in the rear seat. Two men entered the third-row seat of the SUV before two others entered on either side of the hostage. The shooter of the trooper sat in the front passenger seat. The trunk powered shut, and the Toyota backed up, giving a close-up view of the license plate.

"Stop and pause the recording so I can snap a couple of photos of the license plate," said Sam. He intended to run a vehicle registration check on the plate to determine its ownership. Sam noted when the SUV first came into view and when it exited the lot.

"Ray, could you copy the sequence of the events on two separate disks or flash drives, one for me and the other for the state police? I expect them here shortly."

Mitchell agreed while Sam left the office to make a private phone call. The call rang several times before getting answered.

"Detective Ospino," said a sleepy voice.

With a smile on his face, Sam said, "I hope I didn't wake you, detective."

After a sigh, Ospino replied, "What do you want now? I worked into the wee hours of the morning, and I'm tired."

"And a little cranky, I should add. It's nearly ten-thirty on a beautiful Sunday morning, and I thought you would be working this case twenty-four-seven. You promised to call to let me know the status of Trooper Phillips. I also wanted to know if the telephone number I gave you added any value to the investigation."

Sam could hear another sigh from her. "Trooper Phillips lost a lot of blood, but the doctor said, with luck, she should make it. I should tell you that the doctor also said that whoever used the pressure bandages at the scene probably helped save her life. So thank you for that. Regarding the telephone number, it was for a burner phone. We couldn't find any trace of who owned the phone. Now can I get back to sleep? I have a busy day ahead of me."

"Have you or your department learned anything worthwhile about the suspects or the van?" asked Sam.

"Nothing yet. The van had a stolen license plate out of New York, and we believe the van will turn up stolen as well. The van is probably long gone by now. That's it."

Sam quickly spoke before she was about to hang up. "I'm out in the field trying to gather information about the suspects and the van. Why don't you join me before the case gets stale?"

"Uh, what's your name again?" Ospino asked.

"Wow, you forgot me already." Sam was flirting and trying to lighten up the conversation. "It's ATF Agent Sam Caviello, and I'm trying to help you if you'd let me."

"I can't think of any way you could possibly help me, Sam. It's an attempted murder of a state trooper investigation, and you are, what, a firearms investigator?"

Caviello gave a smug chuckle, saying, "I assume you would like to find the van and the guy who shot your colleague. Am I correct, detective?"

Exasperated, Ospino uttered, "I'm tired and need to get another hour or two of sleep."

"Humor me for a moment, please. How can I help you today that would prove I can be of value to you?"

Another pause, followed by an irritated tone. "I'd like to find the van and that fucking thug who shot our trooper. Can you magically do that for me?"

"Well, I can't give you a full glass of magic in a couple of hours, but I can text you where I found the abandoned van and who helped them escape from there."

There was a long pause before Ospino spoke in an angry tone. "That's not funny. I'm not interested in playing games with you. Don't call me again!" She hung up before he could say another word.

Disappointed, Sam thought he might have gone about it wrong with her. He felt he should have been more business-like. He decided to send a text message of apology along with the name and address of the dealership where he found the van. His text recommended bringing a team of forensic techs to dust the van for fingerprints. The message added security cameras at the location caught the suspects on video. It ended by saying, *I'm not kidding. Please meet me here. You won't be disappointed. That's a promise, and it's Sam if you still don't remember.*

Detective Ospino heard the text tone on her cell phone. Hoping it wasn't 'him' again, she felt compelled to check to ensure it wasn't Major Burke reaching out to her. However, it immediately put her in a quandary when she read the message. *Is this guy for real? Could he have found the van that quick?*

Regardless, she knew she would have to check it out. She reluctantly got out of bed and headed to the bathroom. While taking a quick shower, she thought about the message and decided to call Sam back before requesting a forensic team. Once showered and dressed, she hoped she didn't get out of bed for nothing. She retrieved her cell phone and called him.

When Sam answered, being testy, she said, "You better be telling the truth, Caviello."

"Hey, you remembered my name. That's a good start, anyway. Look, Detective, I'm not effing with you. If you would just give me a bit of professional courtesy and come see for yourself, you might end up trusting me and accepting that I can get results. If I were playing games with you and it got out, my reputation would be rubbish. Not only did I find the van, but I also have other leads to find; what did you call the shooter? Oh yeah, that 'effing thug.' I suggest waiting to call your boss until after you're satisfied I'm telling the truth. You can then call him and report what 'you' found. You can have all the credit. I'm here to help, not to take anything away from you." Sam ended the call without waiting for her response.

Sam then contacted the weekend duty agent at the Boston ATF office to run a motor vehicle check for the name of the registered owner of the Toyota SUV and, if possible, text him a copy of the owner's license containing his photo.

In the meantime, Detective Ospino processed everything Sam had told her. She didn't know him or what to make of him, but she couldn't just brush it off if he found the van. He seemed to be a comic and a flirt, but she couldn't help but believe he was telling her the truth after listening to him. She contacted a female friend and colleague on the forensic team and asked her to meet at the address Sam had texted. She held off calling her boss until after arriving at the scene to confirm the finding of the van. Ospino was apprehensive but cautiously excited about finding the first lead on the suspects. She left her apartment, checked her cruiser to ensure she had the needed equipment and drove to the address in Lynn.

CHAPTER
5

It took Ospino thirty minutes to drive to the dealership. Sam and Ray Mitchell were waiting outside the office building when she arrived. Sam directed her to park behind the last row of vehicles near his SUV. When she exited her sedan, Sam introduced her to Mitchell and then pointed to the van. Ospino had a sigh of relief, knowing Sam's claim was no joke. She even gave a subtle smile, unnoticeable unless someone was as fixated on her pretty face as Sam was.

Sam summarized his theory of why the vehicle ended up at this car dealer's lot, what he found in the dumpster, and how the suspects left the area. He told her she could confirm everything after viewing the security camera recording if she had further doubts. She agreed, and Mitchell escorted her and Sam to his office, where she viewed the video sequence of the van's arrival and departure.

When Ospino asked Mitchell for a copy of the video, Sam handed her a copy already made on a flash drive. Again, she felt humbled as critical evidence was handed to her like candy by a guy she had continually brushed off as a nuisance. Looking out the dealership window, Ospino saw the forensic van pull into the lot, so the three of them headed back outside. Ospino stopped Sam as they left the showroom to apologize to him.

"Look, I should thank you for calling me and giving me a heads up on what you found. You could have called Major Burke and taken the credit for yourself. I wasn't pleasant on the phone. I'm sorry for that, but I had a long day and needed sleep."

"I'm only interested in getting these guys for shooting Trooper Phillips. Not to mention, there's a hostage I'm concerned about as well. We need to help the hostage before something terrible happens, like ending up dead. So let me work with you. Trust me. I can help you find these guys."

Ospino saw him in a different light as he spoke. He cared and wanted to help, but she couldn't accept his offer since Sam worked for an outside agency. So, rather than responding to his request, she introduced Sam to the forensic team, her good friend, Detective Andrea Serrano, and Andrea's partner, Charlie Hawkins.

Sam greeted the two and explained what he and Ospino knew.

The technicians nodded like they understood and went to work searching for evidence to identify the suspects. While standing outside the van, Sam told Ospino that the gas station's manager, Roberta, had a security recording of the van from the previous night.

"Why didn't you bring a copy with you?" she asked.

"Well, I felt it was important that you should get the manager's evidence directly. I also thought it was important that you view the video and pay particular attention to when the suspect filled the van's gas tank using a credit card to pay. You might get the cardholder's name from the credit card company. The video will show the gas pump number and when he used the card. Furthermore, one of the suspects went into the store to purchase food items. He picked up a display thermos and returned it to the shelf while he was at the register to pay. You should seize it to check it for his prints. The sooner it's done, the better."

Embarrassed for being snippy again, Ospino simply nodded she understood. Sam then handed her a note.

"What's this?" asked Ospino.

"I ran the vehicle's license plate that arrived last night to pick up the suspects. That's a copy of the owner's driver's license with his local address. Maybe the suspects are hiding there until the heat subsides before they move on. At a minimum, we should check out the address to see what we find."

With a puzzled look, Ospino faced Caviello and asked, "We? What do you mean by we?"

Sam looked bewildered and agitated. "Detective, I'm offering my help. Do you think you can do this by yourself, or is it you don't want to share any glory with anyone?"

Before she opened her mouth to speak, Sam interrupted her. "So that you know, this is all yours. You can tell your boss you came up with it through a tip from a source. I don't need any credit. Tell him I'm only here because I want to help, and you invited me along for the ride."

Ospino wasn't convincing in her response. "You don't have to do that. You did the work. You can take the credit."

"I'm not interested in taking credit. I'm only interested in helping you." Sam took a few steps toward his vehicle. "The note I gave you is your copy, detective. I have my own. I'm leaving, so when your boss arrives, he'll see the scene is yours. I'll find that address and see if those suspects are still around. Remember, they still have a hostage." He turned and walked toward his SUV.

"Wait!" Ospino called out. "You don't have jurisdiction in this case."

Sam turned back to face her. "The guy committed a felony when he shot trooper Phillips with a fully automatic assault rifle, and I'm an ATF agent. Guns are my jurisdiction. I'm going to find that guy. So, if you prefer not to work with me, that's fine. I'll go it alone and won't bother you again."

"Okay, okay." Ospino wasn't quite sure what to say next. Sam waited but sensed she had nothing further to say, so he opened the door of his SUV to get in.

"Okay, can you wait until I get a read from the forensics team and give my boss a heads up first? Then I'll go with you." Ospino couldn't believe she was so rude. *It's not like me,* she thought. She wondered if the expectations of a high-profile investigation were getting to her.

Sam had a look of suspicion on his face before responding. "I don't know if you mean what you said. So far, you haven't given me the right time of day. I don't give a crap about jurisdiction. But, one thing I do know. The best way to find these suspects is through teamwork, working tirelessly together to find them."

Ospino, tired and flustered by her behavior, nodded her head in agreement and apologetically responded, "Okay. Once we finish here, I promise we can go search for that fucking thug together." That remark brought a broad smile to Sam's face. She'd made a truce.

Ospino reached for her cell phone as she strolled back toward the van. Sam heard what she said as she walked toward the technicians.

"This is Detective Juli Ospino. I need to speak to Major Burke. It's urgent."

CHAPTER
6

Forty-five minutes later, the dealership parking lot was in bedlam. Sam counted five additional state police vehicles and eight officers, scurrying around looking like they'd just hit the lottery. Upset about his business, Ray Mitchell complained to Sam that all the police vehicles in his lot were scaring away customers. Sam could only tell him they would wrap up things shortly and leave. When he saw Ospino breaking away from the group of plainclothes officers, he strolled over to her. "Where's Major Burke?"

"He's at a murder scene and won't be free for another hour. So he sent his personal aide, Lieutenant Martin Randell, instead. We'll finish up in a few minutes. We're waiting for a tow truck for the van."

"Any luck with prints in the truck?" asked Sam.

"They found one partial print in the back of the van, a partial on the dashboard, and another on the passenger door. They will go over it in much more detail once we impound the van."

"How about the license plate and the keys?"

Ospino yelled to Detective Serrano and asked if they'd found any prints on the plate. Serrano answered, "Yes."

"Well, today is a good start for finding the identity of those, uh, what did you call them again?" humorously asked Sam.

"Are you always joking with people, or do you just want to hear me say 'fucking thugs' again?" Ospino said with a smile.

Sam chuckled. "That's better. I like seeing you smile. It beats the looks you'd been giving me. Now, let's go and find those, uh, you know."

Ospino began thinking differently about Sam. She felt he was sincere. Not only that, he was a good-looking guy and a hard-charging, no-nonsense investigator. She liked him but hoped he wouldn't disappoint her like the other guys she'd met.

"Your car or mine?" Ospino asked.

Sam saw she was driving an unmarked Silver Ford Explorer. "If we find these guys, I'd rather they shoot up a state vehicle instead of my Acura."

Ospino smiled. "Well, I hope you have a vest and a gun, especially if you think someone might shoot at us. If we are going to be partners, I need to trust you will back me up."

Sam opened the rear lid of his SUV and grabbed his tactical bag. But, first, Sam asked Mitchell if he could park his vehicle in the lot for the day and got his permission. Then while walking with Ospino to her cruiser, he emphatically said, "As my partner, there is no way I'll let anyone harm you, and you can take that to the bank."

Ospino recognized the serious look on his face and believed he meant what he said. She then arranged for two of her colleagues to join her and Sam to search for the suspect's SUV once she finished at the gas station.

Ospino and Sam then traveled south on 1A to the gas station, where Ospino viewed the security recording of the van and the two suspects. Roberta handed Ospino a copy of the video section involving the suspects. Unfortunately, this wasn't enough for Ospino. "I'll need to take the entire original recording. I'll give you a receipt. The court will return it when the case is closed. Also, I'll need to take the display thermos for fingerprint examination."

Roberta asked if it was possible to check it for prints in the store, but Ospino responded, "If the suspect's prints are on the item, it becomes evidence needed for court. I will gladly pay for the item."

With latex gloves on, Ospino placed the thermos in an evidence bag. She then had Roberta provide a sworn statement regarding the evidence taken and left her with a receipt.

From the gas station, Ospino and Sam headed to Lynn to locate the address of the guy in the Toyota who provided safe transport for the suspects from the car dealership. On their way, Ospino contacted the other detectives to meet them at the Walmart parking lot on 1A in Lynn. When they met, Ospino briefed the two detectives, Ed Collins and Kevin Bishop, regarding their search for the owner of the Toyota, identified as Akram Ganani, at his home on 22 Elwood Drive.

The two detectives followed Ospino to Elwood Drive, where they pulled over to the curb in front of number 12 Elwood. Ospino counted down five homes down the street to what should be number 22, Ganani's residence.

"We don't see the Toyota. I'm going to drive by the house to see if his vehicle is in the driveway. You two wait here."

She slowly drove down the street until she approached the house numbered 22. She didn't observe the Toyota in the short driveway, and there was no garage. The two-tenement house appeared to be quiet, with no suspicious activity. Sam recommended they knock on the door to determine if he was home and, if not, inquire where he might be. Ospino agreed, notified the backup team of their plan, and requested they cover the back of the house.

They both parked in front of the house, a two-story duplex with two doors labeled 22A and 22B. Ospino and Sam approached the front doors while Collins and Bishop covered the rear of the house. The black mailbox for 22B had the name Ganani written on it. Sam checked the door and found it unlocked. They walked into the small hallway with stairs leading to the upstairs apartment. Ospino let her colleagues covering the back know they were heading up to the second-floor apartment. As they quietly walked up the stairs, they could hear children's voices bantering and laughing from within the apartment. Ospino quietly notified the backup team children were in the apartment. When they reached the apartment door, Ospino and Sam eyed each other, with Sam nodding for her to knock on the door.

The knock caused the kids to get excited, yelling in their foreign language. A moment later, a woman opened the door dressed in Muslim garb.

Ospino displayed her badge and asked to speak to Akram Ganani. The woman replied that he was not at home.

"Why do you want to speak to my husband?" she asked.

Sam answered, "We believe he may have seen an incident last night that could help our investigation."

The woman looked puzzled. "May I ask what incident you are talking about?"

Ospino answered, "It was an incident involving stolen property and an assault. May I ask your name?"

The woman answered, "Layal Haddad Ganani."

Sam asked Layal where they could find her husband. She answered he was helping friends locate a family member in the city.

"Did he bring his friends here last night to meet you and your children?" asked Caviello. The woman said her husband did not. Instead, he spent the night finding a place for them to sleep before looking for family members today.

"Do you know where he found a place for them to sleep? Maybe we can find your husband there," inquired Ospino. The woman said she did not know.

Caviello asked where her husband worked. The woman replied at a market in the city. When asked for the name and location of the market, she claimed she did not know. Several additional questions brought similar answers. Finally, it became apparent the wife was uncooperative.

"How long have you lived in Lynn?" asked Sam.

"I do not wish to answer any more questions." She began to shut the door when Ospino handed the woman a business card and asked her husband to call her.

Ospino informed her backup team they were leaving. When they all met out front, they decided to find a coffee shop to discuss what to do next.

CHAPTER
7

Ospino used her navigation to locate a coffee shop. They were on their way, driving along Western Boulevard following the navigation's directions, when Sam asked her to take the next left. The left differed from the navigation's route. The detective put on her signal to turn left and took the turn, with her colleagues following behind. She glanced at Sam and noticed his trembling as she approached the next intersection.

"Are you okay, Sam?"

Sam only uttered, "Turn right here."

She made the turn, hoping Sam knew where he was going. "Is there a coffee shop this way, Sam?"

Sam didn't answer. A short distance later, his body shuddered and bounced as he told her to take the next right.

"What's going on with you? Are you alright?"

Again, Sam didn't answer but pointed at a yellowish brick building twenty yards on the right. "Turn into this parking lot."

Ospino had no idea what had gotten into Sam but followed his instructions. Detective Collins, driving behind her, remarked, "What the fuck is she doing? This isn't a coffee shop. It looks like a mosque."

Ospino drove to the side of the building, where she spotted a silver Toyota partially sticking out from the back corner of the building. As she rounded the corner, she was in disbelief when she saw the license plate number. It was Akram Ganani's Toyota.

She glared at Sam. "How did you—" but couldn't finish her question as Sam opened his door and said, "He must be in there. Let's find him."

"Wait, let me park the car before you jump out and get hurt."

She pulled into a parking spot, and both exited the car. Collins pulled in next to her. When he and his partner left their vehicle, Collins asked, "What's going on?"

Ospino pointed to the Toyota.

Bishop was surprised when he saw the Toyota. "Son of a bitch. Why didn't you tell us the wife told you where he was instead of making us believe we were heading for a coffee shop?"

Ospino shrugged her shoulders with both arms in the air, replying, "She didn't tell us anything."

Bishop and Collins gave each other a puzzled look while Ospino tried the building's back door. The door was unlocked.

She had Bishop take a photo of the driver's license containing Ganani's image and asked him and Collins to go through the front while she and Sam entered through the rear.

Ospino waited to give her colleagues time to reach the front entrance before entering. Once inside, she and Sam walked down a short hall to another door and opened it a crack. They saw an empty room resembling a make-shift office with four tables and a couple of chairs at each setting. A computer sat on top of all four. In addition, there were a couple of couches, side chairs, and three coffee tables containing five hookah water pipes.

They both quietly entered the room and meandered toward one of the two doors on the other side. Ospino cracked open the first door they came to and saw a large room most likely used as the prayer room. Ospino knew this room as a musalla, meaning to pray. The room was empty.

She observed Bishop and Collins enter the other side of the room and pointed to a rear open passageway to her right. Collins, a heavyset guy, walked with a heavy foot, which caused Ospino to whisper, "Quiet."

When all four reached the passageway, they could hear a conversation between a few men in their foreign language coming from the second floor. So they advanced to the stairs leading to the floor above. Before heading up, Sam whispered, "Someone should cover the outside in case there is a runner."

Collins and Bishop stared at Sam, hinting that he should be the one to cover the outside. However, Ospino asked Bishop, a younger and fit detective, to secure the exterior of the building. Indifferent, Bishop nodded okay and walked back towards the front entrance. Ospino quietly led the other two up the stairs. When all three were on the landing, they stopped and listened to the voices. They estimated at least three, maybe four men talking, but not praying, from the argumentative voices they heard.

She whispered, "I'll go in the room first, so it doesn't cause a panic from them."

She stepped forward, entered the room, and was surprised to see six men. When all six men noticed her, they looked spooked, staring at their unexpected guest.

"I apologize for disturbing you, but there was no one downstairs. I'm looking for Akram Ganani."

One of them spoke. "We do not know him. He is not here."

Just then, Sam entered the room, searching for Ganani. He immediately spotted two of the six men hiding behind the other four. While walking toward the group, Sam said, "We saw Ganani's Toyota parked in the back of the building."

The elder of the men spoke. "What is the meaning of this intrusion?"

Three of the men moved toward Sam in defiance.

Concerned, Ospino holding up her badge, shouted, "Calm down. We're the police!"

After her announcement, the two men hiding quickly moved toward an exit passageway in the rear of the room. Sam recognized one of them as Ganani, pushed his way past the others, and took off after them.

Ospino radioed Bishop. "Kevin, two runners are heading towards the exit on the left side of the building."

She asked the other four men, "Please sit and stay calm. We are here only to ask questions. Charlie, you stay with them. I'm going out back."

Ospino turned and practically flew down the stairwell, into a back room, and out the rear exit. She saw both runners heading toward Ganani's SUV, with Sam giving chase behind them.

Ospino rushed to step in front of Ganani before he approached his Toyota. Meeting at the vehicle, Ganani attempted to push her out of the way, but she swiped his arm back. He grabbed her by the neck, pushed her up against the SUV, and began choking her. His enormous hands had a tight grip around her neck. He was much bigger than Ospino. Ganani had his weight pushing her against his vehicle, preventing her from grabbing her gun wedged between her and his SUV. Panic set in, and she was gasping for air. She didn't have the strength to push him away. Her vision blurred.

Sam had Ganani's associate on the ground handcuffing him when he saw Ospino was in trouble. Sam left the associate cuffed and ran to help her. When he reached her, he slammed his fist into Ganani's temple, knocking him to the ground in a daze. Then he punched Ganani's face again, opening up a flow of blood from his nose.

A few steps back, Bishop grabbed Ganani's associate and escorted him to where Sam had knocked Ganani to the ground.

Sam was at Ospino's side. "Are you okay? Take small breaths."

Ospino continued having trouble breathing and felt light-headed. Sam turned to Bishop. "Arrest these guys. I'm taking her to the hospital."

Sam picked Ospino up into his arms and gently placed her in the passenger seat of her car. He grabbed the car keys from her jacket pocket and backed out of the parking space, yelling to Bishop, "Get help. I'll call you when I get to the hospital." Being a former tactical team leader, Sam already knew the location of the nearest hospital. He always researched where to go when things went sideways.

He sped toward downtown with his eyes glued to his phone's GPS. He kept asking Ospino to take short breaths while turning on the police emergency lights and siren, speeding past vehicles that pulled to the side of the road. It wasn't long before arriving at the hospital. He drove up to the emergency entrance. He slid out of the car and carried Ospino into the hospital, shouting, "Police officer needs help!"

A doctor and two nurses ran toward him with a gurney. While placing her on the gurney, he informed the doctor, "A suspect strangled her, and she's having difficulty breathing."

The doctor did a quick examination before giving instructions to a nurse and wheeled the gurney into an examination room. Sam was out of breath and immersed in anxiety. He paced back and forth before sitting down, trying to calm himself while waiting for the doctor to return. Then, he thought of Detective Bishop alone with the two suspects. So, he decided to call Bishop to ensure he had help and let him know Ospino was under a doctor's care at the city hospital.

"Everything is cool. Lynn police are assisting, and state officers are on their way." Bishop answered.

"Thanks, Kevin. Would you notify Major Burke about the incident and tell him what hospital is treating Ospino?"

Sam ended the call and impatiently awaited word from the doctor. His concern for Ospino elevated by the minute. He blamed himself for not getting to her sooner to prevent the assault. Not known for being patient, he was a bit jittery and continued covering his face with his hands. He stopped the jitters when he heard the exam room curtain slide open as the doctor walked toward him with an ambiguous look.

CHAPTER
8

Concerned, Sam was anxious to hear the doctor's diagnosis. "She has some neck swelling and pain, difficulty swallowing, and lightheadedness. We will keep her overnight to ensure she fully recovers without complications," reported the Doctor.

"Can I see her?" asked Sam.

"Yes, but keep her from talking as much as possible. Let her rest her vocal cords."

Sam entered her room and quietly told the detective not to speak.

"I apologize for not getting to you sooner."

She replied in a raspy voice, "You saved my life, Sam."

Sam whispered, "Please, no talking—doctor's orders. I'll do all the talking. You just listen. I had Bishop call Major Burke to let him know what happened. Is there a family member you would like me to call?"

Ospino shook her head no, took Sam's hand, and squeezed it tight. Her eyes were moist as she gazed at him with appreciation before asking in a hoarse whisper, "How did you know he was there, Sam?"

"No talking for a while, okay, Detective? Please. We can talk about it tomorrow. The doctor said you have severe neck swelling and should rest your voice. They're going to keep you overnight to ensure no complications develop. Now, please follow the doctor's orders."

She smiled and nodded okay. She wanted to laugh at how Sam treated her like a child. *I'm getting to like this guy. He's cute.* "Sam, my name is Juli, not detective."

"That's a pretty name. I like it, Juli."

They were interrupted as an orderly and nurse entered the room to transfer Juli to an inpatient room. They informed Sam of the room number and floor. Rather than follow them up in the elevator, Sam told her he had to make some calls and would see her in a few minutes. He contacted Detective Bishop to update him on what the doctor had reported. "Have you identified the other runner?"

"Yes. We identified him as Joram Haddad, Ganani's brother-in-law."

"Great, Kevin. Would you run a background check on Ganani, his wife, and Haddad? When you get the information, text me Haddad's DOB and any other information you can find on the other two. I'd appreciate it."

Next, he called his son Drew and briefed him on what had happened. He mentioned he was going to the ATF office in the morning to prepare a detailed report, starting with the Saturday evening events at the gas station, the shooting of the trooper, and everything that had happened today.

"While I'm on the phone with you, could you run some names through immigration to determine their legal status? I'll call you back when I have all the information you need for the inquiry. If it turns out that these persons are not legally in the country, we can pressure them to cooperate with the threat of deportation. I'll get to your place later tonight. We can discuss this further when I arrive."

Sam then called his boss in Boston to fill him in on the day's events and reported he'd be in the office in the morning to prepare a full report. Once done with the calls, he rode the elevator to the third floor and searched for Juli's room. When Sam entered the room, Juli smiled and raised her hand for him to take hold of it. The first thing he said was for her not to speak.

"I want you to rest and recover quickly. I think we make a great team, and I enjoy being with—I mean working with you. So, please follow the doctor's instructions and get better, okay?"

"We do make a great team," whispered Juli.

Sam spent the next forty-five minutes talking her ear off about anything he could think of to keep her from talking. Instead of listening to him talk, Juli couldn't help thinking back to what Sam had said to her in the used car lot where Sam found the van. Sam had said he wouldn't let anyone harm her, and he kept his word. Impulsively, she felt an attraction to him that she hadn't felt for a long time.

Sam finally got a break from blabbering when Major Burke arrived with Lieutenant Martin Randell. Burke first asked Juli how she was doing before congratulating her on finding the van, the videos, and the associate at the mosque. Burke then thanked Sam for helping Juli fight off Ganani's assault.

Unprompted, Juli whispered, "He saved my life, Major."

Burke agreed and said he would address Sam's heroic act in due time. Burke added he posted a uniformed officer outside her room until she got released. "I'd like to stay longer but have to coordinate the situation at the mosque with the local police who arrived at the scene. So, take care of yourself and get better soon. We need you on this case."

Sam walked out of the room with Burke and Randell. "Major. I'd like to continue to work with Juli to find and arrest the suspects who shot Trooper Phillips. I feel partial blame for what happened to her since I called in state police assistance that evening."

"You were doing your job. I listened to the recording of your call. You did everything right. Trooper Phillips should have waited for backup before leaving her cruiser. Thank God she had a vest on, and thank you for going to her aid. Regarding your request, we normally wouldn't have an outside agent working as a partner with one of our detectives, but we could assign you to a task force working on this investigation. With what you have done so far on it, I'd be a fool not to have you continue to work with us. I'm all for it, as long as your agency approves it."

"Thanks, Major. It would go a long way to get the approval if you called my boss and requested my continued help."

Burke said he knew Sam's boss and would call him first thing in the morning. Before Burke left, Sam asked for Trooper Phillips's latest status.

"Her recovery will take a while, but she continues to improve."

Sam returned to Juli's bedside and continued boring her with constant chatter while holding her hand. Juli only reflected on her budding feelings toward Sam and how she would handle it working side-by-side with him. Her thoughts eventually simmered into a dream as she finally fell asleep.

Seeing that Juli had dozed off, Sam tip-toed out of the room and found the cafeteria. He ordered a burger and coffee and took them back to Juli's room, sitting close to his partner and checking his emails while eating. Sam didn't want to leave her, but he had to get back to his son's apartment to prepare his investigative report and deliver it to the ATF office in the morning. He left a note for Juli telling her he had to get some sleep but would return first thing in the morning.

He locked up Juli's car and called Bishop for a ride back to his SUV. While driving to Drew's apartment in his vehicle, Sam got a surprise call from Alli Gaynor, the Hartford reporter he worked with during the Harrington investigation. Sam dated Gaynor a few times after that investigation concluded. He had strong feelings for her, but when Alli accepted a job with a national television station in Washington, DC, he felt the chances of a long-distance relationship lasting were slim. Alli had called to tell Sam she would be in Boston the following week to report on a story and hoped they could get together for dinner. Sam agreed.

Back at Drew's place, Sam helped his son rearrange furniture and helped take out loads of moving boxes to the trash. Next, he prepared his report detailing his involvement in the state police investigation. Then, trying to get his mind off Juli, Sam talked to Drew about the day's events and obtaining the immigration status of Ganani and Haddad. Afterward, Sam joined Drew for a beer and watched the local news before retiring for the night. Sam set the alarm for six in the morning to visit Juli at the hospital for an hour before heading to the Boston ATF office. He was tired but struggled to get to sleep. His thoughts were on Juli and learning what Ganani and his brother-in-law knew about the suspects, especially where they were hiding. He wanted a crack at interviewing both of them to find out where the five suspects were hiding.

CHAPTER
9

Sam woke up after only a few hours of sleep as the alarm clock went off. He showered, shaved, dressed, and scrambled a couple of eggs to have with his coffee. After brushing his teeth, Sam didn't bother saying goodbye to Drew, who was still sound asleep. Instead, he took the elevator to the garage, started his Acura, and drove to the Lynn City Hospital. At the hospital convenience store, he purchased a single red rose.

He found Juli awake, drinking an iced tea and having Jell-O for breakfast. She was happy to see him and spoke with a smile. "Good morning, Sam." The tone revealed an improvement in her voice. He handed her the rose, said she looked great, and that her improved voice was music to his ears.

"I appreciate it, Sam," she softly said with a bit of laughter. "I needed a good laugh after what I went through. Thank you for the rose. It's so sweet."

"I didn't want to leave you alone last night, but I had to prepare a report and help my son move a few more pieces of furniture."

"You have done so much in such a short time. I appreciate what you are doing to help me, not to mention how you clocked that guy who was choking me. I was terrified and thought I would die in that parking lot. I couldn't get to my gun. That bastard pinned me to the car. I was about to pass out when you knocked him to the ground. I want to apologize again for how I sloughed you off when we first met."

"I don't need an apology, only for you to get better, so we can find that, uh, you know, that effing thug and lock him and his flock up."

Juli grabbed his hand again. "I'm bored and want to get back to working the case with you. I've got a good feeling you and I will find him. But, not to change the subject, I want to know how you knew Ganani was at the mosque. Did I miss something when we talked to his wife?"

"You didn't miss a thing. The wife didn't give us any help. But I can't answer your question."

"Why? You don't trust me or just want to keep it to yourself? I won't tell anyone. I promise."

"I didn't say I won't answer your question. I can't because I don't know why or how it happens. It just happens."

"What happens?" said Juli with a puzzled look. "You mean you don't know how you took us there? That seems odd."

Sam knew this was going to be difficult. It's why he kept the bizarre physical sensations he receives to himself. How could he explain what he doesn't understand himself? "It's a, uh, well, uh, just a feeling I get. I don't know why I get it. I just do. And, I do trust you, Juli. If I could explain it to you, I would."

She didn't look like she understood his answer.

"When you're out of the hospital and back to work, I'll try to explain it further, but I'm sure you'll never understand or believe it could happen. So please be patient with me. I'm telling you truthfully that I don't understand it myself."

"Okay, I believe you, but it is strange. When I see Detectives Bishop and Collins again, I know they will ask why we went to the mosque."

Sam knew that trying to explain the sensations he gets was hopeless. Fortunately, Andrea Serrano and her partner, Charlie Hawkins, arrived for a visit, saving Sam from further embarrassment trying to explain the unexplainable. While Andrea and Charlie exchanged greetings and wished Juli a speedy recovery, Sam asked Andrea if she'd found additional fingerprints in the van.

"We did. We found fingerprints on the directional signal, the heater knobs, the outside door handle, the license plate, and partials on a key."

"Great work. How long will it take to get any identification results back?"

"It's a top priority. My guess is we may have results today."

With that good news, Sam said he had to get to his Boston office but would return later in the day.

"Call me first, in case I'm released later," requested Juli.

"I will," replied Sam as he left the room.

Andrea gave Juli an exploring stare with raised eyebrows and a smirk on her face.

"What?" Juli questioned inquisitively.

Andrea didn't answer. Instead, she asked Charlie if he could get some ice cream and coffee for them from the cafeteria. Charlie was happy to oblige and left for the cafe.

Andrea was Juli's best friend, who she trusted dearly. They shared their deepest secrets and supported each other, no matter the circumstances. They could also pass for twin sisters with similar facial and physical features, personalities, and goals.

"Is there something going on between you two, Juli?" asked Andrea.

"What makes you think that?" quizzed Juli.

"When I walked in, you guys were holding hands, and you held a rose in your other hand. I also could tell by the look you both gave each other," said Andrea.

Juli giggled. "I like him. He's cute, funny, a great investigator, and not to mention he saved my life."

Andrea wanted to hear more. Juli described what happened at the mosque and how Sam flattened her attacker and rushed her to the hospital. Andrea wanted to know where Juli's attraction to Sam was heading, but Juli turned their conversation to police business when Hawkins returned from the cafeteria.

*   *   *

Forty-five minutes later, Sam was at the Boston ATF office. He submitted his report and met with the Special Agent in Charge (SAC), Gary Hopkins, and his two assistants, Steve Roberts and Mike Perry. Sam went over the events of Saturday evening and the previous day's event at the mosque.

Hopkins was pleased with what he heard and had good news for Sam. "Major Burke called me about your outstanding work in finding the van and the security videos that led to identifying some suspects. He called you a hero for saving the lives of two state police officers and mentioned he intends to recommend you for a commendation from the department. He also officially requested that you continue to work jointly with his detectives to find those responsible for shooting the trooper."

"I would appreciate it if I could continue to assist them as a task force member. We're making good headway in determining who these guys are and hope to find and arrest them soon."

The SAC responded, "I called the Assistant Director for his approval, and I should hear from him later today. If he approves the Major's request, you'll also have mine. We also want to congratulate you for your heroism and support to the state police."

When the briefing ended, Sam got congratulated by the office staff as he walked through the front office on his way out. Sam's only thought was that word spread quickly within the office. He stopped to see his son, Drew, who worked in the same federal building. He didn't stay long, wanting to get back to the hospital. As he left the building, he called Juli and was surprised to learn she'd gotten released, but her boss ordered her to take a couple of days off before returning to work.

"I agree. You should take a couple of days to recuperate. One way to relax is to join me for dinner later today."

Juli paused before answering. "Oh, Andrea and I planned on dinner tonight." Juli was pleasantly surprised Sam invited her for dinner and definitely wanted to be with him. "Why don't you join us? It'll be fun."

"Wow, you mean I get to join two beautiful women for dinner? What luck."

Juli laughed. "You are so full of it, Sam. So, does that mean you will join us?" When he answered that he would, Juli told him the time and where to meet.

Sam was ecstatic about having dinner with them. He took a few two-step dance movements as he swirled around before calling Major Burke to get updated on the results of their interviews with Ganani and Haddad.

Recognizing Sam's cell number, Major Burke took his call and answered Sam's question. "Ganani denies picking up the suspects at the dealership, claiming someone had stolen his vehicle. Haddad said he knows nothing about the five suspects or his brother-in-law's involvement with them. In addition, the fingerprint analysis identified three of the five suspects. We are currently conducting backgrounds on the three and any known associates."

"I'd like a crack at interviewing both of them. I think I can convince them to talk."

Deciding if he should allow someone other than state police detectives to question their suspects, Burke replied, "I'll have to get back to you on that, Sam."

"Did the detectives learn anything from the other men at the mosque?"

"All claimed not to know anything. None of the men had a criminal record, so we had no reason to hold them. However, a protective search found multiple sleeping carts in a second-floor room with trash receptacles containing empty food takeout bags, water bottles, and coffee cups. We assume the five suspects spent the night sleeping at the mosque."

"Have you identified the restaurant or store where the food and drink came from?"

"We did, and we're going to follow up on it, but presently, the detectives are working on a murder case, putting together evidence and interviews for a search warrant."

"I'm available to help, Major. I could visit the shop within the hour. We should hurry this thing along for the safety of the hostage."

"I prefer state police personnel to conduct interviews, and at the moment, I have no one available."

Sam thought about how he could convince Burke to allow him to assist. "Major, while visiting Detective Ospino at the hospital this morning, Detective Serrano and Hawkins arrived to visit. Might one of them be available to interview those at the store with my help?"

Burke knew Sam was right, that the investigation shouldn't go dormant even for a few hours. He appreciated Sam's help and was confident in his ability to do a thorough job. "Alright, Sam. I'll have Detective Serrano go with you to interview the store manager. However, I have to insist that Serrano complete the report on any interview to keep it in-house."

"That's fine with me, Jack. I'm not in this for any credit."

Fifteen minutes later, Sam received a call from Andrea Serrano asking where he would like to meet. After deciding where, Sam made it clear they needed to convince the store owner or manager to cooperate. "I'm a no-nonsense guy, Andrea. I won't allow witnesses to claim they can't or won't help if they can. One way or another, they're going to cooperate."

CHAPTER
10

Sam and Andrea met at the Walmart parking lot in Lynn. Andrea requested Sam ride with her, so he slid into the passenger seat and thanked her for agreeing to work with him on the interview.

"It's my pleasure, Sam. Juli means a lot to me. I don't know what I'd do without her. So if there is anything I could do for you, please ask. Anything."

"Thanks, Andrea. I'll keep that in mind if I need a favor someday."

"The place we are looking for is Lugassi's, a Muslim grocery store located on the east side of the city, at the corner of Commerce and Summer Street. They offer prepared takeout sandwiches, hummus and falafel, and various drinks. It's a quick ride from here, so buckle up."

Shortly after that, Andrea parked on the side of the street a short distance past the store. They wanted to look for security cameras on the grocery store and the buildings surrounding the area. Andrea spotted one diagonally across the intersection with the camera facing in the store's direction. Sam studied the grocery store for outside security cameras but didn't recognize any. Before entering the store, they agreed Andrea would take the lead if they met with a woman to interview, and Sam would if they met with a man.

Andrea covered her head with a light scarf as they entered the store. She noticed the store hours listed on the outside window reflected the store was open until nine on Saturdays. Once inside the store, Andrea saw a woman behind a counter on her left dressed in a hijab, traditional Muslim garb. Sam scanned the store for security cameras high on the walls and spotted one in each corner and behind the counter where the woman stood. After identifying herself, Andrea asked the woman if she was the store owner.

In broken English, the woman replied she and her husband owned the store. Andrea asked if she was working Saturday night. The woman answered both her husband and she worked until closing.

"Do you remember who came to the store to purchase several orders of prepared foods, water, tea, coffee, and beer to take with them?"

The woman looked apprehensive, not knowing whether to answer the question. Andrea asked if she understood the question. The woman said she should get her husband and walked toward a back room.

"I'm going to keep an eye on her," Andrea whispered to Sam.

Andrea followed the woman but kept herself hidden behind an adjacent aisle. Andrea stopped near where the woman met her husband and listened to their conversation before returning to the counter, as did Andrea.

Sam took over the questioning by asking the husband if anyone came to the store to pick up an extensive food and drink order on Saturday night. Her husband said he did not remember such an order.

Andrea interrupted and pointed to Sam. "He is federal police, and if you lie to him, it is a federal crime in America, and you could go to jail."

The woman looked at her husband, leading them to begin a conversation in their native language.

Andrea then spoke in their native language. "You both are lying. I heard your conversation in the backroom that the Imam sent the two men to get food and asked you not to tell anyone."

The woman and her husband were surprised that Andrea understood and spoke Farsi. It surprised Sam, as well. Andrea let them absorb her response before continuing. "We might overlook your lies if you tell us the truth. No one at the mosque will know what you tell us. It will be our secret. Otherwise, if you lie, we will arrest both of you, and your store will get closed." Andrea pointed to the security camera. We want to see the video for Saturday night."

Sam saw the worried look the woman gave her husband. The husband then nodded affirmatively and led them to the back office. The office was small, with a desk, a four-drawer file cabinet, a small table holding two split-screen video monitors, and two chairs. Next to the table was a closet door that the husband unlocked and opened. The narrow closet had four shelves containing two video recording devices.

While the husband rewound the video footage, Sam saw the store's state operator's permit framed on the wall. He snapped a photo of the license with his cell phone and asked if Bukai and Amena Lugassi were his and his wife's names. The owner answered it was their names. Sam also took several photos of the office area. When the husband found the video segment where the two men entered the store, he played it for Sam and Andrea. While watching the video, Sam recognized the two men as Akram Ganani and his brother-in-law, Joram Haddad. What he didn't see was how they paid. While watching the split-screen monitor, it surprised Sam that the store also had outside cameras that captured the two men arriving in Ganani's Toyota. The camera was sharp enough to see the Toyota's license plate number.

"Mr. Lugassi, how did the two men pay for their order?"

Bukai Lugassi hesitated before answering. His wife nodded to him. "The Imam called and placed the order. He has an account and later sent his assistant to pay me with cash."

"Do you know the name of the man who paid you?" asked Andrea.

"He is called Amir. That is all I know."

"Can you show us when he came to pay you on the video?"

"He paid me outside the Mosque. Maybe two, three days later."

With that said, Andrea asked to take the video while Sam videoed Andrea handing Lugassi a receipt for it. Sam told Lugassi and his wife not to mention their visit to anyone, including the Imam. When Andrea and Sam were about to leave the store, Sam asked Bukai to point out the outside cameras since he and Andrea didn't notice any. Outside, Bukai pointed to each side of the small store sign, particularly to a section that looked like part of the sign. Sam distinguished a small black box that had a hidden camera inside. *Good to know*, thought Sam.

When driving back to Walmart, Sam praised Detective Serrano. "That was amazing. Not only did you follow the woman to the back office to overhear her conversation with her husband, but it shocked them that you understood and spoke the language. It surprised me too."

"I learned to speak Farsi in the Army. I became friendly with the female army instructor, originally from Iran. She taught me the language. Even after being discharged, I stayed in touch to learn more while we spoke Farsi on the phone. I also continued to study the language in night school."

"Well, I'm impressed. All the success today is yours alone."

"Thanks for saying that, Sam, but we did it together, and I hope we can do this again. Hey, I understand we'll be dining together tonight."

"Yeah, I am looking forward to it. Just so you know, I asked Major Burke if I could take a crack at interviewing Ganani and Haddad, but he wasn't keen on it. However, with the information we received at the store, I'll ask him again for you and me to interview them since you speak their language. I think Burke will see the advantage of that."

"I would be happy to do it with you, Sam. I want you to know Juli is glad you both are working together. She trusts you, and I know she wouldn't want me to say this, but she likes you a lot. So, please, don't mention I told you."

"It's our secret, and hearing that makes me feel great because I like her too. I can't wait for her to get back to work to solve this case as a team. I think you should work with us."

Andrea mentioned that she would love to, but she had a daughter and wanted to minimize the risks on the job because of her. "My daughter is the love of my life, and I need to be there for her. Besides Juli and my sister, I trust no one else to care for her, especially if anything should happen to me. My daughter is why I chose forensics instead of working in the field."

Sam understood her reasoning. As they arrived at the Walmart parking lot, Sam offered his hand to shake hers, but she said she'd rather have a hug. He hugged her and said, "See you both at the restaurant tonight."

As Sam drove to his son's apartment, he received a call from his boss, Gary Hopkins. "Sam, the Assistant Director approved your temporary assignment to work jointly with the Mass State Police on their investigation. The AD wants weekly updates on the investigative process."

With that information, Sam felt emotionally satisfied. He feigned a punch in the air with a closed fist. He felt the investigation was progressing toward finding the five men in the van, particularly the one who shot Trooper Phillips.

CHAPTER
11

Shortly after 6:00 PM, Sam entered Bistro Junto al Rio, the upscale Spanish restaurant by the Mystic River. He spotted Juli and Andrea seated at a booth in the rear corner of the restaurant and swaggered his way to them with a smile on his face. After greetings, he sat facing them on the opposite side of the table.

His first words were, "You two look amazing."

The two women responded almost in unison, saying, "You are so right, Sam," causing all three to laugh.

Andrea was in a silly mood, warning Sam she and Juli hadn't been out to an upscale restaurant in months, not because of their heavy workload but because of cheap dates who avoided expensive restaurants. "I'm hoping you are ready for a long extravagant night catering to two sexy women craving delicious food and plenty of champagne." She and Juli laughed until their eyes watered. They'd already had two glasses of champagne each.

Sam liked the way the two women were relaxed and having fun. "It's my pleasure to satisfy your cravings. Select whatever you want from the dinner menu and the champagne list."

Juli and Andrea talked like it would be an expensive night for Sam, but both only ordered three appetizers, quesadillas, tacos, and mole, pronounced moh'-lay, to share. Next, they ordered one dinner, chicken fajita, to split between them. Finally, Sam ordered Lomo Saltado, a Peruvian stir-fried tenderloin dish with cilantro, chili peppers, and tomatoes that they all shared. However, the three bottles of high-priced champagne elevated the bill for the exquisite fun-filled dining experience.

During dinner, Sam touted Andrea for her exceptional work. "Andrea surprised me when she spoke Farsi. We wouldn't have gotten the owners to cooperate without Andrea. I'd like to know more about the special skills you two bring to the state police."

Juli spoke first. "Andrea speaks five languages: Portuguese, Italian, Spanish, Farsi, and English. She is not only one of our best forensic specialists but a fingerprint analyst, document examiner, and controlled substance specialist. She's received Special Forces training in the army and teaches forensics and first aid at the state police academy. She's a wonderful mother to her daughter, Micaela, and a close and trusting friend. She's funny and makes me laugh when I'm down on myself. She's also a good cook, loves food, good champagne, and sex, oops, I mean having fun."

Juli's loose lips caused them to laugh loud enough for those at the surrounding tables to stare at them.

Once Andrea stopped laughing, it was her turn for friendly payback. "Juli also speaks Italian and Portuguese as well as French. Although a female in the mostly men-dominated detectives unit, she is well respected for her hard work and willingness to learn. Juli takes online courses in homicide techniques and hounds me to teach her forensics. She loves Italian and French cuisine the most, champagne, red wine, and all flavors of ice cream, more than Micaela. She dreams of traveling but never makes time for it. She enjoys reading, sexy clothes, especially those showing off her fabulous boobs and tight pants that highlight her round little ass." Sam and Juli laughed hysterically, causing the patrons to stare, with some shaking their heads in annoyance. "Speaking of sex, Juli always talks about having a husband and keeping him active in the bedroom to give her a bus full of kids."

That last remark created piercing laughter from the three of them that the server rushed to interrupt their joyful bantering with the dessert menu.

Sam studied the menu and suggested the desserts for the two very slender but shapely women. They both declined, saying they had to maintain their figures with big smiles on their faces. *They certainly are exquisite,* thought Sam. However, Sam continued to entice them with his description of what sounded to be delicious delicacies. Finally, the two women gave in and agreed to share one dessert. They each took two spoonfuls of the molten chocolate lava cake with a side scoop of hazelnut gelato.

When finished, Andrea had a question for Sam. "Tell us a little about you. Are you married, Sam?"

"No. I'm not married but divorced with one son who is an agent with the State Department in Boston. After finishing college, I started my career as a middle school teacher, but I always dreamed of having an exciting career in federal law enforcement. As a result, I applied for a federal investigator's position, took the exams, and was fortunate to get hired by ATF. Currently, I'm the supervisor of the Hartford ATF office." He summarized several criminal cases he and his agents had conducted over the past several years that impressed the two detectives. After dining for more than two hours, Andrea excused herself to answer a phone call.

When she returned to the booth, she had a disappointed look. "I have to call it a night. I promised my sister I'd pick up Micaela by nine." After hugging Juli and Sam, she thanked him for a great time and whispered, "Could you drive Juli home, please? And no funny stuff when you get to her apartment. Just kidding. She's crazy about you, so have fun."

When Andrea left, Juli also thanked Sam, telling him she appreciated treating her and Andrea to a great night out. She didn't want to leave the restaurant, so she revealed more about her friendship with Andrea.

"Andrea and I have similar backgrounds. We met in the Army and were two of only five female candidates to qualify for the Special Forces training. We completed the rigorous training among the men, even though all the guys would say gross shit throughout the tough exercises. During overseas assignments, we also faced harassment but fulfilled our commitment and received honorable discharges. Our enlistment obligation was for four years, but Andrea got discharged earlier because of her pregnancy."

Juli said she took a couple of months off after being discharged but stayed in touch with Andrea. During her time off, she visited her uncle in Southborough. "My uncle, Luis Castillo, retired as a colonel in the Mass State Police, convinced me to apply to be a state trooper since the department was adding fifty recruits. I was reluctant to be a trooper since they're similar to the military—made up of mostly men. Being a minority woman, I felt I might have to deal with harassment and teasing as I did in the army. However, my uncle assured me the state had tightened harassment laws, and he would hand-select my training officer. As a result, I immediately contacted Andrea and pleaded with her to apply along with me. She agreed, and we made it through the academy with high marks. During training at the police academy, we both decided not to have any close relations with the male cadets as recommended by my uncle. Our class had six female cadets, and we formed a woman-only clique for support and motivation. After we finished training, Andrea and I enrolled in night and weekend college courses in criminal justice and forensics during the first six years on the job. A couple of years after receiving our degrees, my uncle recommended me for promotion to a detective. I begged him to get Andrea promoted to a forensic detective. He made it happen, given that he was second in command of the state police. Andrea has a daughter, Micaela, who will be eight years old in a couple of months."

"Is Andrea married?" asked Sam.

"No. Andrea got pregnant while in the army but never married. Once discharged and having Micaela, she lived with her sister while attending the police academy. Her sister and husband, who live in Framingham, cared for Micaela until she completed her training. Andrea then found an apartment in Framingham to be close to her sister."

"What about you, Juliana? Any special guy in your life?" Juliana sighed and admitted she'd had a few dates, but nothing serious. "I always dreamed of finding someone special to spend my life with but haven't found him yet."

"That surprises me. You are a beautiful woman, smart, strong, and good at what you do. I can keep going on and on with superlatives. Why have you avoided dating?"

"I work many hours, and guys generally shy away from woman police officers, and I try to avoid dating police officers. I've been hit on by several, including some who were married. So I've learned not to date where I work."

Sam was careful about how to respond. "I didn't mean to pry. I respect your privacy. I'm attracted to you. I hope that telling you doesn't affect our working relationship. I enjoy working with you and hope we can continue to work together as friends. The suspects in this investigation are dangerous, and I want you to know I'll have your back every step of the way."

Juli smiled with her head nodding in the affirmative. "I know you will be there for me, Sam. I trust you with my life, and I'm more than pleased we're now working together."

Sam said nothing for a moment, only staring at Juli's gorgeous turquoise-colored eyes. "How did you end up with such beautiful eyes?"

"My mom was a beautiful blonde with dazzling blue eyes. Unfortunately, she died of cancer when I was only twelve years old. I miss her so much. We were the perfect mom and daughter."

"I'm sorry for your loss. Let's get you home safely, as Andrea ordered."

Juli lived in East Boston in an old five-story brick building facing the Mystic River and the Boston skyline. Her uncle had used his influence to arrange for her to secure the in-demand rent-controlled apartment. Parking was at a premium in the area, with most on-street parking reserved for residents only.

"Sam, if you drive past the building and take the next right, there's a driveway entrance to the back of the building where we might find an open spot in the small lot," claimed Juli.

Sam managed to squeeze his vehicle between a Mini Cooper and the dumpster. Juli then used her passkey to enter the back basement door leading into a small foyer with stairs leading up to the first floor. From there, they took the elevator to her fourth-floor apartment.

Juli led Sam into her apartment. "Wow, I'm impressed," said Sam, "You did a great job furnishing the place, and you have a fantastic view of the river and city skyline. Very nice. I'd trade my apartment for yours."

Julie thanked him and asked if he would like a glass of wine, coffee, or water. He chose water. They sat on the living room sofa, staring out the window, taking in the city's skyline. Sam asked how she felt, but Juli brushed that aside and wanted to know more about him.

"Well, where do I start? I grew up in a beach town in Rhode Island. Looking back to those days, I'd say my family was below what people would call middle class. My mom didn't work. My dad first worked at a mill and part-time doing his own trash collection business a couple of days a week until he got hired at the Electric Boat, a company that builds submarines in Connecticut. My family lived in an apartment above my grandmother, who owned the house. My father's brother, my uncle, lived across the street. My uncle was a weekend lifeguard at the town's beach and took me there often during the summer. I have a fond memory of him. He saved my life from drowning. My older brother, his friend, and I were at a pond across the road from the ocean side beach. My older brother and his friend jumped into the deep part of the pond and dared me to jump in with them. I was only nine years old and didn't know any better, so I jumped into the water. Of course, I couldn't swim, but luck was with me. My uncle came looking for us when it was time to go home. He saw my predicament and pulled me out, saving my life."

"Why didn't your brother help you?"

"He was only twelve and probably froze, not knowing how to rescue a drowning person. Growing up, I wore hand-me-down clothes, was a slightly above-average student in school, and believe it or not, I was a shy, quiet kid back then. My closest friends were other neighborhood kids. We would meet at the corner of Oakland and Tower Hill Streets during the summer months. Kids who knew us referred to us as the Oakland Street boys. We played baseball in a field across the railroad tracks and basketball on a small one-basket dirt court in the neighborhood. My mom and dad often fought over money because my dad liked to gamble and usually lost a good part of his paycheck. I was the only one from my small group of neighborhood friends who finished college. Looking back on my life, finishing college was the best decision I have ever made."

Juli wanted to ask about his marriage that led to a divorce but instead quizzed Sam again about how he knew Ganani was at the Mosque. "You promised me you would explain further."

Sam sighed. He preferred not to talk about experiencing the eerie physical feelings that he'd considered a curse when first encountering them, but he accepted them as a gift in time. He trusted Juli and decided he would attempt to explain the best he could what he didn't fully understand himself.

"I trust you will keep this to yourself and not repeat what I tell you, Juli."

She promised, so Sam reluctantly began. "What I'm going to tell you is only what I think was the reason I began getting those feelings. I could be completely wrong about it, though. Anyway, I was one of three children, all boys. I was the middle son. My older brother, Jim, was three years older, and my younger brother, John, was five years behind me. When I was eight years old, I became very ill from what I later learned was an unidentified virus. I was in an ICU unit for days in a local hospital not known for having world-renowned doctors. My family couldn't afford specialized doctors or big-city hospitals."

He paused momentarily, convinced he shouldn't be telling this story. "I was too young to know what happened there in the hospital. My brother Jim told me my doctor called my mother to the hospital, telling her he felt I wouldn't make it through the night. My father drove my mom and Jim to the hospital, but he never came in to visit but just waited in the car. He wasn't what I would call a loving father. When my mom and brother arrived, the doctor was waiting at the nurse's desk and told my mother I had just passed."

Juli looked shocked, not knowing what to say.

"My mom became faint and needed medical attention before regaining her composure. Minutes passed before she felt strong enough to enter my room. Again, I'm telling you only what I learned from my brother years later. I remember nothing about that day. According to my brother, my mother entered the room, slowly walked over to where I lay in bed, and hovered over my body, sobbing as any mother would. At some point, she leaned over to kiss my forehead. As my brother told me, it was at that moment my eyes popped open, and I whispered, 'Mom.' She screamed and was about to faint when the doctor by her side held onto her."

Juli put her arm on Sam's shoulder when she saw his glossy eyes. Juli tried to comfort him the best she could. Sam composed himself and continued. "I learned the doctors and the staff at the hospital that night were in total denial. The hospital staff went completely protective, keeping the event quiet. For years afterward, my older brother would jokingly claim I arose from the dead. I was too young to realize or understand what had occurred. Later in life, I learned my father contacted an attorney who negotiated a non-disclosure settlement that didn't amount to a lot of money but was enough to satisfy my father's gambling debts and buy a newer car to replace the junk he drove. My mother refused to talk about that night and re-live that terrible event. Of course, my father was missing in action. I only know I began experiencing these bizarre feelings as I got older. It took a long time for me to realize they were not a curse but signs that helped me find things and avoid risky situations."

Sam took a moment to drink some water. "An early example that I can think of was while in high school, I attended a party with a friend, Maggie, who I had a crush on. Most of the kids at the party were underage, but they had alcohol and smoked pot. Not me. I was still a shy kid whose only fault was throwing snowballs at passing cars at night with a couple of my friends. Later in the evening, one of the popular football players, who was 16 and had a car, invited Maggie, his friend, and another girl to go for a ride to the beach. I begged Maggie not to go with him since he was high on pot and drinking. However, she wanted to go. When Maggie got into his car, I experienced a weird feeling that I couldn't describe to this day. Another kid and his girlfriend joined them in the car. The next morning, I learned the driver went off the road at high speed, crashed into a tree, and rolled down an embankment. The only survivor was the driver, with a fractured leg and cuts and bruises on his head."

Juli looked troubled by what she heard.

Emotionally, Sam finished his story. "As I experienced these bizarre feelings, I became tormented, believing I possessed some kind of plague. I didn't know why it was happening to me. However, the more I experienced these strange feelings, the more I understood they were not a curse but an awareness to grasp and apply to the situation. For example, when a four-year-old neighborhood child went missing, the police and neighbors searched for her. I joined the search and was the one who found her hiding in her parent's bedroom closet. The parents, the police, and even my friends asked why I looked in their house. At first, I thought of telling them of the phenomena I felt that led me to her, but instead, I told them it was only a hunch since my younger brother often hid in the closet. I didn't want anyone to know I had experienced these strange feelings. I figured they'd probably laugh and call me a freak or a liar. So, anyone who questioned me, I simply told them I followed a hunch that turned out to be a lucky one."

Sam faced Juli and noticed her beautiful eyes were watery, with a single teardrop sliding down her cheek. She gazed at him with empathy, pulled him towards her, and kissed him passionately. He was in awe, but only for seconds, as he put his arms around her and returned the passionate kiss. Their tongues met and intertwined. She moaned as he kissed her cheeks, nose, and neck. They were both in a euphoric state, touching, feeling, and kissing each other while panting heavily.

Sam was unsure how far he should go, but he began unbuttoning her blouse while kissing her. Now fully aroused, he pulled her blouse open, reached around to undo her bra, but she stopped him.

"I can't, Sam—I mean, we shouldn't."

Sam looked up at her. Her eyes, still tearing, met his. "I want to, but I'm afraid. I'm not ready."

Sam touched her face and wiped the tear from her cheek. "It's okay. There is no rush."

He hugged her as she placed her arms around him and held him tight. Then, Sam gently pulled away, looking into her eyes. "Juli, everything is fine. Besides, it's getting late. I should go so you can get some rest."

"I'm sorry, Sam. Don't get mad, please. I want to, but—"

Sam interrupted while cupping her cheeks with both hands. "I'm not mad. We'll take it slow. I care about you, and you need your rest." He then stood and shuffled toward the door.

Juli didn't want him to leave feeling rejected. Once again, Sam, understanding her reluctance, said, "I'm okay with it, Juli. Get some sleep, and I'll call you tomorrow. Maybe we can meet for lunch?"

"I'd like that, Sam," she said as they kissed again.

Sam left and drove to his son's apartment, only minutes away. When there, he thought about his feelings for Juli and knew he had to keep them in check. When he entered Drew's apartment, he dropped those thoughts and asked his son how things were going with his new job.

"Looks like I'll be able to help you. I filled my boss in on our involvement the night the trooper got shot, and you are now working with the state police. He requested that I help in the investigation where I could. My boss had assigned me to a senior agent, Eric Mills, as my OJT instructor for my first year in Boston. He asked Mills to indoctrinate me on the procedures used to gather information on the immigration status of foreigners."

Sam gave Drew some fatherly advice on the dos and don'ts of government work. "Be patient, listen and learn from agent Mills. He's been on the job for years and knows what to do. Be a good learner. Let him do the talking and ask questions when you're unsure about a procedure. No question is a dumb question when you're learning how to get the job done the right way." They talked for nearly an hour about the job, sports, and spending more time together while both were in Boston.

Sam asked Drew to hold off on the immigration status inquiries he'd asked him to do since the state police had already contacted ICE for the information. Later, when watching Comedy Hour on television, Sam told his son about his feelings for Juli. Drew thought it was great that his dad was getting on with his life after the divorce.

Now twenty-four years old, Drew initially wanted to serve his country by joining the Marines following high school graduation. Sam, however, convinced him to join the Marine Corps Reserves and have them pay for his college tuition under the GI Bill. So, taking his father's advice, Drew joined the reserves, finished his basic and specialized training, came home, and began college as a criminal justice major at a Connecticut State University. Once Drew graduated college, he followed in his father's footsteps in a law enforcement career that made Sam one proud dad.

CHAPTER
12

Sam drove to state police headquarters the following morning, where Detective Andrea Serrano was waiting for his arrival. They met with Major Burke and Detectives Bishop and Collins, who interviewed Akram Ganani and his brother-in-law, Joram Haddad, without gaining their cooperation. Ganani was formally charged with assault on a police officer, while the state police only detained Haddad for forty-eight hours as allowed by law. Both men claimed they were in the country legally on a visa.

Major Burke and the detectives had already read Andrea's report on interviewing the Lugassi's grocery store owners. They then watched the security video showing Ganani and Haddad picking up the groceries to bring to the mosque. After viewing the video, Burke informed Andrea and Sam that he learned only that morning that Ganani's wife, Layal Haddad, was issued a student visa five years ago and did not renew it after it expired. Also, Joram Haddad entered the country over two years ago under a temporary work visa and had overstayed it. It's common among students and those who got a work visa to remain in-country illegally after their visas expire. It's only a misdemeanor to overstay a visa, so unless these subjects committed a crime or got arrested, ICE wouldn't search for them for deportation.

Burke mentioned it was a different situation for Ganani. "There is no record of Akram Ganani entering the country legally. That and his arrest for an assault puts him in jeopardy of deportation. We could charge Haddad with aiding and abetting if we could show the food Ganani and he obtained at the store was for the five suspects we believe may have spent the night at the mosque."

The five of them brainstormed the best method to re-interview the two men. Sam and Andrea explained what options they had previously discussed, and the two detectives added their suggestions until they reached a consensus on the interview plan.

Andrea and Sam decided to interview Haddad first. They presumed him to be the one more likely to cooperate. Andrea and Sam entered the interview room, where Haddad sat cuffed to a bar on the top of the table. Sam brought a can of Coca-Cola, a sandwich, and a chocolate bar from the vending units for Haddad. He asked Andrea to remove the handcuffs from Haddad during the interview. Detectives Bishop and Collins observed from the adjacent room through a one-way window.

Sam began by dictating Haddad's right to remain silent. Haddad, who spoke English well, said he understood. Sam continued. "Joram, we know that your visa to work in the U.S has expired. We know you did not renew the visa, so you violated the immigration laws, and ICE can deport you. If you cooperate with us, we could help you stay in the U.S. by renewing your visa. I want to show you the video of your brother-in-law driving his Toyota into a car dealership where he picked up five men and a person held hostage. Your brother-in-law brought these men and their hostage to the mosque to spend the night. Then, you and Akram brought food to those five men from a grocery store."

While eating his sandwich, Haddad shook his head, saying, "No. I did not do that."

"Joram, I am a federal agent, and if you lie to me, it is a crime. I can arrest you, send you to prison, or deport you."

Haddad continued shaking his head no. Sam then had him view the video from the grocery store showing him and Ganani purchasing food and drink.

"You can see the store's name on the bags and the cups you and Akram bought in this video. We found the same bags and cups at the mosque where we arrested Akram and you. I will ask you again and hope you do not lie to me. If you continue to lie, we will hold you for ICE to pick you up and deport you. Do you understand, Joram? If you tell us the truth, we can help you stay in the U.S., but you have to tell us the truth. Your brother-in-law, Akram, is in big trouble. He will spend years in jail and then get deported. So will your sister Layal. You can also help her stay in the U.S. if you help us. We want to find the five men Akram picked up in his Toyota and brought to the mosque. If you help us find where they are, you can go home, live with your sister, and protect her and her children."

Haddad sat back in his chair, considering what he should do. Sam nudged Andrea with his knee signaling it was her turn.

Andrea took over and spoke Farsi as previously planned. "Joram, your sister, and her children could stay in the United States if you help us find the five men. They shot a police officer, and they hold someone prisoner. Akram helped those five men to escape and hid them at the mosque. We will send Akram to prison for a long time and then deport him for helping those five men. You cannot help Akram, so it does not benefit you to protect him, but you could help your sister and yourself."

"If I help you find these men, how do I know you will not deport Layal and me?" asked Joram.

"We will have the prosecutor give you a written promise that no charges will go against you and your sister. Plus, we will help you and your sister renew your visas."

Haddad was hesitant to say anything against his brother-in-law but realized he could not help him. However, he wanted to help his sister and himself stay in America, so he finally agreed to cooperate.

Sam piped in, asking him if he knew where the five suspects were hiding and if he could show them the location. Joram nodded yes. "I could show you where they are now."

"Good, Joram. Tell us where they are now," asked Sam.

"I helped Ganani set up sleeping carts for these men and women at the mosque."

"Yes, we know they were at the mosque. But where are they now?" insisted Sam. "For us to help renew the visas for you and your sister depends on you telling us where they are now."

Joram looked at Sam carefully, considering his options, before speaking again. "The Imam asked me to use his van to help Ganani bring them and supplies to a farm. So I helped load the van with long black bags, heavy wooden boxes, and food and followed Ganani to the farmhouse. Ganani drove the woman, three men, and the girl they held, while the fourth man rode with me. So there were five of them and the girl."

"Can you tell us anything about these five men and the girl?"

Joram shrugged. "There were only four men and one woman. The five were all Iranians. The woman was friendly with one of the four men, who seemed to be the leader. Akram told me the woman was the driver for the other four."

It surprised Sam that a woman drove the van. He asked, "What about the girl they held as a prisoner? Can you describe her?"

"She was a young American girl who did not speak. They kept her in a separate small room. She was white, my height, medium body, and needed to use an inhaler for breathing."

"Do you know the names of the men and the woman?" asked Andrea.

"No. I only heard what one of the men called the woman. They called her Melika," answered Joram.

"Tell us about the farmhouse. Who owns the farm, and where is it?" asked Sam.

Joram held up his arms, signaling ignorance. "I do not know who owns the farm. I only helped Akram bring them food and drive them to the farm. I heard the Imam give Akram the address, so I put it on my phone, so I don't get lost."

"Can you describe what they carried to the farm?" asked Andrea.

"Yes. Water, beer, tea, blankets, the long black bags, and the wooden boxes. I do not know what was in the bags or boxes. They were heavy. The Imam gave us all these supplies."

"How did you pay for the food at the store?" asked Sam.

"Akram said the Imam called the store for the food. We did not pay. Akram said the Imam took care of paying. That's all I know."

"Did you help unload the provision and bring them into the farmhouse?" asked Andrea.

"No. Akram helped the four men carry everything into the house. They told me to wait in the van until they finished unloading everything. When they finished, they told me to go back to Lynn."

Andrea thought back to the woman with the four men. "Joram, tell me more about the woman, Melika."

"I don't know much. She was average but pretty and friendly with one of the men."

Once Andrea and Sam finished the interview with Joram, Andrea prepared a written statement for Joram to read and sign.

Sam and Andrea met with Major Burke and Detectives Bishop and Collins. Burke thanked her and Sam for their job convincing Joram to cooperate. He then directed Detectives Bishop and Collins to re-interview Ganani now that they had leverage to use on him.

"After Ganani's interview, we'll plan for the four of you to have Joram Haddad bring you to the farm's location. Once you scope out the farm with photos, we'll begin a twenty-four-hour surveillance and get background information on the owner and blueprints for the structures on the property," directed Burke.

Sam and Andrea left Burke's conference room with Andrea whispering, "We did good, Sam. We're a good team."

"Yes, we are, so let's you, Juli, and I have dinner again soon to celebrate."

"Great. I'll ask my sister to watch Micaela."

"Bring Micaela along to celebrate with us. I'd love to meet her."

Andrea looked around the hallway and, seeing no one, hugged and kissed him on the cheek. "I love that idea. I told Micaela about you, and she is excited to meet you. I'll contact you when Burke tells us to have Haddad show us the farm's location."

Sam left the headquarters just before noon and called Juli to arrange a place to meet for lunch. When she answered, he said, "Good afternoon, Juliana. I hope you slept well."

"I tossed and turned for hours before I finally passed out. I didn't roll out of bed until fifteen minutes ago. Where are you?"

"I'm just leaving state police headquarters. Andrea and I did another super job. We got one of the two guys arrested at the mosque to cooperate. I'll tell you all about it when I get there. I should be at your place in about forty minutes. Do you have a place in mind to have lunch?"

"I do. I'm preparing lunch as we speak to eat at the apartment instead of going out. I want to explain about last night and why I reacted the way I did. I hope you will understand."

"Lunch with you sounds great, but you don't have to explain anything about last night."

"I need to. I owe you that much."

"I'll text you when I'm close and meet you in the back of the building again."

*   *   *

"Yeah, this is Tony. Whooz this?" asked Tony Dellagatti, who answered the phone while leaning against the Somers, Connecticut, prison wall.

"It's Forster, Tony," replied Harrington.

"Oh, hey, boss. I heard they gave you sum big time. The feds socked it to ya. How ya doing?"

Harrington hates getting reminded he received a ten-year sentence for planning to frame and murder a federal agent.

"I thought with ya there and me here, calls ain't allowed," said Tony.

Forster shook his head in disbelief. "Everybody's listening in, Tony, so be smart, will you. Right now, I need someone to do a job, you know, the work I wanted you to do. Think back about the job I wanted you to do after what happened to Dickie. You know what I mean. I want to repay the debt owed to that guy.

"Oh, yeah, that guy, boss. I'm also stuck here in jail because of that guy, ya know."

Harrington thought, *Is this guy on drugs or what? Sometimes he can't get his head out of his ass.*

"For chrissake, Tony, I know you're not in a hotel room. So, listen, Rach is pregnant and can't help. I'm hoping you might know someone you trust that can do the work. I'll pay the going wage, whatever it costs. You know anybody on the outside?"

Dellagatti knew Harrington wanted revenge against Agent Caviello. He took a few minutes to think of anyone he knew who might agree to do the job. *I'd like to get that bastard myself,* Tony thought. "Yeah, I might know a guy who can do it. If he can't, he'll know who can. I'll try gettin' in touch with him. I'll have to let ya know. I need a few days. Can ya call me back?"

"Yes. But when you reach out to this guy, be careful what you say. The contract is a business thing, Tony. You tell him the customer wants a job done and ask the cost. It's a business contract. Understand?"

"Yeah, boss, like a business thing. I'll get right on it. Call me back."

Harrington couldn't help but think that *Tony doesn't know a thing about a business other than beating a guy to a pulp. That's a business thing to him.*

CHAPTER
13

The drive from Drew's apartment to Juli's was a short eight minutes. He entered the back parking lot and drove into the only visitor spot available. He had texted Juli when he was five minutes out. She was waiting at the back door for him. They greeted each other with a kiss before heading up to her apartment. Once in the apartment, Juli asked, "Are you hungry?"

"I am," sensuously answered Sam.

"What? You have a suggestive look on your face, Sam."

"I do? I mean, I do."

She laughed. "That's just what I thought." Feeling guilty about the night before, she grabbed his hand and led him to the bedroom.

For over two hours, they enjoyed making love, fulfilling their cravings for each other. Eventually, Sam rolled to her side. "Wow. That was amazing. I was hungry when I arrived, but not so much now. But, let's take a break for a glass of wine."

She gave him a devilish smile. "Okay, we can break for a glass of wine. I'll even let you try my special salad if you promise to return here for more of the same. "

"I'll take that deal."

Juli's special salad was delicious. She made the salad with an array of fruit, three kinds of lettuce, and pecans, all covered with a yummy dressing. The red Cabernet wine hinted of chocolate and berry fruit, followed by a velvety finish. They sat on the two stools at the kitchen counter with her feeding him the last pieces of fruit with her fingers. Sam couldn't get over how beautiful Juli was. He guessed she was five feet, four inches tall, and weighed between one-hundred and fifteen to one-hundred and twenty pounds. She had a model's figure, a slim waist, nice curves, and small hips. While they ate, Sam filled her in on his and Andrea's success interviewing Joram Haddad. Juli was excited to learn they had found the suspect's hiding place and wanted to call Major Burke immediately to tell him she was ready to get back to work. However, seeing it was late in the afternoon, Juli felt it could wait until morning, so she led Sam back to the bedroom, where they relaxed among the linen sheets and soft pillows.

"This is my case—I mean our case—and it's time to get those— uh— you know, effing thugs."

Sam laughed at Juli's more subtle choice of words instead of using the F-bomb to call the thug who shot the trooper. Sam asked if she felt comfortable discussing what had frightened her about intimacy the night before. The smile on her face turned to a frown.

"Juliana," he said compassionately, "it may help to talk about it. If you have anxiety that's locked inside you, let it out. I'll keep your secret."

Juli nodded in agreement. "I didn't get much sleep last night after you left. I felt empty and regretful. The truth is, I'm a little messed up about something that happened two years into my enlistment. The army deployed me to Afghanistan as part of a specially-trained reconnaissance squadron. My squad advanced into enemy territory to collect needed intelligence critical to the combat troops in the field. We made periodic movements into known or suspected enemy positions, sometimes resulting in confrontations with the enemy, and at times, it resulted in a firefight. The assignment usually lasted a few days, but sometimes they went a week or longer before we could head back to camp to relax and regroup. I was in a relationship at camp with a civilian contract technician named Tim. I was in love with him and thought he loved me too. So before going out on another mission, I told him we should get married when I get discharged. He didn't respond but only said he was late for a meeting with the Colonel and that we could talk about it later."

Juli paused a moment deciding on what to say next. "Once out on the mission, my squad took a break to rest. One of the guys I was friendly with sat with me while resting. We talked about what we had plans to do after completing our service. I mentioned to him I wanted to get married and have kids. He sat quietly for a moment before asking if I had plans to marry Tim. I was hesitant to tell him because of the curious look he gave me. I didn't say anything until he blurted out, 'You know Tim is married, right?' I was stunned at what he asked. I didn't know how to respond, so I just got up and walked away. Later, I searched for Tim back at camp and heard he transferred out of the unit at his request."

"That's horrible, Juli. I'm so sorry," said Sam.

"Unfortunately, it happened to me a couple more times with guys I thought loved me but learned of their deceit only after sleeping with them. It happened with a trooper separated from his wife, who later decided to return to her. Then again, I dated another guy I thought was sincere until I slept with him. He then turned out to be a control freak with a mean side. It frightened me, so I broke it off."

"I'm sorry that happened to you, Juli."

Juli's face crumpled as she looked away from Sam, trying to hide her tears. Sam immediately reached out and held her, whispering in her ear, "I'm not like them, Juli. We can take it slow with this relationship. I'll earn your trust. I promise."

"I do trust you, Sam. I just didn't want that to happen to me again, and I didn't want you to think I'm an easy mark for sex."

"I don't think that way and never will."

"Not even when I led you to the bedroom earlier?" Juli asked with a bit of humor in her voice.

Sam smiled. "Especially not then. I give you permission to do that anytime you want to."

Juli giggled and let out a sigh. "It feels good to laugh now. But, I have to admit, I'm a little stressed out from telling you all this. I think I need more wine, now."

"I agree. Let's have more wine. Then, I know a way that you can release more of your stress."

"Yeah, how will you do that?"

Sam pushed her down onto the pillow and started kissing her.

Juli didn't hesitate to go with the flow. She felt different about Sam. He treated her like a princess and was such a gentleman. She was crazy about him. They made love again until they finally took a break for more wine.

CHAPTER
14

Sam slowly got out of bed and headed to the bathroom the following day. He was exhausted from the bedroom activity and didn't get much sleep. He glanced at the alarm clock, seeing it was 8:45 AM. He leaned over, kissed Juli, and whispered it was time to get out of bed and get to work. She moaned and turned over, complaining, "I'm too tired. You wore me out."

Sam whispered, "Oh, and here I thought it was you who wore me out. You could stay in bed if you want to. I'm going to take a shower."

"Oh, okay. I'll join you."

Mmm, now I know the secret to get her out of bed, thought Sam.

After a long shower together, they had breakfast and coffee and discussed plans for getting back to work. Sam suggested she contact Major Burke and let him know she was ready to report back to work.

"Also, let him know you are aware of the interview results with Haddad and want to participate in the farmhouse surveillance."

As Juli sipped her coffee, she curiously received a call from Major Burke.

"Yes, Major," Juli listened attentively, "Yes, I'm ready to return to work," Juli excitingly replied. "Major, I heard Joram Haddad cooperated and can show us where the suspects are hiding." She listened as she squirmed in her chair with a wide smile. "Yes, Major. Yeah, I want in. Thank you, sir. Okay,—fine. I'll wait for their call. Thank you. Bye."

She stared at Sam with a surprised look on her face. "Wow. That was freaky. I'm back on the investigation. He told me Andrea and Bishop would contact me for a place to hook up. They'll have Haddad with them, and I should arrange for you to join us. It was almost like he was listening to our conversation when you suggested I call him. Does that have anything to do with those things, uh, those feelings you get?"

"Not a chance."

*　　*　　*

Andrea and Detective Bishop were waiting to meet with Juli at the Revere state police troop E facility. In the back seat of Andrea's van was Joram Haddad. Juli and Sam arrived a short time later. Based on the MapQuest information from Haddad's cell phone, they decided on the best way to get to Haverhill. Andrea took the lead, with Juli following in her unmarked sedan. Juli and Sam talked the entire distance, sharing additional background about each other. Sam also asked Juli about the father of Andrea's daughter.

"Andrea started dating a soldier after they met during training in the states before her second deployment. She hadn't been with a guy for months, and how can I say it? Uh, she needed some love and intimacy. Let's just say her need sometimes is immense, especially after too much alcohol. They had sex the night before she got redeployed, and she wasn't on the pill. Afterward, she hoped for the best when deployed, but it didn't turn out that way. A few weeks later, she learned she was pregnant. She got sent back to the U.S. and assigned to a desk job. When she was only three months shy of fulfilling her military commitment, the army gave her an early discharge."

"What about the father of the baby?"

"He avoided her when he found out she was pregnant. Andrea later learned he already was planning to marry his high school sweetheart during his next military leave."

Sam had no comment. Their trip to the Haverhill area took just over an hour with traffic. They followed Andrea into a diner's parking lot, with Juli rolling up parallel to Andrea's van.

With their vehicle windows down, Bishop related their plan from there.

"Haddad remembered Ganani stopping at this dinner for take-outs before getting to the farmhouse. He remembers the farm should be located a half-mile up Brewers Road on the right side. So I'll tap the radio mic twice as we pass the driveway to the farmhouse."

Five minutes later, Juli and Sam heard the radio mic taps from Bishop as they slowly drove by the farmhouse. The unkempt old farmhouse sat more than a hundred yards from the road at the end of a dirt driveway. Several small pine trees ran along the left side of it. As far as one can see, a dense forest covered the right side of the driveway beginning at Brewers road. A wooden structure similar to a carport sat in front and more to the left of the house. The open front of the carport contained two vehicles, a van and an SUV. It had room for another car. On the opposite side of the house was a barn facing the right back corner of the house. It didn't have the typical two wide barn doors on the front. Instead, it had a single door and a window on either side, like the front of a typical home. Sam estimated the distance between the farmhouse's rear corner and the barn structure's front door to be about thirty yards. The rear of the barn couldn't be over twenty-five yards from the dense tree line covering the whole right side of the property. The rear and left side of the farmhouse was wide open farmland.

As Juli drove by the farm, Sam took a video of the property with his phone. Then, a hundred yards up the road, Juli pulled alongside Andrea's van. "Let's head back to the diner for lunch," advised Bishop. "We'll take additional photos of the farmhouse from the van afterward before heading back to headquarters."

"What about Haddad?" asked Juli.

"We'll park the van outside the diner's window with Joram in the passenger seat so we can keep an eye on him. I'll bring him a menu, have him select something, and bring it out to him when it's ready. In the meantime, we'll eat and discuss what we'll report back to Major Burke. Burke will expect recommendations from us when we get back."

Once in the diner, Sam decided to bring the food out to Haddad in the van. When he did, he asked Joram how he was doing.

"I'm fine. Thank you for the food."

"Thank you for helping us. I'll make sure you don't have any issues with the law after this." Sam handed him a fifty-dollar bill. "Is it cool if we call you again after today? We might need your help again, and I'm sure you can use some extra money."

"Yes. I do not have a job. Thank you for giving me this."

Sam nodded in recognition of Joram's gratitude and returned to the booth where the waitress had already served their lunch. Bishop began with his thoughts on what they should do. "I believe we should hit this place hard with our tactical teams. We don't know how long these bastards will be here. They could leave tomorrow, and we may never find them again."

Andrea didn't comment. Juli said she wanted to get these guys before they moved. Bishop added, "I'm sure Burke will want to move quickly on these guys."

Sam listened and absorbed what the detectives discussed. Since he was once the Boston Special Response Team leader, Sam pointed out critical elements in preparing for a raid on a house possibly filled with armed men. "I agree we shouldn't wait long before nabbing these guys. However, we know little about the house and the barn interior, which also looks like a house. We're not sure if they have any security devices surrounding the place to warn them before anyone approaches. I'm sure your tactical teams will want to study the area and determine the interior layout of both structures. Without more intel, the teams would go in blind. I'm sure it will take two tactical teams, one to hit the house and the other to hit the barn simultaneously. They'll need to know where the nearest hospital is if the raid goes south. Also, we need to notify the local police department. There has to be an operational plan carefully worked out, and it could take a few days, not a few hours."

Juli agreed. From her military experience, she knew definitive plans were necessary before they conducted a military operation. "It would be helpful if we had intel on these guys regarding if any had combat training. We have no idea if we could encounter well-trained soldiers."

"Points well taken," said Bishop. "What should we recommend to Burke?"

Sam spoke first. "We need to have the tactical leaders in on the conversation. I would recommend a short surveillance period to gather as much intel as possible. One way to do that is to watch the place for movement inside the house and barn, including the overnight. We don't know how many suspects could be in the two structures. There are two vehicles in the carport. We should find out who they belong to and where they came from."

Bishop interrupted, saying he used the van's 35mm camera with a telescopic lens and got the plate numbers of the two vehicles.

"That's great. Hopefully, a motor vehicle check will tell us something about the owners. Then, I would have three or four guys in camouflage on foot enter the property at night, taking photos of all sides of the buildings for escape routes. Also, we need to determine if any security cameras or devices surround the property. Another recommendation would be to use any available unit with thermal imaging devices capable of detecting bodies inside both buildings." added Sam.

"Good shit, Sam. I think you should be with us when we meet with Burke," said Bishop.

Juli agreed, but Andrea followed with a suggestion. "I don't want to spoil your enthusiasm for the four of us to meet with Major Burke, but I think two of us should remain here to surveil the farmhouse to watch for any movement after two of us leave here."

"Are you volunteering?" asked Bishop.

"I'll stay," volunteered Sam. Juli followed by saying she would too.

Bishop responded, "That's settled. Andrea and I will head back to headquarters and provide Burke with a worthwhile list of recommendations. We'll be in touch with Juli after our sit-down with him. Good luck." Bishop left the booth and walked toward the exit. Andrea moved more slowly, allowing more space between her and Bishop. She winked at Sam and Juli as she walked to join Bishop.

"Have fun, you two. Try not to do anything I would do."

CHAPTER
15

After Bishop and Andrea left, Sam realized Bishop had stuck him with the bill. Juli offered to split the bill, but Sam wouldn't allow it. So they left the diner and drove back towards the farmhouse. Sam mentioned Andrea's comment about not doing anything she would do.

"Did you mention anything to Andrea about last night?"

Juli grinned before answering. "Well, maybe a hint or two. Besides, Andrea and I share everything, our grieving, despair, and regrets, our failures, successes, and good times. I enjoyed our time together last night so much I had to share it with her. I'm sorry. I hope you're not angry."

"How could I be angry about that? I only hope you didn't describe the evening in much detail."

"I only told her little details, but I can't tell you what they were, okay?" Juli said with a suggestive smile on her face.

"Oh, little secrets between friends, huh?"

"Yeah, something like that."

"Got it. Let's get back to work." They staked out the farmhouse from behind thick brush next to what appeared to be a breakdown area at one time. They only observed a guy walk from the farmhouse to the carport and walk back into the house two minutes later.

Juli's cell phone rang after nearly three hours of staring at the house. She answered the call from Andrea, who reported that Major Burke agreed to have tactical team members survey the property after sunset using thermal imaging devices borrowed from emergency services.

Once the call ended, Juli repeated the information to Sam. "The team will arrive just before dark to relieve us for the night. They want us back here at six in the morning to relieve them, and we'll get relieved at noon. We're to report to headquarters to take part in operational plans to raid the farmhouse within a day or two. We received a report the license plates on the two vehicles in the carport were stolen from New Hampshire a couple of weeks ago."

"At least we are moving forward with a plan. I'm bored sitting here. Let's take a ride back past the farmhouse. I'd like to check out the road on the other side of the woods near the barn. If there is a back exit on the barn, the suspects could escape from it into the woods. I'd like to know the escape routes in preparation for having to give chase," asserted Sam.

Juli asked, "Isn't that what the tactical team will check on when they arrive?"

"No doubt, but I'd like to get a look for myself since it might be my ass on the line. Plus, I want to check if any security devices are on the house and barn."

Juli agreed and warned Sam to be careful of tripwires since her squadron encountered a few on patrol.

Juli drove past the farmhouse and took her first left onto Country Farm Road. An old fieldstone wall lined the wooded area on the left side of the road. She slowed to a crawl until coming to a stop at a distance they estimated would be even with the barn. They agreed to stay in contact via their cell phones. Juli dropped Sam off while she returned to the previous surveillance spot to observe any movement on the property.

Sam walked into the woods through an opening in the stone wall. He figured the gap was wide enough for a vehicle to fit through it. The previous farmer must have cleared some trees and brush leading toward the barn. Sam figured the cleared area could have been a way for a tractor to get from the road to the farmhouse years ago. He also thought it could be a way of escape by a vehicle hidden in the barn.

Sam strolled among the trees, looking for tripwires or any device on the ground or attached to a tree. He moved towards the barn in baby steps, not noticing anything that looked like a security device. He tried keeping a tree between him and the barn to avoid detection as he moved forward. At the end of the tree line, Sam stopped behind a wide tree trunk, giving him an unobstructed view of the rear of the barn and the house. There were three windows on what Sam figured was a second level of the barn and no windows or doors on the ground level visible to him. The farmhouse had a typical back door, three windows on the first floor, and three on the second floor. The middle window on each floor was smaller, most likely a kitchen window on the first floor and a bathroom window upstairs.

He carefully canvassed the back of both structures, looking for security cameras or other observation devices, but noticed none. He called Juli, noting his findings, and asked if there was any activity on her end, with her answering no. He asked her to give him twenty minutes to assess the situation further and take photos before heading back to the road.

After taking several photos, he cautiously moved toward the back of the barn. Once at the barn, he pressed his ear to the barn wall, attempting to hear any sounds from within it. He heard none. He drifted from one corner of the barn to the next, feeling the structure and listening for sounds inside the barn. Once he reached the left corner of the barn, he took a quick peek at the side of the farmhouse. Two standard-sized windows on the bottom floor and two on the second floor were all he could see. Not wanting to take unnecessary risks of being seen, he moved back into the woods. As he retraced his steps towards the road, he received a call from Juli. "Sam, someone left the house, entered the carport, and backed out in a grey SUV. It's now heading up the driveway. Where are you?"

"I'm heading back to the road, but you have to tail the vehicle to see where it's heading. Leave plenty of space between you two. Keep the communication open so I know where you are going. You can pick me up later."

She stated she couldn't see which way the SUV turned out of the driveway.

"Stay put for a minute. Then, if it doesn't pass by you, assume it turned the other way and step on it to catch up."

Juli waited, but the SUV didn't pass her, so she turned onto Brewers Road and headed past the farmhouse. "Sam, it didn't pass me. I'm past the farmhouse now trying to catch up."

Now nearing the road, Sam saw a grey SUV pass by on Country Farm Road. "Juli, a grey SUV just passed by where you dropped me off. Head back this way and pick me up."

Once he saw the SUV drive over the small hill and out of sight, he ran across the street to wait for Juli. A minute later, Juli screeched her tires to a stop to pick him up and sped away.

Once driving over the hill, they spotted the SUV about a half-mile ahead. Juli stepped on the gas pedal to gain some distance before slowing down for the approaching intersection. The SUV had taken a left turn at the crossing. It was out of sight as Juli made the turn. She drove straight ahead for a short distance, where they came upon it parked in front of a small commercial building called the Crescent Drive Plaza that housed a market and a liquor store.

"Juli, park around the side of the building to screen your car from their view. I'll go into the liquor store, and you go into the market. Let's see what goes on inside and take a photo of the person if we get a chance."

Juli entered the market and glanced to the right, not seeing anyone other than the female cashier dressed in dark grey Muslim attire at the register counter. No one was in the aisle straight ahead. She grabbed the hand-carry basket and walked to the right, where there were two additional aisles. She saw a woman wearing a sweatshirt with a hood over her head and black jeans. She recognized it was the same outfit worn by the person leaving the farmhouse. Juli skipped the middle aisle and walked over to the cooler in front of the last aisle. She reached in to pick up two bottles of

Coca-Cola before walking swiftly down the third aisle, rounding the corner to come up behind the woman wearing the sweatshirt. Juli observed the woman reading the label on a can she'd taken from the shelf. The woman then placed it back on the shelf, selected two other cans, read the labels, and carried them to the register's counter.

Juli continued up the aisle, carefully placed the can the woman first held into her basket, and peeked around the corner of the aisle. Juli saw the woman was now at the cooler. Juli pretended to be looking at other groceries while the woman returned to the register with two milk containers and a six-pack of Coke. The woman spoke in a foreign language with the cashier for several minutes. Juli assumed they knew each other by the way they carried on. Finally, the woman left the store carrying two grocery bags and the Coke to her car.

As Juli walked to the register, she noticed the woman didn't get into her vehicle after placing her bags inside. Instead, she walked toward the liquor store. While the cashier totaled her purchase, Juli carefully held onto the can the woman first took from the shelf so the cashier could scan the barcode. Then, Juli placed it into the grocery bag herself. She would later have the can examined for the woman's fingerprints. While waiting for her change, she texted Sam that the woman was heading to the liquor store.

Inside the liquor store, Sam held one bottle of red wine while looking over several others. He glanced at the woman as she entered the store and pretended to look for additional bottles while watching her. He noticed the woman spoke in a foreign language to the cashier. The woman waited for the cashier to bring over an empty wine box and selected wines for her as they chatted like they were friends. The cashier chose four different beer labels while she gathered several bags of chips from a rack near the register's counter. Sam figured she was planning a celebration party at the farmhouse, or maybe a supply for several days. After totaling the woman's bill, the cashier told Sam in English that he'd be back in a minute. The cashier loaded the woman's purchase into a cart and wheeled it out to her car. Sam rushed to the glass door and took photos of the woman and the cashier as he loaded her bags into the trunk of her SUV. The cashier returned to the counter, where Sam waited to pay for the bottle of wine. He then left the store and met Juli, already waiting in her car.

They pulled out of the shop's parking lot and followed a distance behind the woman's SUV. They watched her turn right at the end of Country Farm Road onto Brewers Road and back to the farmhouse. Juli glanced at her watch, wondering when their replacements would arrive. She and Sam were tired and hungry. Sam suggested when their replacements come, they should stop to eat on the way back to Boston.

Juli said she had a better idea for them with a sensual smile. "Let's stop for takeout to bring to my apartment. We can enjoy the meal with the wine you purchased and have some fun afterward." She chuckled, but Sam didn't respond. "Well, Sam, if you don't want to, we can...."

"I didn't say I didn't want to. I'm game if you are."

"I thought you would like that idea."

"Juli, just being close to you is great."

"That's sweet, Sam. You're very special. I want you to know that."

"You're very special too, Juli, and I'm in for more fun tonight."

Juli gave him a beautiful, sensual smile. "I knew you would see it my way." That caused them to laugh.

After the joking subsided, Juli wondered why the tactical team members were late getting there. They continued their surveillance, observing no movement. Another twenty minutes went by before her cell phone rang. "Juli, this is Lieutenant Randell. Something came up, so the team members won't be there tonight. Two troopers will relieve you there shortly. Major Burke has scheduled a morning briefing at eight-thirty sharp in the conference room. Have the agent there as well."

The change of plans perplexed Juli. "Randell said two troopers are coming to relieve us instead of the tactical team members. Something doesn't sound right."

CHAPTER
16

It took another forty-five minutes before their replacements arrived. Two troopers arrived in an unmarked sedan and dressed as civilians. Since it was late, Sam recommended they have dinner close to her apartment at a restaurant and skip the fun at her place until another time.

"We're both tired and need to sleep. I also need to spend time with my son. We could repeat having fun another time. Anticipation makes it more exciting."

Juli frowned in disappointment. "I understand."

Sam spent the night at Drew's apartment. When in bed, he decided to be cautious with his relationship with Juli since he would be returning to Hartford when the investigation was over. He liked her a lot but worried the relationship was moving too fast. The last thing Sam wanted was to hurt Juli.

*   *   *

Sam arrived at the state police headquarters at eight-forty-five the following morning. After displaying his identification to the desk officer, they buzzed him into the lobby. Juli was waiting to greet him and guided him to the conference room. Inside the room, Sam noticed officers filled most of the chairs surrounding the sizeable rectangular table, including the additional chairs lined up towards the back of the room. Juli pointed to the two empty chairs near the head of the table. Andrea sat to the right of the two empty chairs. Once seated, Sam nodded to Lieutenant Randell seated across from him. The two chairs at the head of the table remained empty.

Several minutes later, Major Burke entered the room, greeted everyone, and sat at one of the empty chairs at the head of the table. Burke first had everyone individually stand and introduce themselves. All were state police detectives or tactical team members, except an Assistant Distant Attorney (ADA) and Sam. Major Burke then described the investigation that began with the shooting of Trooper Phillips. Finally, he summarized the progress made in the investigation to date.

Burke looked around the room for questions, but there were none, so he continued. "Detective Ospino recovered fingerprints of three suspects. We received fingerprint results late yesterday identifying those three, all Iranians. One, a woman identified as Melika Hajim, who we now believe drove the van. She came to the U.S. four years ago under an approved student visa. She attended Boston University and dropped out of sight after graduating. We identified another suspect as Ameen Nazari, who entered the country on a work visa three years ago, working for a hi-tech company called Interphase along the Route 128 corridor. His visa got re-approved once. Then, when the company no longer needed him, he disappeared. Finally, we identified the third suspect as Rashid Al Madari. Al Madari's name caused a call from the FBI. We'll learn more about him from the FBI when they arrive here.

Burke paused again when his cell phone vibrated. He looked at the screen and didn't answer it. He continued. "We have the farmhouse property under surveillance. We originally planned to have our tactical team execute search warrants there. However, the call from the FBI postponed any issuance of a warrant. The Boston FBI Special Agent in Charge, members of his staff, and an Assistant U.S. Attorney requested a sit-down today at eleven o'clock. We expect they will request to take over our investigation. We scheduled Colonel Greg Matthews to be here at ten this morning. We will brief him on our operational plan and response to the FBI. Sergeant Frank Moore, our SWAT team tactical leader, will brief the Colonel regarding recommendations provided by Detectives Ospino, Bishop, Serrano, Agent Caviello, and the tactical team. We will go around the room for additional ideas before our ADA Arnie Carlson provides the legalities and authorities we face in dealing with the FBI and the suspects."

At 10:05 am, Colonel Greg Matthews entered the room. For thirty minutes, Matthews listened to Major Burke and tactical team leader Sergeant Frank Moore provide a list of recommendations under consideration to employ in an operational plan for raiding the farmhouse.

ADA Carlson followed with suggestions in dealing with the FBI to ensure the state gets to prosecute the shooter of Trooper Phillips on the charge of attempted murder of a police officer. The ADA felt we should charge and prosecute the other four suspects, Ganani and the Imam, with conspiracy and aiding and abetting the shooter. The Colonel asked for a clarification on several recommendations to his satisfaction that ended the session. Major Burke dismissed everyone except those he wanted to return for the briefing with the FBI after a ten-minute break. Those included Lieutenant Randell, the tactical team leader, his assistant, the ADA, Detectives Ospino, Bishop, Collins, Serrano, and Sam.

A few minutes before eleven, those invited back to the briefing sat around the conference table in designated seats. Major Burke was waiting at the front entrance to greet the FBI. Shortly after that, Burke entered the room and introduced the FBI Special Agent in Charge (SAC), Austin Taylor, Supervisory Special Agent Vondell "Dell" Haskins, the Hostage Rescue Team (HRT) leader Jesse Carter, and Assistant U.S. Attorney (AUSA) Donna Ranero.

SAC Taylor greeted those seated before he began his briefing. "Rashid Al Madari, identified as an Iranian terrorist, has been red-flagged by the FBI going back three years, and it troubles us to learn of his presence here in the U.S. In conversations with Major Burke, we have the identities of others associated with Al Madari. Additionally, we learned from you that he and his associates held a hostage and shot Trooper Phillips. The fact he and his associates shot a state trooper and are holding a hostage has the U.S. government's full attention. We are grateful for the fine work of your department in identifying the suspects in this violent group and their location."

Taylor took a drink of water before continuing. "Using the description of the hostage we learned from your investigation, the FBI began a search for any kidnappings of young American females. We found four missing young women in the northeast, one of which we believe may be the young woman being held hostage by these suspects. She is the daughter of a naval officer who helped plan the bombing of a remote camp in Iran where our intel reported a top Hezbollah leader and his closest combatants trained."

Taylor paused to allow everyone in the room to absorb what he said. "Two of the other three kidnapped Americans are also daughters of naval officers. We haven't identified everyone killed at that campsite, but we've estimated that it was between fifteen and twenty, including several young women combatants who were part of the training. Based on our intel and internet chatter, our profilers interpreted the kidnapping of young American females as reprisal for bombing young women at their training camp. They believe this radical group plans to kill American women on U.S. soil."

*   *   *

"Yeah. Whooz this?" asked Dellagatti.

"It's me, Tony. Have you been able to find a contractor who can do the job?" asked Foster Harrington.

"Oh, hey, boss. Yeah, I got hold of the guy— the business guy. He can do it if it's local, but if not, he can't leave the area because of a personal problem. I didn't use any names, but he understood the work. He said if it's local, fine, but if it's out-of-state, it would cost extra."

Harrington knew it was going to cost him. "What's he talking about on the tab?"

Dellagatti replied, "He wants twenty big ones if it's not local. Half before and the rest when they finish the job."

"That's a big number. Any way you can get him down a bit?"

Dellagatti answered, "Not if it involves travel, boss. It might even cost more depending on how far, ya know. Do ya know where the work has to get done? If it's not nearby, the guy has more work to do, like travel, the cost of staying over, and such. So, what do ya want me to do?"

"You still remember my private number?" asked Forster.

"Yeah, I member it."

"Well, I had the number changed. The last four numbers are 3-0-0-0. So remember it."

"Got it, boss."

"Rach has the phone now. Give me a couple of days to talk to her. Then have your guy call her on that new number for the details and the first installment. Understand?"

"Yeah, boss, give him ya old number that now ends with 3-0-0-0 and call her for whatever and the first payment. Anythin' else?" asked Dellagatti.

Harrington answered, "Yeah. When he calls, have him say it's for Dickie, so she will know what it's about."

"Got it. Where are ya, boss?"

"Tony, don't ask questions I can't answer." He ended the call.

CHAPTER
17

The information the FBI gave the officers seated around the conference room table concerned them. Agent Taylor cleared his throat before continuing. "I assume most of you feel we're here to steal your thunder and take over your investigation. That is not the case. The FBI is here to supplement your department's impressive progress in uncovering what the government now believes is a terrorist threat against American citizens, right here at home. We propose establishing a task force to work jointly with your department to stop whatever plan these radicals have to harm Americans."

Taylor then turned to AUSA Donna Ranero, who concurred with the FBI's response.

"We propose our office coordinate with the State DA's Office to ensure these men and their associates get prosecuted for their criminal acts to the fullest extent of federal and state laws. We can make prosecutable decisions jointly to promote the severest consequences for each of these suspects, especially where we can prosecute both under federal and state statutes."

Sam and the state officers sat listening to the federal officials promise to work as a team and share whatever credit was due. Still, after the arrests and prosecutions, they knew the news headlines would highlight the success of the FBI and U.S. Attorney's office with a short blurb somewhere buried in the story where the feds credit the state police for their assistance. When the federal spokespersons finished their pitch, a short period of questions and recommendations were open for discussion.

Questions revolved around who would have the overall command and control of the operation to lead the raid at the farmhouse, who would handle the press conferences, and what court would prosecute most of the suspects. AUSA Ranero answered those questions.

"We will determine prosecutions based on where we can get the severest punishment for the crime. Our focus is on immediate close-up surveillance of the property to establish the safest plan in securing the suspects without harming the hostages or injuring our officers. We will hold press conferences jointly."

The focal point of the conversations then turned to the FBI's tactical leader agent Jesse Carter and the state's tactical leader Frank Moore. Sam listened to both men who, as yet, hadn't laid eyes on the farmhouse. Since time was of the essence, SAC Taylor interrupted the discussions, saying he and Major Burke agreed to continue the conversation tomorrow morning in Boston at the U.S. Attorney's Office on the fourth floor of the Federal Courthouse.

Sam raised his hand to get noticed. When he didn't, he spoke out saying he had input to share. When Sam got their attention, he passed to the two tactical leaders photos taken from the road out front of the property the day before. First, he pointed out the carport and the woods running along the backside of the barn. Then, he referred to a second photo.

"Country Farm Road runs parallel to the woods on the east side. Notice the opening in the stone wall. I walked through that opening into the woods yesterday, carefully checking for tripwires and security devices. I found none. I walked to the rear of the barn and closely canvassed the rooflines of the house and barn for security devices but saw none. I caution that just because I didn't see any doesn't mean there aren't any."

He directed them to the photos of the back of the barn and house and gave his thoughts on potential escape routes. He also recommended using thermal imaging devices to help determine the location and number of occupants in the farmhouse and the barn.

Sam continued with the observations and recommendations. "Capturing images at night will hopefully tell us how many occupants are in each building and maybe identify where they hold the hostages. The suspects might spend their daytime hours in the farmhouse but retire to the barn, providing them more time to escape. If you can identify persons with little or no movement, it may point to where they have the hostages. We should know the configuration of the barn inside. They may have set it up for defensive purposes. I studied the farm's layout and believed the best approach would be for one tactical team, under cover of darkness, to advance from the road along a berm, giving you cover up to the back of the carport. Then, I would have a second-team advance through the woods to the back of the barn and around to the front door. As state building codes require, there are no alternative exit doors on the sides or back of the barn. That caused me to believe there is a secret escape route that we must consider. Also, since the closest hospital is nearly ten miles from the farm, it would be wise to have multiple ambulances with trained EMTs at the site or on standby. Finally, I recommend having fire apparatus, an explosives ordinance team, and a cadre of uniformed police officers for traffic control surrounding the whole area."

Jesse Carter, the HRT leader for the FBI, asked, "Do you have any specific intel indicating we will encounter a firefight?"

Sam responded, "When we interviewed an associate, he described at least six or seven heavy long black tactical bags and two closed wooden boxes transported to the farmhouse. He didn't know what was inside those provisions and couldn't carry anything into the house. When you review the security camera video from the used car lot where the suspects abandoned their van, you will see they carried four tactical bags. You can guess what they probably contain since they shot Trooper Phillips with an assault rifle normally carried in those types of bags. Regarding the boxes, I would prepare for anything."

Carter contended, "The boxes simply could be provisions, clothing, blankets, food, or water?"

Sam countered, "Yes, they could, but they could also be weapons, ammunition, body armor, even explosives. So we should prepare an operational plan for the worst-case scenario."

Carter stared at Caviello and asked, "Who are you again?"

Major Burke cut in and answered. "He is ATF Agent Sam Caviello, an integral part of our team. Sam initially spotted the hostage in the van at the gas station. He observed the shooter gun down our trooper with an assault weapon and provided life-saving aid to her while calling for the ambulance. We credit him for finding the abandoned van that led to learning the identity of some of our suspects. I should also mention he is a former leader of ATF's Special Response Team in Boston. We owe him a tremendous amount of gratitude."

The FBI SAC reacted by saying, "Well, we certainly would like Agent Caviello to participate in our joint operational team."

"I'd be disappointed if not invited. I'll be there and prepared for what I believe will be a battle," answered Sam.

Finally, the briefing ended by one in the afternoon after Major Burke and Taylor agreed to share twenty-four-hour surveillance at the farmhouse and had supervisors from both sides work out a schedule.

Juli whispered to Sam to follow her to a vacant office, where she gave him a quick hug and said, "Your suggestions and recommendation to the Feebs were awesome, Sam. You're amazing. I got annoyed when their agent questioned who you were. Anyway, can you meet Andrea and me for the celebration dinner tonight? Andrea said you suggested it to her earlier?"

"Absolutely. Do you have a place in mind?"

"Yes. It's a restaurant near my apartment. You'll like it. We invited Andrea's sister, Mariana, and her daughter Micaela and I'd like you to invite your son. We want to get to know him."

"Thanks, I will. Right now, I need to get to the ATF office to update my boss and stop in to see my son. I'll call you later."

While driving to Boston, Sam got another call from the reporter, Alli Gaynor, who had asked if he could meet for dinner during the upcoming week.

"I'll do my best, Alli. I have a briefing tomorrow that could put me on hold for a few days or possibly more. I'm assisting the state police in an investigation that I can't discuss right now. I'll call you as soon as I can."

"I'll be in Boston for the better part of next week, and I'm dying to see you, Sam. So I hope we can get together. I have a lot to tell you about my job in DC, and I want to know all about what you've been doing."

"That sounds great. Unfortunately, I'm involved with something big and don't know how long it will last. I have your number. If you don't hear from me a couple of days after arriving, please call me." While driving to Boston, Sam took a moment to reflect on the investigation and his conversation with Alli. *Everything's happening now, and there's no way of knowing when or if I'll be able to meet her.*

Sam called his boss and asked to meet to bring him up to speed on the state investigation. When he arrived there, his boss, Gary Hopkins, was briefed on the status of the state investigation. Hopkins asked many questions, some of which Sam couldn't answer, but one, in particular, he reluctantly answered.

"I should have known the FBI would insert themselves into the state's investigation. If they're planning on raiding the farm, could you suggest our tactical team take point?" asked Hopkins.

"I'll mention it to the U.S. Attorney tomorrow at the briefing, but I wouldn't count on them agreeing to have a third team added to their operational plan. I'll do my best." Once the briefing was over, Sam's only thought was it probably would be better if the ATF team stayed out of it.

After meeting with his boss, Sam called his son, whose office was in the same building, to let him know he was on his way to see him. He left the ATF office and took the elevator to the seventh floor, where his son, Drew, was waiting for him at his office's reception desk. First, Drew introduced him to the Special Agent in Charge, Pat O'Shae, who asked him to stop in his office for a chat once he finished with his son. Next, Drew introduced Sam to the administrative staff and the agents in the office, including his training agent, Eric Mills. Once the greetings and small talk finished, Sam took a few minutes to update Drew on the investigative progress of the state case.

"By the way, when you introduced me to the admin staff, who was the young woman with blonde hair sitting in the far cubicle?"

"She's a new hire. Her name is Madison, but she goes by Maddie."

"She's a doll. Is she married or has a steady guy?"

"Dad, she's too young for you."

Sam chuckled. "I'm not interested in her. I'm asking for you."

"I don't think it would be a good idea to date a colleague in the workplace."

"So you're interested but concerned about workplace dating? I think dating those you work with is becoming commonplace. Unless the agency or your boss has a rule against it, go for it. Just keep the romance outside the workplace. Look at me. I'm doing it. The detective assigned to the shooting and I have become an item. If you remember, her name is Juli Ospino. I'm joining her and her best friend, another female detective, for dinner tonight. Juli wanted me to invite you to join us. She'd like to get to know you, and I'd like you to be there. We could ride over to the restaurant together."

"Yeah, okay, but you're not trying to fix me up with Juli's friend, are you?"

"No, she's in her thirties and has an eight-year-old daughter. But, if you would like to invite Maddie to join us, that would be great."

"I don't think so. Maddie's new to the office. Maybe I could join her for coffee sometime."

"Good plan. I'd like to see you have friends here in Boston and not all male friends."

"Yeah, I hear you."

"I'll see you at the apartment around six."

Before leaving the office, Sam stopped to chat with Drew's boss, Pat O'Shae. Pat praised Sam's son as a fast learner and a promising young agent. Sam thought O'Shae had a down-to-earth manner and seemed like a nice guy and an ideal boss. O'Shae suggested they meet for lunch sometime while Sam was still in Boston.

"I look forward to it, Pat." But as Sam left the office, he wondered when he'd find the time.

CHAPTER
18

Just before six, Sam and Drew were on their way to the restaurant when Sam asked his son if he had any concerns about his father dating Juli.

"Not in the slightest. I saw that you and mom were growing apart. The breakup was mutual, and you both are still on friendly terms. Mom is dating, so you should get on with your life too. I remember you had your eye on that detective. I'm only surprised it happened so fast."

"Miracles happen. I like Juli a lot and hope our relationship continues."

Drew mentioned he was familiar with the restaurant they were going to. "Agent Mills and I lunched there last week. It's a popular place in the neighborhood with good food and drinks but lousy parking. It shouldn't be too busy on a weekday, though. Wait till you see the view overlooking the river and the Boston skyline."

Drew was right. Parking was at a premium, causing Drew to park half a football field away from the restaurant. Sam saw Juli's car parked near the restaurant front and figured she had arrived early. It was a beautiful day. The sun shone brightly, with few clouds in the sky and a slight cool breeze blowing across the river.

The restaurant hostess greeted them and asked if they had a reservation. Before answering, Sam pointed to the table where Juli was waving at him. Seeing that, the host escorted Sam and Drew to Juli's table by a window with a beautiful view of the river and the city skyline. Juli, Andrea, and her sister Mariana greeted Sam and Drew with hugs. Next, Sam turned to Andrea's daughter, Micaela, and said hello.

Juli and Andrea nearly finished a bottle of Champagne. Mariana was driving, so she didn't drink. "We arrived early and ordered three bottles of champagne at the happy hour price. The other two bottles are on ice," said Andrea.

Juli grabbed a bottle from the ice bucket, already uncorked, and filled Sam and Drew's glasses. Sam held up his glass and said, "To Juli and Andrea's continued success with the investigation at hand and all those that follow. Also, good health, long life, friendship, and happiness for all of us." They all sipped the champagne.

Dinner was delicious. The champagne perfectly matched the salmon with skillet potatoes and asparagus for the women and fresh Halibut with the same potato and veggie for Drew and Sam. They enjoyed fresh focaccia bread with the meal and a special Tahitian vanilla bean vinaigrette dressing over a blend of green lettuce covered with tropical berries, pomegranates, and walnuts. The dessert was a rich, creamy New York-style cheesecake with strawberry topping. Micaela enjoyed sharing the salad, small pieces of fish from everyone's plate, and her own hot fudge sundae. She also enjoyed the constant attention given to her by Sam and Drew.

Everyone shared a little about themselves to get to know each other and told funny stories about their younger days. They enjoyed the lively chatter, which lasted nearly two hours. Sam picked up the tab with a generous tip as they toasted one last time with the remaining drops of champagne. Earlier, Sam had told Drew he would hitch a ride with Juli to her place and probably spend the night. Andrea and Micaela drove back to Framingham with Mariana.

Back at Juli's apartment, Sam and Juli drank chardonnay wine while feeding each other grapes like in the days of ancient Rome. They laughed and joked around while watching television repeats of the sitcom Friends. When Juli excused herself for a trip to the bathroom, Sam changed the station to watch the Red Sox game already in the sixth inning. Not long later, Juli walked back into the living room wearing a skimpy negligee. She stood there waiting for Sam to notice her.

When he did, he was in awe. "Wow. I see you're not interested in watching TV anymore."

"Well, you can watch TV if you'd rather."

"Uh, no. I kinda like watching you better."

She put out her hand for Sam to take and led him to the bedroom.

She helped Sam undress and, while doing so, asked if he'd like to shower first, but when he finished undressing, she added, "Oh, on second thought, it looks like you're ready to go."

It was another long night of passionate love, talking, laughing, and learning more about each other as the bright moon glow beamed through the window. The beam glittered on Sam and Juli as they slept.

Sam had set the alarm for six-thirty to ensure they would make it to the federal courthouse in time, but neither moved an inch when the alarm sounded. When it kept buzzing, Juli sluggishly shut it off.

Sam was the first to crawl out of bed. "Oh, boy. I'm not sure I'm going to recover soon." He shook Juli to get her to wake up. "I'm heading to the shower. Want to join me?"

Hearing that, Juli didn't hesitate to get out of bed and follow Sam into the bathroom. Unfortunately, the shower fun wasn't quite as intense, not because of the lack of energy but the lack of time.

*   *   *

Rachel Peterson was busy running the Harrington construction business while learning by on-the-job training from Gus Walker, her dad's confidante. Running the business wasn't easy, but she was bright and putting in long hours to make the company profitable again.

Her husband, Ron, did what he could by watching their daughter, Olivia, cooking and cleaning their home. Rachel's mom also babysat Olivia, and sometimes Rachel brought her to the office to watch with the help of her Executive Assistant, Susan Michaels.

Rachel spent most of her days on the phone and the computer. At times, when she needed a break, she walked around the paths on the company grounds. She was about to pour herself another cup of coffee when her dad's private cell phone rang.

"Hello." There was silence for an instant. "Who's calling, please?"

"This is Sonny. I'm calling for Dickie. I need half now and the details. Let's meet in person."

Rachel was a little nervous about having any connection to the plan her father had to get even with Sam Caviello.

She bluntly responded to his request. "That's not how it's going to happen. There's a lunch wagon parked near 2100 Riverdale Road in New Haven. Be there the day after tomorrow at ten in the morning before the crowd gathers for lunch. There will be a guy reading a paper on the bench nearby. Call him Leo. You tell him Tony D sent you. He'll have an envelope for you, and don't call this number again until you complete the job." She hung up.

CHAPTER
19

Sam rode with Juli to the federal courthouse in Boston. They were twenty minutes early, so they went to the courthouse cafeteria for a quick breakfast. They saw Andrea sitting with Detective Kevin Bishop when they entered the cafe and joined them at their table.

Juli had a grilled corn muffin with their coffee. Sam ordered two scrambled eggs with wheat toast and coffee. Andrea talked non-stop about the great time she, her sister, and Micaela had during last night's dinner.

"Andrea, Micaela is so adorable. You're doing a great job bringing her up," said Sam.

"My sister gets most of the credit for that. She has two daughters, twelve and ten, and they are the dominant influence on Micaela."

Before nine o'clock, the four arrived at the U.S. Attorney's Office and got escorted to the large conference room. Sam saw fifteen chairs squeezed around the twelve-foot conference table, and the twenty-five folding chairs circulated the back of the table. AUSA Donna Ranero introduced the U.S. Attorney, Lucas Steward, and asked those in attendance to stand one by one and introduce themselves. Sam counted sixteen FBI agents, twelve tactical team members from the state police, seven uniformed state police officers, three state command officers, and six from the U.S. Attorney's office. He was the lone ATF agent.

Lucas Steward provided only opening remarks before handing it over to Donna Ranero, FBI SAC Taylor, and his tactical team leader, Jesse Carter. Ranero and Taylor covered the topics for the first hour before the tactical teams planned their strategy during the afternoon session. Sam was disinterested in listening to the fed's procedures on how agents and police need to conduct themselves during a raid, emphasizing the policy on the use of excessive force. They used a PowerPoint presentation on case studies and court precedent decisions. Sam had seen similar presentations often during his time with ATF. He understood state officers might need the information presented, but for the most part, state laws frequently mirrored federal law based on Supreme Court decisions.

Finally, a discussion began between the tactical and investigating officers. The group discussed the possible number of combatants and their weaponry and devices. Also, the dialogue included copies of the farmhouse and barn floor plans and when to conduct the raid with the best chance of surprising the suspects. Generally, entry into a home or building would often happen in the early morning hours when suspects were sleeping and unprepared to respond quickly. However, this was a unique situation since the raid targets were terrorists. The tactical team leaders outlined how and when they would survey the farm to determine entry points, obstacles, escape routes, equipment needs, and the number of personnel required.

They assigned the administrative staff to establish contact persons for local police, the fire department, utility companies, and medical facility locations. In addition, they chose two agents to select an appropriate staging area nearby for the command post vehicle and prepare the best sites where state police cruisers would secure all roads. Also, where to assign local and state police to protect nearby schools.

The number of personnel involved in preparing for the raid was mindboggling. The plan called for the tactical teams to enter the farmhouse and barn and secure all suspects and property. Then, the search and evidence collection teams would enter both premises and do their job. They assigned additional tactical teams as a backup in case they encountered fierce resistance from the suspects. Medical personnel was to be on standby in case of injury. At the close of the day's discussions, the FBI informed all raid participants to reconvene at ten the following morning at the FBI office in Chelsea for an updated briefing to outline the final operational plan, personnel assignments, and the date and time of the raid would begin.

During the day's briefing, Sam attentively listened to the preparations discussed, but he felt everyone should know about any missing factors before executing the plan. His past observations of the barn troubled him since the structure lacked the typical design. Therefore, he decided to find out more about the interior floor layout and knew where to get the information. After the meeting, Sam stopped by Lucas Stewart's office regarding his bosses' request to include ATF's tactical team in the raid plan.

"Lucas, you considered adding additional tactical units, if needed. However, it would be beneficial to use a second FBI tactical team instead of outside agencies like ATF. The reason for this is not all tactical teams train the same. They use different signaling and communications equipment, and their distinctive procedures could cause problems communicating, affecting the overall performance." Stewart agreed it was a good point and would discuss it with the FBI leadership.

* * *

Sonny exited his car parked near 2100 Riverdale Road and walked toward the lunch wagon. He surveyed the area to ensure there were no police nearby. He observed a guy sitting alone on a bench reading a newspaper several yards past the lunch wagon.

He studied the guy before approaching and speaking to him. "Uh, I presume you're Leo, right?"

The guy sitting on the bench looked up at Sonny. "Yes, I'm Leo. Do I know you?"

"Tony D sent me, and I understand you have something for me."

Leo nodded affirmatively. He reached for a brown paper bag tucked behind him and handed it to Sonny. Sonny opened the bag and counted ten wrapped thousand-dollar bundles and a sheet of paper identifying the target. He was content with the bag's contents and uttered, "Nice doing business with you, Leo. Hope to see you again in a week or two." He turned and walked back to his car.

CHAPTER
20

S am arrived in his SUV the following day at the FBI office in Chelsea. He searched for Juli in the crowded room and spotted her talking with Detectives Bishop and Collins. He moved closer to get her attention, motioning her to meet with him. She excused herself and followed Sam out to the corridor.

"I'm still concerned we don't have enough information about the barn's layout. I called the town building inspector's office and arranged to review the barn's building plans. I know the FBI already has a copy, but I suspect they made changes not reflected in the blueprints that could affect the raid's operational plan. The farmhouse interior probably has a standard layout for houses built during those years, but the reconstructed barn we saw on surveillance does not match a typical barn's blueprints. The entry team needs to know what's on the other side of the barn door when they enter."

"Let's head up there now," suggested Juli. Sam agreed.

They arrived at the town hall an hour later. They entered the building department and asked for Harold Bennett, the building director. Bennett appeared from his work cubicle and met them at the front counter. "You must be Agent Caviello."

Sam identified himself and Juli as a state police detective.

"It took me nearly an hour in the basement archive room to locate the folder containing the permits and plans for that house and barn. Come to this side of the counter where I'll spread out the plans so we can look at them together." Bennett pointed to the farmhouse schematics first. "The farmhouse was originally built in 1958 with no additions or major alterations other than the addition of a carport used for farm tractors. They added the carport in 1960. Unfortunately, the inspector for the construction of the house passed away a few years back. The owners sold the property in 1986. Fire destroyed the original barn in 1989. The new owner had it rebuilt in 1991."

He pointed to the plans that reflected a structure similar to most barns, with two wide barn doors in the front, one window on each side, and an exit door on the south side near the rear.

"Does the same person still own the property?" asked Juli.

"No. Getting on in age, the owner became ill and eventually passed away sometime during 2014. He had no family besides his wife and one son who lived in California. His wife lived there for a year, maybe two, before putting the property up for sale and moving in with her son. The property sat unsold for quite a while. It eventually got sold and purchased by its current owner late in 2017. As I recall, the new owner didn't move in right away. I remember the property was unoccupied when the barn got heavily damaged by another fire a few months after purchasing it. According to the fire marshal, the fire was suspicious, but the DA ruled there wasn't sufficient evidence to prove it was intentionally set. It took the owner quite a while to settle his claim with the insurance company. Finally, in early 2019, they began construction to rebuild the barn."

"Can you tell us the new owner's name?" asked Juli.

"Let's see. Here it is. His name is Shadrad Abedini."

"Were you the inspector overseeing the construction?" asked Sam.

"No. I was the department director at the time. According to the record, the inspector was Tucker Ferguson."

"Is he working today?" asked Sam.

"Tucker retired at the end of 2019, not long after submitting the final inspection report on that property. After retirement, he got married, and the scuttlebutt was his wife had money and was much younger than him."

"Does he still live in the area?" asked Juli.

"Tucker moved to New Hampshire near the shoreline with his new bride."

"Do you have a number and address for him?" asked Sam

"I'll have to look it up on my cell phone."

Once he found it, Bennett gave Sam and Juli the number and address. Since Sam planned to pay a visit to Ferguson, he wanted to take the building plans and inspection reports with him. Bennett said that could be a problem since he would have to get an okay to release them.

"We can't wait for that, Harold. This is an emergency situation. I'll give you a receipt and return them to you tomorrow. No one will know they left your office," promised Sam.

Sam and Juli arrived at Ferguson's New Hampshire address an hour later with the building plans in hand.

"This is some swanky home in an upscale town near the ocean. It had to cost him a bundle," remarked Juli.

"Yeah. It seems that way, but right now, the more important thing is to get some answers from him. Lights are on in the house. Let's ring the doorbell."

Once the doorbell rang, it only took seconds for the door to open.

"Mr. Ferguson, I'm Special Agent Sam Caviello, and this is State Police Detective Juli Ospino. May we come in and ask you a few questions about a construction project you worked on when you were a building inspector a few years back? We met with Harold Bennett before arriving here, and he told us you were the inspector on the project. I have the building plans and the inspection report you signed and would like to discuss them with you."

"Was there something wrong with the plans?" asked Ferguson.

"We don't know. Since you were the inspector, we're hoping you could point out any possible changes to the building made but not reflected in the inspection report. May we come in and show you the building plans?

I'm not an engineer or building inspector. I hoped you could explain the building codes required for the structure and the procedures for final approval of the project."

"Couldn't Harold have explained all that to you at the town hall?"

"He couldn't answer our questions and recommended we talk to you since you were the inspector. It shouldn't take long. We would appreciate your help. May we come in and explain further?" requested Sam.

"If it's only going to take a few minutes. I'll do my best to help you where I can."

Ferguson showed Sam and Juli into the large living room. The room had designer furniture arranged in a U-shape around a long glass-top coffee table. The room contained a large-screen television mounted on the wall above a fieldstone fireplace that warmed the room from the glowing flames crackling high within the hearth. The only framed family picture sat below a tall ceramic lamp on the end table.

"Can I get you both something to drink? Coffee, juice, water, anything?" asked Ferguson.

Juli began to say no thank you, but Sam interrupted and asked for coffee.

"I can brew some. We have a Keurig. It'll only take a couple of minutes," answered Ferguson.

"We'll each have a cup, thanks, Tucker," said Sam.

When Ferguson left the room, Juli whispered, "I didn't want coffee."

Sam reached for the family photo on the end table and showed it to Juli. "I wanted to show you this photo of him and his wife with Tucker out of the room."

Juli looked surprised. "Oh my God, she looks Middle Eastern. You think she's Iranian?"

"If she is, we need to know if she's connected to the farm's owner." Sam took a picture of the photo after quietly placing it back on the end table.

Ferguson returned with two cups of coffee, a container of half and half, and several small packets of sugar on a tray. Sam thanked Ferguson for the coffee and started a conversation about the town and the house, trying to get Ferguson in a reasonable frame of mind. "How long did you work at the building department, and how are you enjoying retirement in New Hampshire?"

"I worked at the department for thirty years, the last ten as a lead inspector. Retirement is better than I thought it would be, which I attribute to being married to a lovely woman."

"Well, congratulations to you and your wife on your marriage."

Pointing to the framed picture, Juli asked, "Is that a picture of you and your lovely wife?"

"Yes, and thank you. I'm a lucky guy to have met Tsarina, especially at my age. We wanted to live closer to the shore and found a home that was a short walking distance to it. We take walks along the beach when the weather permits. She's visiting her cousin now. They like to get together every month."

Sam said he'd like to spread out the building schematics he brought on the long coffee table. Ferguson removed the tray to the kitchen, and when he returned, the building plans were all set up for him to review.

Sam pointed to the building plans for the barn. "I'm particularly interested in the blueprints for the barn built on this farm."

Once Ferguson recognized the documents, he frowned with a crinkled face, a curled lower lip and clinched jaw. Concerned and with uneasiness in his voice, he looked at Sam and asked, "Why are you interested in asking about this property?"

"I just have some basic questions about the barn's foundation. Also, I'd like to know more about the front doorway? From the road, it looks like the barn has a single standard door found on a typical home rather than two large barn doors, as shown on the approved blueprints. In addition, it appears there is a second-floor level. Also, it seems that the barn lacks the required fire exits."

Awkwardly, Ferguson rebuffed answering Sam's question. "Hmm, all I can say is they constructed the barn according to code, and it passed inspection, as you can see from the Certificate of Occupancy. Harold could easily have explained that rather than have you drive here for me to tell you."

"Harold couldn't answer if the foundation got poured as a slab or like a full basement found in most homes. He couldn't answer that because he wasn't the inspector. He also couldn't explain why the front door was different and why there weren't any fire exits. It seems the barn doesn't comply with code."

Ferguson was silent as he examined the documents, apparently considering his answer.

"Why is the federal government concerned about a barn constructed in a small rural community back in 2019?"

"Tucker, you were the inspector for the construction of the barn. Could you describe the depth of the foundation?"

"As the plans show, it was a six-inch slab with wire mesh and a crushed stone base with concrete piers under each supporting post, all according to code."

"So you are telling me that the foundation was a slab of concrete and not an eight-foot deep basement type foundation that you would ordinarily find in a home like yours here?" asked Sam.

"That's what it shows in the plans. You can see that for yourself," replied Ferguson.

"What about the barn doors, the apparent second floor, and the lack of exit doors?" asked Juli.

"Again, as the blueprint shows, the barn had standard-width dual barn doors, with a second-level loft and an exit door in the rear corner, all according to code," said Ferguson.

"And this is what you examined and approved?" asked Sam.

"That's my signature on the bottom of the final inspection report," Ferguson answered.

Sam removed two close-up photographs of the front and side of the barn taken from the road. He had photos of all sides of the barn but didn't want Ferguson to know he took them from the woods while he was on the property.

Sam showed the two photos to Ferguson. "These photos of the barn taken recently do not match the plans and what you tell us. The front of the barn looks more like a house, with a single door and two first-level windows."

Ferguson shrugs his shoulders and states, "That's not how it was when I inspected it. I can only guess the owner must have made changes later on. Now that I think back, I remember the owner telling me he was thinking about hiring summer farmworkers from the islands, and he would need to have a place for them to sleep. So maybe he made some minor changes. You should have Harold look for a recent application for new or added construction."

"Harold told us these were the latest and only plans since 2019. Do you remember the owner's name?" said Sam.

"I don't remember the names of all the owners. I deal mostly with the contractors. The owner's name should be on file or on your documents. I don't know what else I can tell you. If there are no more questions, I have to get ready to pick up my wife at her cousin's place."

"Okay, Tucker. We are sorry to bother you. Thanks for your input and the coffee. Have a good evening," said Sam.

Once in Juli's car, Sam recommended finding a secluded area to watch the house to see if Ferguson left to pick up his wife or travel straight to the farmhouse. "Do you think he was straight with us, Juli?"

"Hell, no. When Tucker saw the building documents were for the farm, he looked like a deer caught in the headlights."

"Can you request your department to do a background on Shahrad Abedini? Let's also find out if Ferguson's wife, Tsarina, is related to him."

"I'll call it into our intel unit first thing in the morning."

Juli and Sam observed Ferguson pulling out of his driveway and heading south ten minutes later. Sam used binoculars to capture the vehicle's registration. A while later, Juli and Sam agreed that Ferguson was heading in the farm's direction.

CHAPTER
21

ATF Agent Jennifer Clarkson was busy reviewing investigative reports behind the desk typically occupied by Sam Caviello. In Sam's absence, Jennifer was the designated supervisor while he assisted the Massachusetts State Police.

At nine in the morning, agent Rick Ziglar walked into her office. Ziggy, as his colleagues called him, was five-foot-six and weighed one hundred and fifty pounds. He was an ex-Marine Corps captain who served in Afghanistan. He was short but built like a bulldog. He actively exercised by running five miles most days of the week and occasionally pumped iron at a local gym. On the job, he was a workhorse, being one of the most productive agents in the office, and why Sam assigned him to the Connecticut State Police Drug Task Force. Ziggy was an easy-going team player who was an ideal representative working jointly with the state task force. He was married with two boys in college and a daughter in high school and was well-liked among his colleagues. The office staff enjoyed Ziggy's sense of humor and considered him an amateur comedian.

"Zig, what a surprise. What the hell are you doing here? Did you get lost finding your way to the task force office?" asked Jennifer.

"Ha-ha, that's funny, Jen. You just miss me and are jealous because you're stuck behind the desk rather than in the field. I'm here to fill you in on a potentially big case. One of the task force officers, Ruben, and I stopped to have a beer at a café in New Haven last night. When we walked into the café, one of Ruben's CIs was sitting at the bar and saw us come in. He wandered over to us when we sat at a table in the back. The CI mentioned an associate asked if he could do a contract hit. The CI hangs out in the New Haven area, where he enjoys a reputation for taking on jobs no one else will do, including murder for hire. However, the CI claimed he never did that kind of work but only bragged he knew people who would and he'd take a finder's fee. Because he was leaving on vacation for two weeks, Ruben asked that I verify what the CI claimed and felt the feds could better handle a case like this, so he introduced me to the informant. His name is Joey Dawkins."

"Any mention who the target is and how it's supposed to go down?"

"No. Dawkins said he only knows the guy as Sonny, who asked him if he would be interested in doing a hit for five grand. So I told Dawkins to find out as much as he could about the hit, including who's the target."

"Five grand doesn't sound like a lot for killing someone," said Clarkson.

"Agreed. Dawkins asked Sonny why he wasn't doing it himself since the guy had a rep for doing hits. Sonny told him he was on probation, showed his ankle bracelet, and said he couldn't leave the state. He told Dawkins the hit was on someone in Boston. Dawkins told him he was too busy with other jobs, but he knew who might be available to do it."

"So, did Sonny buy that?"

"He was interested. I asked Dawkins if he would introduce an undercover agent to Sonny. Initially, Dawkins didn't want to be a snitch. I suggested he tell Sonny he has a trusted friend who knows a guy recently released from prison who needed money and would do the job. I told him to tell Sonny he had never met this other guy, but he trusted his friend, who wouldn't recommend someone who wasn't. Dawkins agreed to try it but couldn't promise it would work."

"Sounds like a good case if we could put it together. But, of course, you'll first have to sign up Dawkins as an ATF informant. I assume Dawkins is looking to get paid."

"We haven't discussed money yet, but Ruben told me that's how Dawkins works. So I'm sure he'll want to get paid. I worked on a similar case three years ago. You were in training at the time. It involved a guy looking to have his daughter killed because she agreed to testify against him for felony charges. I did the undercover, playing someone with expertise in explosives. He wanted to rig his daughter's car, so it would go off when she started it."

"Are you doing the undercover if Sonny agrees to meet?"

"No. It would take up too much of my time, and it would be unfair to the guys I work with at the task force. Besides, I already talked to Pete, and he agreed to do it."

"Pete is working with the Hartford police drug unit. Are you sure he has the time to get involved with this?"

"He told me he could do it, so he's our man if we can meet with Sonny."

Pete Macheski, half Polish, half German, enjoyed working undercover, especially with the Hartford drug unit targeting drug dealers who carried guns for protection. Pete was the most productive agent in the office. He lived just over the border from Hartford in the Springfield, Massachusetts area and was married with three boys. Pete generally wore jeans, worn-out t-shirts, and old sneakers, playing the part of a street player looking to buy drugs or guns. His hair was primarily grey at age 44, and he stood just under six feet tall, a little overweight, like some guys his age.

"Okay, Zig, let me know if Sonny agrees to meet. We'll have to coordinate with Boston. Since Sam is working in Boston, I could ask him to coordinate it with the front office. Anything exciting going on in the task force this week?"

"Just surveillance on a drug dealer. We're trying to get enough PC to get a search warrant for where he deals his drugs. You know, Jen, you look pretty good behind the boss's desk. Maybe you should think about taking the job permanently."

"No, thanks. I'm not spending any more time behind a desk than I have to. I'd much rather be working out in the field. Sam can have this job. It sucks."

Clarkson was another favorite of Sam's. She was one of the top three producing agents in the Hartford office. Statistically, Pete led the office with the most cases sent for prosecution, with Ziggy and Jennifer right behind him. All three did most of the undercover assignments. However, Jennifer was more successful working undercover in the inner cities. Being an attractive woman of color who spoke fluent Spanish, she easily won acceptance by gang members and minorities compared to white males. Sam had a colleague-friendship relationship with the three agents and often socialized with them outside working hours.

"Well, I'm out of here, Jen. I just wanted to run this by you. I'll let you know if this works out, and we can meet with Sonny. I've got to run. If I get lost remembering how to get to the task force office, I'll call you, ha-ha. See ya, Jen. By the way, if Sam decides to stay in Boston, you'll be a shoo-in to take over the job."

"Yeah. If Sam doesn't come back, I'm throwing your name into contention for the job, wise guy."

* * *

"Do you think Ferguson is heading to the farmhouse to warn the owner we were asking questions?" asked Juli.

"We'll certainly find out soon enough. We're only about twenty minutes from the farm," answered Sam.

Minutes later, Juli slowed down and pulled off to the side of the road when she saw Ferguson pull into the Crescent Drive Plaza that housed the convenience and liquor stores. It was the same plaza Sam and Juli had earlier followed a woman to after leaving the farmhouse. They observed Ferguson wait outside until a woman came out of the grocery store and got into his car. The car didn't move for several minutes.

"That's strange. Do you think that was Ferguson's wife? I thought he said his wife was visiting her cousins," said Juli.

"Maybe her cousin owns or works in the store. What's important is to know if Ferguson's wife is involved with anyone connected to the farmhouse. It looks like he's heading out. If he heads back home, let's call it a night."

Juli followed not far behind Ferguson until his car drove into the driveway of his residence. Sam decided they should call it a night and head towards Boston.

"Are you spending the night at my place, Sam? If so, we can get takeout at Jonathon's Grille on the way."

"Yeah. We could do that, but we need to get up early and determine what the FBI has planned for their operation. So, let's limit any fun time and get some sleep so we're not late for the meeting."

"I guess I wore you out so bad your forty-something-year-old body needs hours of sleep to recuperate?"

"Only when the thirty-something-year-old used up so much energy she can't get up the next morning."

They looked at each other, knowing how the night would turn out. "I promise, I'll get up when the alarm goes off. Does that satisfy you, Sam?"

"Oh yes," said Sam while smirking. He enjoyed the banter.

CHAPTER
22

Sam rolled out of bed and noticed it was after seven o'clock. He walked gingerly to the bathroom. His only thought was Juli didn't know when to stop. Not that he didn't enjoy the night, but she promised he could get some sleep. The last time Sam glanced at the clock, it was after one in the morning, and she swore she'd get up when the alarm went off, but she didn't.

After showering alone, he made enough noise in the kitchen, making breakfast and perking the coffee, until Juli finally woke up and showered. Then, after a light breakfast, they drove separately to the FBI office for the scheduled meeting. The tactical FBI leader, Jesse Carter, began the briefing by pointing to enlarged photographs and sketches from the teams' surveillance of the farm the night before.

"Using thermal imaging devices, we estimated seven persons were inside the farmhouse and two in the barn on the second level. Therefore, we may have to contend with eight potential armed assailants and one hostage. However, more than one hostage could be inside. We took observation points at nearly every angle of the property. Team members and I agreed with Agent Caviello that the best choice for a covert approach to the farmhouse would be along the berm that runs from the road to the back of the carport. Also, the second team will enter the woods from Country

Farm Road and advance to the barn. We observed no security cameras or devices during our surveillance. We're drafting a search warrant affidavit for a search warrant for the farmhouse, the barn, and all vehicles on the property. Are there questions or comments so far?"

Ospino got their attention. "Agent Caviello and I visited the town's building department and reviewed the building plans for the house and barn. I took photos but haven't had time to have them printed for everyone."

"We have those schematics already," replied Carter.

Ospino added, "A fire destroyed the barn in late 2017, and they finished rebuilding it during 2019. We interviewed Tucker Ferguson, the building department's inspector, for the reconstruction. Agent Caviello and I strongly feel the plans for the barn are fake. When Ferguson realized we were inquiring about this property, his attitude and tone changed dramatically. Plus, shortly after he retired, he got married. At his home, we saw a photograph of him and his bride. We took a photo of his wife, first name Tsarina, who looks like she's from the Middle East. I have our department conducting a background on her. Ferguson is sixty-six years old. His wife looks to be mid-to-late thirties."

FBI supervisor Dell Haskins asked, "So, you think there's a connection between his wife and the suspects?"

Sam answered his question. "It's just a hunch, but Ferguson got disturbed when we asked about the property. It seemed like a weird coincidence that his wife is Middle Eastern. It will become an important part of the equation if we find out she's connected to the suspects. It all points to Ferguson probably submitting a deceptive inspection report. This morning I contacted the current building department director to find out the contractor who constructed the barn. I plan on meeting the contractor to see if he made any major changes to the barn not shown on the blueprints. I believe there were major changes, and it's critical we find out before we hit the place. We should know what's on the other side of the door we enter. Once I get a call back with the name and number of the builder, I'll visit him this afternoon."

Haskins looked back at Jesse Carter and SAC Austin Taylor. Haskins stepped forward and said, "Our position is to act without further delay. We believe the suspects could have more than one hostage and plan to harm them soon. The tactical teams are going over the operational plan this afternoon. We expect a judge to approve the search and arrest warrants by the end of the day. I will conduct a briefing of all participants tomorrow in anticipation of executing the warrants the following morning. So let's break and get back here in twenty minutes. We'll review the operational plan draft and consider any recommendations before finalizing it."

Lieutenant Martin Randell called out the names of the state police officers to meet in the adjourning room after the break. Surprisingly, he left out Sam's name. Ospino, also surprised, searched for Sergeant Moore to protest Sam's exclusion from the meeting. But she saw Moore huddled in conversation with FBI Agent Jesse Carter. She then searched for Sam, but he was on a phone call.

"John Pittman Construction, can I help you?"

"Mr. Pittman, this is federal agent Sam Caviello. I've studied building schematics for a barn that your company constructed in 2019 in the Haverhill area. I want to meet with you to determine if there were any last-minute changes in the construction plans that don't appear on the Certificate of Occupancy at the town hall."

"The inspector would have to include any last-minute changes in the final approved construction documents before filing them at the building inspector's office," insisted Pittman.

"I understand the procedure. Do you maintain a copy of the final schematics, including any construction changes?"

"Absolutely. My copy should match the documents filed at the town hall."

"I visited the building department and reviewed the documents with Harold Bennett. I have a copy of what got filed at the town hall that I would like to compare to what you have."

"Are you insinuating that our records violated the town's building codes?"

"No, sir, I am not. I only want to know what changes they made to the original construction plans. I do not suspect your company, but the owner might have made changes. I need to confirm that today."

"Well, I'm at a construction site in Concord, New Hampshire. Where are you?"

"I'm in Boston. Are you based in Concord?"

"No, my office is in Nashua."

"Can I meet you at your office later today?"

"That I cannot do. I have to be at this site until late today to prepare for an inspection tomorrow morning. So the earliest I can make it back to the office would be between two and four tomorrow afternoon."

"Can you text me your office address? I'll contact you tomorrow afternoon to coordinate my arrival."

When Sam hung up, Juli asked him to join her for coffee in the break room. The FBI break room had two large coffee urns next to assorted pastries. After filling their cups with coffee, Sam followed Juli to the hall for privacy.

"I asked why Lieutenant Randell didn't include you in the meeting. He said it was for FBI and state police officers only. I told him you are an important investigative team member, but Randell said the FBI wanted this to be an FBI-Mass State Police operation. I tried to convince him you should be part of this, but the Lieutenant stood firm. I'm sorry."

"You have nothing to be sorry about, Juli. So that you know, I have an appointment tomorrow with the owner of the construction outfit that built the barn. Have you heard anything back on Ferguson's wife?"

"No. But I'll call my office after the meeting."

"Great. Let me know when you hear anything. I'm going to leave and call my son to meet for lunch."

On his way to Boston, Sam contacted Drew, and they agreed to meet at the sports bar across from the federal building.

It was challenging to find a parking space on the city street near the restaurant, so Sam parked in the first vacant ATF parking space he saw in the federal building garage. Then, he walked across the road to the restaurant and saw Drew already seated at a booth.

"How are things working out with your training officer?" asked Sam.

"So far, so good. I've taken part in several security details, but I'm eager to get involved in a criminal investigation. I'm lucky the boss assigned me to Eric. He's got the most experience as an agent in the office. He's given me good tips on handling security details and lists of the right people to call for information. How's the case going with the state? I assume you're still working with them."

"Well, now the FBI got involved. Unfortunately, the Feebs want to push me out of the case, so it's an FBI-state police investigation with no other outside agencies to share the credit. I'm still doing background work to help, but I could be back in Hartford if they lock me out. But, hey, it's great being in Boston where you're working. It gives us a chance to get together and help each other out in our work. Have you had a chance to invite that new blonde employee for coffee yet?"

"Uh, not yet. I'm in no hurry. Unfortunately, her desk is close to the rest of the admin staff, so I'll wait until she's alone at the printer."

They both ordered burgers and a Coke. Since Sam didn't have much time to spend in Boston, he ate in a hurry while Drew described his typical workday in more detail.

"Well, it's a busy day for me, so I have to leave. Good luck with work and having coffee with that blonde. Be careful. I'll see you soon. Love you."

CHAPTER
23

The informant, Joey Dawkins, sat at the bar in the New Haven Café. He ordered a beer and looked around for Sonny. They had agreed to meet, but Sonny wasn't there yet. He glanced at agents Ziglar and Clarkson seated at a separate table a distance from agent Pete Macheski, who sat alone in the back of the cafe. Another fifteen minutes passed before Sonny finally entered the café and joined Dawkins at the bar.

"Another beer for me and whatever my friend wants," Dawkins said to the bartender. Dawkins was not wearing a recording device. He refused to get recorded and later identified as a participant in an eventual court proceeding.

Sonny took a sip of the scotch on the rocks and asked, "So, what's up, kid? Why am I here? You find someone to do the job?"

"Hey, man. Relax. Enjoy your drink and calm your nerves. I've got a guy, but I wanted to talk first. A friend of mine knows a guy who will do it. My friend vouched for the guy, but I wanted you to know upfront that I don't know him personally. My friend said the guy did time for attempted murder. He got released a month ago and needs cash to travel to a warmer climate. If you want to meet him, he's sitting alone in the back wearing a black jacket."

Sonny looked back at the guy. "What's his name?"

"I only know he goes by KC."

"You trust your friend who vouched for him?"

"One hundred percent. I trust him with my life. We've done a lot of shit together. He's not a rat, but as I told you, I don't know this guy."

"Well, let's go talk to him. See what he has to say."

"Wait. Once I give the intro, I'm out of it. The less I know about the hit, the better."

"Let's go meet him," asserted Sonny.

Pete Macheski, wearing a listening device, saw Dawkins and Sonny heading towards his table. Agents Clarkson and Ziggy sat at another table using earpieces to listen to the conversation between Pete and Sonny.

"KC, this is Sonny," declared Dawkins.

"Hey, Sonny. Have a seat and let's talk," said Macheski, playing the undercover role of KC.

"I'll leave you two to talk. I have to go pick up my girlfriend," said Dawkins.

"So, Sonny, I understand you have a job that needs doing. Tell me about it, and what's the payoff?"

"I can only tell you that I have a name, address, and a photo of the guy. My problem is I don't know you other than you're a friend of a friend."

"You mean Joey didn't vouch for me?" replied Macheski, pointing toward Dawkins.

"Not exactly. He only vouched for his friend."

"Well, I can't give you references any more than you'll give me yours. I'm sure you know I just got outta the joint and need cash to head south. I need a new place to operate where no one knows me. My gal moved south after I got sent to the joint. I need cash to get there, with enough to hold me over for a few months."

"What's your name so I can ask around?" asked Sonny.

"What's yours so I can ask around about you? You're not a cop, are you?"

Sonny didn't answer but only sat back in his seat with a not-so-friendly look.

"Listen, the name 'Sonny' obviously isn't your real name. You're thinkin' the less I know about ya, the better it is for ya. Well, that works both ways, ya know. The less ya know about me, the better it is for me. If I get caught doin' this job, there's not much I can tell the cops about who paid me, ya know. But I'm here, ready to do the job. If ya want references, ya'll have to visit the cemeteries where the people I knocked off are permanently sleepin.' If ya don't trust me, say the word, and I'm outta here."

Sonny was sitting on ten grand. He knew he needed to get the job done before it got canceled, and they demanded the money back.

"The job needs finishing by the end of the month. Otherwise, it gets canceled."

"That's not much time. What's the payout?"

"Five grand," said Sonny.

"And when I complete the job?"

"That's it. Five total."

KC laughed out loud. He moved forward, looking Sonny straight in his eyes. "Not interested. Sell that to some junkie who does'n know what he's doin'. You have a name and an address. What's that tell me? Nada. I have to find the guy, watch him, study his moves, get the timin' down when it's best to do it, and much more. It's not a five-minute job, my friend, ya know that. So, why ain't ya doin' it?"

Sonny shows him the ankle bracelet, saying he can't leave the state.

"What? Ya mean the hit's not here in the area?"

"No, it's in Boston."

"No fucking way, man. I can't do it for five Gs. I've neva taken less than ten grand plus expenses. I just got out of the can. I don't have wheels, man, so how do I get there? I've been riding the bus for chrissake. I'd have to rent a car or borrow yours. Ya, obviously gettin' a cut to find somebody to do it. That's a slice of my take, man. I need a piece (gun), a car, and time to set up the thing, which means spendin' a few days in Boston. Three hundred or more a night for a room, times two nights, a car rental for a week, and a good piece with a silencer will cost another bundle. Then, of course, I have to eat. All that adds up to two grand or more in expenses on top of the ten grand."

Sonny wasn't happy. He hoped to keep fifteen grand out of the twenty, but he didn't have time to negotiate. So Sonny sat back trying to figure out how much money he would make on the deal, and it wasn't much. He studied KC figuring if he was on the level. *The guy seems to know what he's doing. Unfortunately, it leaves me with only eight Gs, but I don't have much choice.*

"How soon can you complete the job?" asked Sonny.

"Once I have half the money and all the details, six days, tops. Also, I need to know where we meet to settle up after finishing the job."

"How will I know you finished it?"

"I'll take a picture. Plus, if someone finds the body right away, which is unlikely, I'll bring the mornin' paper that reports it."

"I don't have the cash with me." Sonny needed time to figure out how he could increase his stake. "So we'll have to meet again tomorrow."

"I'm staying with a friend in Springfield. Here's my number. Call me when you have the cash. That's twelve big ones. Six upfront and six afterward. Let's meet halfway, near Hartford."

"I'll call you by ten in the morning," replied Sonny.

CHAPTER
24

The following morning, Agent Pete Macheski waited in the designated room at the Springfield, Massachusetts ATF office, where they'd set up an undercover phone listed to a fictitious person. The plan called for Pete to give Sonny an out-of-state number to call. Using an interstate call to arrange a murder makes it a federal offense. When Pete saw it was fifteen after ten and there was no call, he got concerned that Sonny had gotten cold feet about trusting him. Pete planned on waiting most of the morning. However, ten minutes later, the phone rang. Pete let it ring four times before answering it.

"This is KC."

"It's Sonny. At five this afternoon, let's meet in Hartford at Macky's Grille on Franklin Avenue."

"You have the six Gs?"

"I do."

"I'll see you at Macky's at five."

*   *   *

It was 1:30 PM when Sam called John Pittman, who advised he'd be at his office in Nashua between three-thirty and four o'clock. Sam decided to head to Nashua and stop for coffee on the way. At three-forty, he arrived at Pittman's office and parked next to a pickup truck with the Pittman Contractor's logo on the driver's side door. Sam entered the office and introduced himself to Pittman, who was behind a counter reviewing construction plans.

"John, I brought the approved plans from the building department so we can compare them to what you have in your records."

Pittman took the building sheet numbers from the plans Sam brought with him. Then, Pittman searched his computer for which file cabinet stored the matching set of plans. Once he found the matching project, he spread the sheets on his long table and compared his plans against the building departments. It didn't take long before he realized something was amiss.

"This can't be right. I remember this job, and their plans are the initial ones, not the final updated plans."

"Can you tell me the changes made, John? Start with changes to the foundation and then the layout of the barn's interior."

"The initial plans called for a slab foundation. When my crew and I arrived to start construction, we saw the concrete company had poured a basement foundation. That wasn't the only surprise. They formed the foundation to include walls for an underground tunnel that led from the former basement bulkhead exit of the house to the barn's basement. The rear of the barn's basement wall had an opening for a bulkhead exit. I questioned the owner about why he had a full basement foundation built for a barn."

"What were the owner's name and response to your question?"

"It's on one of these sheets. Hold on. Here it is. His name is Shahrad Abedini. The owner claimed he planned on hiring farm workers and originally planned on having bunk beds and a place for them to eat in the house's basement. But later, he decided he didn't want them to have access to the house, so he changed the barn's plans to have them sleep and eat in the basement. He claimed the reason for the rear basement passageway was for them to have an additional fire exit. There was a backhoe parked in the back of the barn's foundation. I assumed it was there to dig a ditch for eventual steps leading to a bulkhead door as part of the rear fire exit."

"What about the construction of the barn? Can you describe the changes made?" asked Sam.

After reviewing the two sets of plans, Pittman shook his head. "Are you sure the plans you brought are the final ones recorded at the town hall?"

"Yes. Not only that, but I also interviewed the inspector who signed off on the recorded plans. You probably remember him. His name is Tucker Ferguson."

"Yeah, Ferguson. I remember him. He was the inspector on another small project I did for the town. But unfortunately, neither of the plans you brought reflect the changes we made to the barn."

"Describe the changes to me?"

"What you brought me only shows the original configuration for the barn. It was a typical barn layout. It had an open first floor and a second-level loft with a small door opening for lifting hay, or whatever, into the loft. It wasn't until after we put up the walls and roof the owner requested additional interior changes. That caused a delay because I had to draw up new blueprint layouts for the crew to follow."

Again, Sam asked Pittman to explain the changes.

Pittman pointed to where they made changes on the blueprints as he spoke. "Abedini wanted the loft extended from eight feet to fifteen feet long because he decided to use the barn for housing and dining for the hired help. He wanted us to construct three small bedrooms on the second level, with a landing, and three similar rooms directly beneath them on the first floor. The owner figured he would have a minimum of six workers, one for each room, and he wanted to use the rest of the first-floor space as a combination dining and TV room."

"Any windows or fire exit doors on the two floors?"

"They changed the typical double barn door to an oversized front door you would typically find in homes. Next, by code, the second-floor windows were egress-sized with a plan to attach an escape ladder the owner claimed would be added later. Finally, we installed a fire exit door in the middle of the first level on the north side of the barn."

"John, any other changes made or anything else you can remember that seemed odd to you?"

"I can't think of anything, but something is not right here. I'm going to have to call Bennett."

Sam quickly asked him not to call. "I prefer you not to discuss with anyone what we discussed today. We have an ongoing investigation regarding possible kickbacks and fraudulent building approvals. Unfortunately, we don't have all the facts and haven't identified those involved yet. I'd like this to remain between the two of us. Do I have your word on that, John?"

"My company only did what the owner asked for and never would be involved in any fraudulent dealings with the owner or the building department. I've been in business for over twenty-five years without issues. You can ask anyone we've ever done business with."

"I'm not questioning that, John. We're not looking at your company for violations, but we need your discretion on this matter."

"Well, you have it. Can I get your business card?"

"Yes, sir. I'll write my cell number on the back. Please call me if you can think of anything else that seemed strange to you or your crew members."

"Now that you mentioned my crew, there was something one of them said to me after we finished up at the farm. Rather than give you the wrong information, let me call and have him refresh my memory.

CHAPTER
25

"Pete, this is Ziggy. I just got a call from Joey Dawkins. He's getting cold feet. Sonny told him about meeting with you later today in Hartford to seal the deal. Sonny warned Dawkins it better not be a setup, or Dawkins won't see daylight again. Dawkins is worried we're going to arrest Sonny today."

"No. The arrest will happen after the final payoff. That won't happen for five or six days after calling Sonny to tell him I finished the job. After the final payoff, we'll bust him. You were working at the task force when we made that decision. Didn't Jennifer bring you up to speed?"

"Yeah, she told me, but I wanted to be sure before telling Dawkins no arrests are happening today."

"Okay, Zig. We want nothing to fuck this up now. We need to know the target in Boston and who put out the contract. I'm only about ten minutes from the meeting place. Is the surveillance team in position?"

"Yeah, we're in position. Jen contacted the state police colonel, who assigned two detectives to work on the surveillance. I'll talk to you later," replied Ziggy.

Just after five, Pete walked into Macky's Grille, looking for Sonny. He didn't see him at the bar, so he walked toward the rear of the dining area when he noticed Sonny waving his arm from a booth in the back. Pete walked to the booth and sat across from him.

"So, you're not a cop, are you KC?" were the first words out of Sonny's mouth.

"Wow, nice to see ya too. There's no 'how ya doin'', or 'are ya ready to do the job,' but 'are ya a cop?' Listen, man, tell me now if ya don't trust me to do this thing. I'll walk outta here, and ya could find somebody else. I need the money, though, and I'm ready to get it done this week. So, are we goin' do this or not?"

While Sonny stared at KC, he thought, *Joey better be right about this guy.* Sonny wasn't born yesterday and had a plan to find out more about KC. Ultimately, Sonny reached into his coat pocket and handed over a thick envelope.

Pete opened the envelope and fanned the six bundles of hundred-dollar bills. "Now we're in business, man." Inside the envelope, Pete also noticed a sheet of paper. He unfolded it and stared at an enlarged copy of the target's Massachusetts driver's license. Pete didn't show any emotion seeing who it was, even though he knew the target. "Anything else I need to know about this guy? Like where he works or hangs out, and does he live alone?"

"You got what I got. That's it," replied Sonny.

"Okay, Sonny. I need to get on this right away. The sooner it's done, the sooner I can bounce. I'll be in touch."

Pete slid out of the booth and walked toward the exit, thinking, *I can't wait to tell the rest of the guys who the target is, but it won't surprise them.*

Pete got into his car and drove off. When he did, two older vehicles, one a junkie-looking pickup truck and an older Toyota Corolla, discreetly followed a distance behind. Pete drove through a couple of neighborhood streets to ensure he didn't have a tail. However, he noticed the old pickup staying with him, so he decided to lose it. Pete took a left at the end of the street and slowed down to watch if the truck also turned his way. The pickup turned toward him. He also noticed a second car taking a left behind the truck.

Pete called Ziggy, telling him he might have a tail so he won't meet up near the airport road. Instead, he would meet at the office once he shook his shadow. After ending the call, he signaled to take the next left he came to and noticed the truck also signaled for a left turn. So instead of turning left, Pete continued straight until seeing a CVS pharmacy up ahead at the corner of the next street on the right. He pulled into the pharmacy parking lot. Pete saw the truck pull over to the side of the road and park while the old car drove slowly by the pharmacy.

Pete entered the CVS and stayed close but hidden near the entrance. Seconds later, the pickup truck drove slowly by the pharmacy. Pete saw the truck's passenger scanning the pharmacy as it passed by. When the truck was out of sight, Pete rushed out the door, slid into his car, backed up a bit, and then drove the wrong way down the one-way corner neighborhood street. The street curved to the right and then left before coming to the stop sign. Pete didn't notice any vehicle following as he turned right and accelerated to a familiar street on the left that led to I-91. He entered the road and pressed down on the gas pedal until he came upon the I-91 north entrance. He swerved onto the ramp, entered the interstate, and floored the gas pedal. Next, Pete took the left entrance ramp for downtown Hartford, continued straight until circling the rotary near the city park, drove onto Elmwood Street, crossed Main, and entered the garage at the federal building. Pete swung into an open parking space and loosened his tight grip on the steering wheel while feeling smug, thinking, *That was easy losing those amateurs.*

Still sitting at Macky's Grille, Sonny reached for his phone that rang. "Yeah, what did you find out?"

"We lost him," answered the guy in the old pickup truck. "He stopped at a pharmacy. We pulled over and waited for him to come back out. We drove by the pharmacy when he didn't, but his car was gone. He must have driven down the wrong way on a one-way street at the corner."

That made Sonny suspicious of KC, thinking maybe he was a cop who was savvy enough to evade the tail. Now, it was his turn to rethink his next move and avoid getting trapped by the police and going back to jail.

* * *

Pittman ended the call with his crew member. "I remember now. My guy was driving by the farm after we completed our job there. He noticed the backhoe was excavating a ditch from the barn toward the woods, maybe thirty or forty yards long."

It didn't surprise Sam. He knew precisely the purpose of the excavation. "John, I would like to get a copy of your plans. I need it to show the state police. I promise I'll return it to you within a day or two."

"I may have an extra copy in the cabinet. It'll take a few minutes."

While Pittman searched for another copy, Sam noticed it was close to five o'clock. Pittman returned with a copy and turned it over to Sam.

"Thank you, John. You've been a tremendous help."

Then, as Sam was about to leave the office, he thought of something that needed clarification. "John, you mentioned a side exit door on the first floor. Do you remember if your crew actually placed a door there?"

Pittman took his time answering. "Yeah, I remember the owner telling me he changed his mind about the type of door he wanted. He said he had a friend who would give him a special price on the door and installation. Now that you mentioned the fire door, it reminded me of another strange request from the owner. He wanted three-foot square holes in the floor of each closet on the second and first floors, with a ladder going from each closet down to the basement. I have to say that was a strange request. The owner said it was an additional way to escape during a fire."

Sam replied, "Yeah, I think I know why he needed the extra means of escape. Thanks again, John."

"Wait, I just remembered one other strange request. The owner wanted to know where to get ¼" high strength steel three feet by four feet nearby. I told him he should check with Home Depot, Lowes, or any building supplier."

Sam had an idea why they wanted the steel. He thanked Pittman again and left the office with the document in hand. As he drove back to Boston, he called Juli.

"Hi, Sam. How did it go with the contractor?"

"Juli, contact Frank Moore and tell him they had to rethink the operation. The blueprints approved and confirmed by Ferguson are fake. There is a full basement in the barn and a tunnel that leads from the barn into the woods. I'm sure it's an escape route."

Juli responded, "That's not the only revelation about Ferguson. It turns out his wife is the sister of the farmhouse owner, Abedini."

CHAPTER
26

Sam arrived at Juli's apartment within the hour. The first thing he wanted to know about was the response from Frank Moore.

"He hasn't gotten back to me yet. He informed the FBI, but the FBI was adamant about not putting off the raid for another day. Frank believes the FBI has information they are not telling us. He also mentioned they called in a second FBI tactical team that arrived last night."

"This is insane. You can't send in teams without knowing what they'll be facing on the other side of the door. They don't have an accurate floor plan showing the possible positioning of the suspects inside and where they hold the hostages. Not to mention an escape route."

While they continued their discussion, Juli's cell phone rang. She answered and listened to Frank Moore's instructions. Before she said a word, he hung up.

"That was Frank saying the plan is a go for tomorrow morning. They want us at the Lowell FBI office by three in the morning for a briefing. The arrangements and operational plans are all set. There will be no further delays. Whatever you learned about the barn layout, they want you to update them during the briefing."

Sam couldn't believe it. Perhaps the FBI learned of a plan to harm the hostages tomorrow. He wished the FBI would have shared what they knew so all participants in the raid had all the information.

"What's Frank's number? I have to fill him in on what Pittman told me, and maybe it will convince them to put the raid off for another day."

Juli gave Sam the number, but Sam only got Frank's voicemail, so Sam left a message for him to call back. Juli said she prepared a delicious salad with sliced apples, avocado, red onions, pecans, thin slices of grilled chicken, and a tasty dressing she copied from a Food Network website. Sam brought a dry Riesling from the neighborhood liquor store to accompany the meal, but they decided to drink water since they had to be sharp for tomorrow's event.

During dinner, Sam and Juli had a list of things to do in preparation for any circumstance they might face during the raid. Their checklist included having a clean weapon, enough ammo, an armored vest, a helmet, goggles, a first aid kit, and a flashlight, to mention a few.

"Juli, I know you know this already, but please maintain good cover and avoid the line of fire at all times. We have three tactical teams, so stay in the background and away from the gunfire." Sam didn't want Juli anywhere near a gun battle.

"Sam, I'm Special Forces trained, remember?"

"I remember, but that doesn't guarantee you are invincible from getting shot. I care about you and promised I wouldn't let anything happen to you. I want us to leave the farm tomorrow and come home safe."

"I know, Sam. I'll be careful. Our tactical guys are top-notch and will take care of business."

"I'm sure they're well trained and are good at what they do, but I'm troubled about the changes made to the barn and hope they recognize the potential for problems there."

"Are you having one of those feelings or whatever you call them?"

"No, I'm not. When you went on patrol in the Army, I bet you faced situations where you had a feeling something bad might happen."

"Every time I was on patrol, I felt that way. We never knew where the enemy hid or if one of their snipers had one of us in their crosshairs."

"Well, that's the feeling I have about this operation. Anyway, let's stop talking about it. It makes me nervous. Promise me you will stay back and not get involved with any firefights. Please."

"I promise I will be careful and not do anything stupid. I'm assigned to backup the guys in blue and can't hide from that responsibility. I know you wouldn't either."

Sam knew she was right. He would insist on being part of the same backup team as Juli so he could watch over her. "Just do me one favor. If hell breaks loose, stay close to me. Okay?'

"I will, I promise."

Sam's cell phone rang. He answered the call from Frank Moore. Sam spelled out all the changes made to the barn and what he believed to be an escape tunnel. "Frank, the changes tell me this group is prepared and ready for a fight. I have the revised blueprint layouts. I suggest the teams—"

"Sorry to interrupt, but I'm swamped with calls and need to get some sleep soon. Bring the plans to the briefing. We'll study them and make the appropriate changes in our approach to the barn. We still have the operation set for six, and it's a go. Don't be late for the briefing."

*   *   *

Two FBI surveillance teams were still watching the farmhouse. The team observed two vans arriving at the farmhouse around eight that evening. They saw two men, including the driver, exit the van parked near the front of the house and carry what appeared to be grocery bags into the house. The two men remained in the house while the other van drove back toward the road. The FBI team leader, using binoculars, could only see the driver leaving in the vehicle. The other van remained parked several yards away from the front door. The team leader radioed his observations to Jesse Carter, the FBI tactical team leader at the Lowell FBI office.

"Roger that. Have one team follow the van. The other should remain on surveillance," requested Carter.

The black van that left the farm drove east and then turned onto Country Farm Road. One team of two agents in a sedan tailed the van a distance behind. The van drove up the steep hill and disappeared over the hill's crest. As the FBI sedan reached the hill's peak, the two agents saw a large truck pulling slowly out of the driveway of a farmhouse on the right. The truck blocked both road lanes as it made a wide turn. Seeing the truck blocking the road, the driver of the FBI sedan sounded his horn to no avail. The large truck slowly straightened to clear the opposite lane. The FBI driver then put the gas pedal to the floor to pass the truck, trying to catch up to the van under surveillance. However, as he pulled into the passing lane, he saw an oncoming vehicle with blinding high beams heading toward him. The agent tapped the brakes and yanked the steering wheel to bring them back behind the truck, nearly slamming into its rear end. Both agents fixed their eyes on the truck's rear as the oncoming vehicle passed by, with neither agent noticing it. When the road cleared, the agent floored the gas pedal and passed the truck that blocked them.

"Where's the van?" the agent driving shouted. "It couldn't have made it to the intersection that fast."

The black van the FBI was following had made a quick U-turn while the large truck pulled out of the driveway blocking the road to prevent the FBI from pursuing it. It was a prearranged plan to ditch the tail. The black van's driver laughed as he passed by the FBI's sedan, heading back in the opposite direction with high beams glaring. At the bottom of the hill, the van stopped at the wall opening leading into the woods. The side door slid open as four men exited the van and dashed into the woods carrying long black tactical bags. The van then drove off. The four men carrying tactical bags moved through the woods and entered the rear door of the farmhouse unseen by the FBI team that remained to surveil the farmhouse.

Inside the farmhouse, Shahrad Abedini, his sister Tsarina, and the Imam began a briefing for the regiment of fourteen trained men and women. Rashid Al Madari, their field combat leader, was also present.

Abedini gave the men a short inspirational call for courage following the briefing.

"The Americans are fools. They come to our country to kill us and destroy our way of life. They killed my sister's 15-year-old daughter and Rashid's young brother, only 14 years old, while they trained to fight for our country. Many of you who volunteered to help us also lost sons, daughters, or loved ones on that day. Now, we kill their daughters in their country. They know we are here. The Imam learned they would attack us tomorrow morning. We saw police here last night preparing for their attack on us. We are ready for them. We applaud all of you as our heroes and martyrs, and after we shame them, we will celebrate our victory. Rashid will give you final instructions. Go in prayer."

The Imam, Abedini, and his sister left the room. Abedini guided them to the barn's basement, through the tunnel, and out its exit into the woods. They walked in the woods for a distance until they reached a predetermined spot near Country Farm Road. An associate was waiting in a car across the street, parked in the driveway of an old colonial house. Abedini signaled his aide, Ameen Nazari, who drove across the road, picked them up and drove them to safety.

CHAPTER
27

Sam drove with Juli to Lowell the following morning, arriving a few minutes early. When they entered the office, Sam searched for the break room, where he found a coffee urn and poured himself a cup. He sipped the coffee while selecting a blueberry-filled donut from the dozens of donut-filled boxes in the break room. When Sam entered the large briefing room, he spotted Juli seated next to Frank Moore. He then spotted an empty seat next to Major Burke.

"Good morning, Major."

"Morning, Sam. You called Frank Moore last night and recommended they delay the operation."

"Yes, sir. The changes made in the barn give the suspects a better defensive position. I'm concerned we could face a serious gun battle. I hope I'm wrong."

"So, the finalized layout recorded at the town hall is phony?"

"What the inspector recorded at the town hall is bogus. Detective Ospino and I interviewed the inspector at his home. We brought the official records we borrowed from the town hall. The inspector became rattled when we asked him about the accuracy of the approved plans. However, he claimed the recorded documents were legit. I interviewed the contractor and compared his final construction plans to what the inspector approved and filed at the town hall. They look nothing alike."

Austin Taylor, the FBI agent in charge, interrupted Sam's conversation and welcomed everyone to the briefing. He summarized an updated intelligence report warning they overheard terrorist chatter regarding an imminent plot to kill young American girls on U.S. soil.

"We have a brief window of opportunity to prevent this from happening. We have the search and arrest warrants in hand and plan to execute them at six this morning. So before I turn the briefing over to Dell Haskins and Jesse Carter, I suggest you save your questions and comments until we finish explaining the operational plan and assignments. Thank you."

Agent Carter directed all to a PowerPoint presentation on the large screen as Supervisory Agent Haskins described the farm's location. Next, Haskins pointed to several photographs depicting the farmhouse, carport, and barn. Several photos showed each structure from various angles. Next were pictures of the interior layouts of the farmhouse and barn. They illustrate the configuration for the first and second floors of the farmhouse. Then, Hawkins pointed out each room to familiarize all participants with the layout. He showed the floor plan for the barn next. As Hawkins was about to describe its configuration, the state police tactical leader, Frank Moore, interrupted and reminded him of the changes to the barn discovered by the ATF agent.

"Right, thanks, Frank. Is the agent from ATF here?" asked Hawkins.

"I'm right here, Dell," said Sam, now standing.

"I'm sorry. So many people and so many names to remember. What's your name again?"

"It's Sam Caviello."

"Sam, would you summarize the changes made to the barn?"

Sam moved towards the front to speak with the rolled-up schematics under his arm.

"You don't have to come to the front. Just summarize changes you believe they made," instructed Hawkins.

Sam simply held up the schematics still rolled up in his hand. "What I have in my hand are the *true blueprints*," Sam emphasized the words true blueprints. "They show major changes made to the barn, not changes I *believe* they made, but changes confirmed by the builder. The documents that the town's inspector approved are fraudulent. The owner of the farm is an Iranian. The inspector who signed off on the plans submitted to the town retired shortly afterward and married the Iranian farm owner's sister, who is half his age."

Sam's disclosure gained the immediate attention of those in attendance. They began whispering between themselves at the revelation. Next, Sam summarized all the changes to the barn. As he continued to outline the changes, he mentioned the floor cutouts in the closets with ladders leading to the basement. Hawkins interrupted Sam. "What's the significance of the ladders in the bedrooms going to the basement?"

"The short answer is, they're for the suspects to escape."

"An escape to where?" quizzed Haskins.

"If you allow me to finish, I will answer all your questions. I met with the contractor yesterday, who made all the changes at the owner's request. He told me one of his crew members rode by the farm a few weeks after completing the project and saw a backhoe digging a tunnel from the back of the barn's foundation towards the woods. I should add that the contractor also mentioned that the owner asked him where he could find one-quarter inch thick, three feet by four feet high-strength steel sections. He didn't mention why he wanted the steel sections, but one reason would be to use them as bulletproof shields."

Sam noticed Haskins and Carter whispering to each other, not paying attention while Sam described the possible intended use of the steel sections.

"I emphasize there is no doubt in my mind that the changes were intentionally kept secret by the inspector to conceal them for devious reasons. We need to understand why the owner made the radical changes to the barn. I, for one, believe he made the changes to be ready for an attack."

"Anything else, Sam? We are on a tight schedule," asked Haskins.

"Just one more thought. These changes appear to be a readiness blueprint for battle, including the escape route for the leaders to use after the battle begins. We should study the changes long and hard. The inspector likely informed his wife or the farm owner that the government was looking at them. As a former ATF special response team member, I suggest we seriously consider these changes by taking the time to revise the operational plan needed to ensure our team members go home safe."

The FBI SAC, Austin Taylor, spoke. "Do you know if the contractor plans on contacting the building department or the inspector about the inaccurate inspection report?"

"I asked him not to contact anyone, and he agreed he wouldn't," conveyed Sam.

Haskins looked at Jesse Carter, nodding for him to speak. Carter, the FBI tactical leader, told Sam the team would study the documents he brought and revise their plans where necessary. "We brought in a second tactical team as a backup. Thanks for your input, Sam. We have all the personnel and equipment resources we need to proceed with added caution. I want all the tactical team members to remain in the room to review the barn's layout. Then, we'll decide what revisions we need to make to the operational plan for the barn. The rest of you take a break until we call you back into the room. Sam, you can stay. We may need to get additional details from you."

Sam provided answers to all questions concerning his interviews with Ferguson and Pittman during the fifteen-minute revisit of the operational plan concerning the barn. As a result, the tactical team members agreed to changes in their approach and entry to the barn, including adding additional backup tactical officers there. However, Sam still felt uneasy about the operation. He was ready to assist in any way necessary, but his continued focus was on ensuring the safety of Juli and rescuing the hostages.

CHAPTER
28

T he caravan of law enforcement vehicles began their early morning journey towards the farm just after four that morning. Every officer had their assignment and instructions. Sam requested they assign him to the backup team at the barn. He had studied the barn's layout and had Juli familiarize herself with the modifications. The FBI arranged to use an out-of-business truck dealership as a final briefing area. The dealership was located three miles from the farm. They would hide all vehicles and personnel from view inside the vacant maintenance building for last-minute instructions before the commencement of the raid.

Participants got acquainted with the Incident Command vehicle parked there and its staff of FBI agents, the state police commander, Major Burke, and the federal prosecutor, Donna Ranero. The command staff had communication with raid team members. They designated the team assigned to hit the farmhouse and their backup team as Alpha One, and the team and their backup set to hit the barn as Bravo One. Charlie One made up a three-person tactical team assigned to a lookout post for escapees along the tree line.

Command members had a list of contact names for all nearby hospitals, police emergency services, and state police districts in the area. Also stationed at the command site were an FBI armored vehicle, a state police EOD bomb disposal vehicle, and three ambulances with nine EMT members. In addition, fire personnel remained on standby only four miles away.

At five forty that morning, all personnel in full tactical gear and weaponry advanced to their positions. The Alpha One tactical leader, Jesse Carter, was confident most suspects were sleeping in the farmhouse while guards in the barn held the hostages. The plan called for the leader of two entry teams to advance to their targets simultaneously. Behind the leader were two team members carrying body bunkers and one clutching a battering ram.

Sam and Juli were part of the backup team at the barn. Andrea Serrano was part of the three-person evidence collection and forensic support team that remained a reasonable distance from the entry teams. State Police cruisers were assigned to block all traffic on Brewers Road and Country Farm Road.

Once the command staff heard from all teams that they were in position and ready, they would receive the signal to activate the raid plan.

*   *   *

At five the same morning, a soft-sounding alarm and dim flashing lights went off inside the barn. All windows had shades that prevented any light from escaping to the outside. The alarm and flashing lights awakened all the militants. They slept ready for action with their clothes on and their equipment and weapons close by their side. The two women who guarded the hostages were responsible for getting them up and ready to move. The two men assigned to remain awake and on guard ran around to ensure everyone was up and ready. Rashid Al Madari, with his wife Malika by his side, went over last-minute instructions to the combatants. Al Madari reminded them of the young men and women murdered by the American bombing.

"It is our time to take the lives of Americans on American soil, so they do not forget we will always revenge any attack against our brothers and sisters. So you must fight to your death like the martyrs you are. I will lead you in battle and to victory."

*　　*　　*

Both Alpha and Bravo teams advanced toward their selected targets. The Alpha team moved in a traditional alignment, often called a snake sweep. They moved silently to the rear of the carport, temporarily stopping and hiding behind the parked van near the front of the farmhouse. As they advanced, the team members focused their weapons on the windows and front door. The Bravo team simultaneously moved along the north and south side of the barn from the woods stopping at the front corners, close to the front door.

The Alpha and Bravo team leaders signaled that they had reached their destination. The two teams moved toward the house and barn doors from their stationary position. The agent on each team lugging the battering ram approached the door, followed by the team leader holding a distraction device. The plan called for the officers carrying the battering ram to slam the doors open, followed by the team leaders throwing a distraction device into the house and barn. The agents carrying protective body bunkers would be the first to enter, followed by the rest of the team.

Sam was positioned next to last in line as part of Bravo's backup team, with Juli positioned behind him. As the two entry teams gathered at both doors, Sam's body shuddered with an eerie feeling encompassing his entire body. Juli noticed his tremors and whispered, "Sam, are you alright?"

"Yes, but apprehensive about this operation."

"Are you getting a sign?"

"Maybe, but it could just be the feeling we normally get when serving warrants, not knowing what we're about to face. So do me a favor and don't move toward any gunfire, okay?"

"I can't run from my responsibility."

"I'm not asking you to run from your responsibility. Just stay close to me and be careful."

"I'll do my best. You be careful too."

When team leaders signaled their position at their target, Alpha One leader Carter signaled to command that they were in place and ready.

"Alpha One, you have a go," ordered FBI Supervisor Dell Haskins.

"Bravo One, this is Alpha One. Status check."

"Alpha, we are a go."

"On my three count. One, two, three."

CHAPTER
29

The alpha team hit the farmhouse door seconds before Bravo's team. The sound was deafening when the agent slammed the door with the battering ram.

Boom — Boom — Boom! The detonation blasts sent an explosive percussive sound throughout the farmhouse, causing a piercing shock wave engulfing the Alpha team. The ignition pushed out a barrage of air and gas at a tornado-like speed, causing shocked team members to stop in their tracks for seconds before a rush of wind flung them in the air while pelted by steel fragments and surrounding debris at tremendous force. The fragmentation hit like bullets within milliseconds, causing immediate severe injury and death. Another secondary blast followed from the van parked in front. A horrific conflagration and thermal heatwave generated the front of the house to catch fire. Agents and police nearby heard horrifying screams from those scorched by the savage blistering heat caused from the caustic blast wave.

"What the hell?" said Frank Moore as his Bravo team was a second away from hitting the barn door. Bravo team members at the door turned to see the blast and flames emerging from the front of the farmhouse. They stared in disbelief, losing focus on their job at hand. Then, distracted for a moment from their objective, a barrage of bullets pierced through the barn's front door from automatic gunfire from inside. The projectiles hit four officers gawking at the blast scene with their backs to the door. The other team members quickly backed away as bullets splintered through the marred door. The four officers hit included the officer holding the battering ram, the officers carrying a protective bunker, and Frank Moore, the Bravo team leader. It devastated the other tactical officers that backed away from the door, seeing their leader and other members lying on the ground. For a moment, they became confused, numb, and disorganized.

Sam witnessed the two horrific scenes and whispered to Juli. "They were ready for us, just as I feared."

Alarmed by the blast and shots fired, Agent Haskins at the command center keyed his mic. "Alpha, Bravo teams, what's the situation?"

Juli didn't hear any immediate response, as everyone among the entry teams was in a state of shock.

"Command, this is Detective Ospino. Explosives and automatic gunfire hit Alpha and Bravo teams at entry. The scene is entirely chaotic. We have large-scale injuries and casualties and need medical assistance immediately."

Juli started to move toward the barn, but Sam grabbed her by her tactical belt. "Where are you going?"

"Our team members are down, and we need to get them out now. So I'm going there to help."

"They have eight guys right there to pull them from the doorway. So you'll only get in the line of fire."

"They look like they are in shock. Someone has to do something now."

"Okay. I'll go with you, but don't get near the doorway until the gunfire stops."

Bravo team members were not eager to advance into the destructive path of the door until Carlos Reyes, the assistant team leader, pulled himself together and took command. "When the gunfire pauses, the last two in line on the south side pull our downed guys to safety."

"Carlos, Tim has been hit in the arm. He's bleeding badly."

"Have him retreat to the rear. EMTs should be coming shortly."

Sam, Juli, and other backup officers joined the team on the south side of the door and helped get all five wounded officers to a safe distance. Juli and Sam checked the pulse of the four critically hit. "These two have a pulse," Sam shouted. Juli shook her head regarding the other two team members. Tim was wounded but not critically.

"These two are gone, but let's pull them further away," added Sam.

Juli then checked Tim's arm. She reached into her first aid pouch and took out a compress bandage and scissors. She cut open a section of Tim's shirt near the wound and ripped the rest of the long sleeve off him. Juli pressed the bandage on the wound as Sam handed her tape to wrap it in place. Juli clicked her mic again. "Command, this Ospino again. We have severely injured officers down. We need EMTs on the scene now!"

Andrea, part of the evidence collection team and safely positioned below the berm, began jogging to Juli and Sam's location after the blast. "Are you guys okay?" she shouted as she approached them.

Surprised to see Andrea, Juli responded, "We're okay. What's the situation at the farmhouse?"

"Oh my God, Juli, I couldn't stand listening to the crying and screaming any longer. I think most of the team are seriously injured or dead. Where are the medics?"

Sam pressed on his mic. "Command, this is Agent Caviello. Where are the medics? We have many injured and need them now, not later!"

Command finally responded. "It's crucial we find the best path for the medical personnel without endangering their safety. We've called in additional medical assistance to the scene. It will take time for them to arrive."

"I suggest two EMT teams follow the berm to Alpha One's position. The farmhouse is on fire, and I'm confident no suspects remain in the house. The third team should enter the woods at Charlie One's location and head to the south side of the barn. We have that area secured. Get them here now. The farmhouse was booby-trapped and used as a ruse. They're using the barn as their strategical stronghold, with multiple suspects firing fully automatic weapons at the Bravo team. There's only one way into the barn, and they have all the firepower pointed in that direction."

"Roger that, Sam. We'll send the EMTs in as you recommended." responded a voice from the command post.

"We may need the armored vehicle to launch tear gas into the barn. Otherwise, the gun battle could go on for hours," recommended Sam.

Silence. There was no further response from the command staff.

Sam saw what remained of the Bravo team. "Juli, the Bravo team has three members on the north side and four on the south side of the barn door. I'm going to move to the north side, to even the sides. Watch over these guys until the EMTs arrive."

"I'll join the guys on the south side."

"I want you to stay away from the gunfire. Please, Juli. Wait for the EMTs to get here! It'll only be a few minutes."

Juli didn't want to stand by without helping. She let Sam move around the back of the barn. She then asked Andrea to wait for the EMTs and rushed to join her colleagues on the south side of the barn.

Sam cautiously moved around the backside of the barn while radioing the Charlie team. "Agent Caviello to Charlie One. Any movement in your area?"

"Negative."

"Roger that. I'm moving around the back of the barn to join the Bravo team on the north side."

As he maneuvered around the barn, he purposely focused north for possible suspects exiting along the tree line, but he saw no movement. He stopped at the front corner, checking the back of the farmhouse to ensure no suspects were at the windows. The house was ablaze, so Sam felt confident if any suspects had been inside, they were gone now. He then cautiously stepped towards the front of the barn to join the three officers hugging the barn wall. As he did, his face turned grim in disappointment, seeing Juli had joined the four team members on the opposite side.

"Hey, Sam. I'm Carlos. These guys are DaShawn and Greg. The three of us discussed forcing the door wide open. Then when the suspects stop shooting, we take alternating turns to peek and shoot from both sides of the doorway and hopefully nail them one by one until we get them down to a manageable number. When that happens, we storm in with force using the protective shields by the first two inside."

"Sounds like a plan. So let's do it," responded Sam.

After they slammed the door wide open with a ram, the automatic gunfire from inside the barn began again. The gunfire paused after the bombardment of bullets shattered the door and frame into wood splinters. Carlos signaled the four guys on the opposite side to start their plan on his two mic clicks. When he saw the team members on each side were ready, he clicked his mic twice. The first two tactical team members, one on the north side and one on the south side, positioned low at the doorway, peeked around the doorjamb, aimed and shot three times, and then quickly moved back. The south side officer held up one finger, meaning one suspect was down inside. The north side officer held up his closed fist, indicating zero hits. Both officers reported some suspects were behind some sort of metal barricade. The suspects fired a slew of rounds back at the team members, kicking up chunks of wood and drywall. When the firing stopped, Carlos could hear the suspects reloading their weapons. He gave the second two officers the signal to peek and shoot. Standing in a high position, the two team members fired three rounds each and then moved back. Again, the south side officer held up one finger, and the north side officer raised one finger. That totaled three down.

After the suspects stopped firing again, Carlos waited longer for the next team to fire inside. He asked if anyone who had already shot had an estimate of the number of shooters remaining inside. The first two officers estimated about ten. When it was quiet again, he signaled to get ready for the next two, including Sam. Hearing the click of the mic, Sam and the south side officer went low to shoot. Sam had his weapon in full auto and unloaded a barrage of bullets from one side to the other side of the barn until his gun was empty. The suspects then fired back with another mass of rounds before reloading again. Carlos could hear fewer weapons reloading inside and saw the south side officer signal that he shot two.

Sam signaled a definite two. Carlos subtracted four from ten, leaving six at the most inside. Carlos asked Juli to peek high and give an estimate to confirm the remaining number of suspects inside. As she did, automatic gunfire from inside began. She pulled back and estimated between five and six suspects remained.

Carlos decided for all team members to make crisscross entries, with the first two using bunkers. He had the team get in their original lineups. His decision to send Juli to the back of the line disappointed her. Carlos then held up his magazine, reminding his team to reload.

"I'll signal the first team with the bunkers to crisscross in and fire while advancing to their far corners. The second team will crisscross midway to the corners. The third move straight in and low. The fourth will remain at the door frame and fire from there. Everybody ready?"

Carlos saw all seven display a thumbs up. Then, with the adrenalin flowing high, the team members were ready for showtime.

CHAPTER
30

Carlos used his fingers, giving a three count to the first two officers who crisscrossed into the barn, keeping low to the left and low to the right. They took immediate gunfire at their bunkers. The gun battle began. Two more officers crisscrossed into the barn a second later, followed by the third team, including Sam. The last two, Carlos and Juli, began firing near the door opening.

"Ah, shit! That hurt." Sam cursed after a round hit his left arm and rib area. He dived onto the floor and fired a three-shot burst at a suspect in the open at the top of the stairs, causing the guy to tumble halfway down the stairs, still clutching his weapon.

"That's for hitting me, asshole," whispered Sam. The scene was tense, with gunsmoke filling the room and the loud crackling of bullets zinging by in all directions. Sam could feel the pain from his wounds and the cries from others getting hit, some fatally. Sam could only spot four suspects, one firing from behind a shield on the first floor and three on the second-floor landing behind a shield. While lying on the floor, Sam carefully aimed at the closest suspects firing from behind a metal plate on the second floor. The suspect ducked behind his shield to reload. Sam waited for the suspect to expose himself. When he did, Sam took careful aim and pulled the trigger. The bullet hit the suspect in the ear, causing blood to splatter against the far wall as he collapsed to the floor.

Sam could see two suspects remaining on the second floor. He stood up and moved toward the stairs when he saw the last suspect on the first floor taken down. That left two shooters on the second level. A barrage of gunfire from team members nailed one of the two remaining as Sam moved toward the stairs. The last shooter moved low and quickly from the far side of the landing to the center, shooting down in full auto from behind a metal barrier. The suspect then disappeared into the middle room. Sam took slow steps up the stairs with his gun pointed up and ready to fire. Halfway up the stairs, the guy Sam first shot lay wounded but still alive on the stairs. The suspect grappled for his weapon.

"No, you don't," Sam said as he fired a round into the suspect's face, saying, "Time to sleep, dirtbag." He took another step up the stairs when he saw the lone shooter return from the room and fire down to the first level. He quickly turned his weapon toward Sam and began unloading the rest of his rounds at him. Sam immediately dropped to hug the stairs. Bullets splintered four railing balusters flying over Sam's back. As the suspect reloaded, Juli entered the barn, fired her weapon, and hit the suspect in the thigh. The suspect fired back in her direction and fled back to the room behind him. Sam had gotten a good look at the suspect and recognized him as Al Madari, the same guy who shot Trooper Phillips.

That's the guy I want, thought Sam. He lifted himself up to move after the guy but stopped when hearing a weak female voice calling his name. He turned and saw what he feared the most might happen. Juli was down on the floor with her head leaning against the wall.

"No, no, no, no! Please, no!" he screamed as he nearly tripped while racing down the stairs. He rushed to Juli's side. The barn was now quiet, with no further rounds fired. There was anger and emotional pain throughout Sam's torso. Carlos joined Sam with two other team members moving to her side.

"I'm here, Juli. Stay with me," shouted Sam. He noticed Juli was bleeding from the neck, the right hip below the vest, and the center mass below her vest.

He pressed his mic, "This is Caviello inside the barn door. Detective Ospino's hit. We need an EMT here now! Now, Goddamn it!"

Juli was motionless, staring at Sam and whispering his name.

"Carlos, bandage the right hip. Jason, compress a bandage below her vest." Sam had a compress bandage already on her neck. "Hold on, Juli. Stay with me, okay? Help is on its way. Please, baby, stay with me."

After hearing the broadcast about Juli, Andrea ran to the barn. She safely peeked around the open entranceway and entered when seeing Sam and the team giving aid to Juli. Andrea moved to Juli's side. "Juli, honey, I'm here. Stay with us and stay awake."

"She's been hit in the neck, the hip, and below the vest, Andrea. We need medical help right now!" yelled Sam.

Andrea called out on her radio mic. "This is Detective Serrano. I need an EMT at the barn door now! Officer down, 10-999, we need help now!"

Seconds later, she heard a response. "We're on our way, detective."

"Help's on the way, Juli. Stay awake. Look at me. Don't close your eyes. I'm right here with you." Sam couldn't hold back his emotions as his voice quivered and his eyes blurred with tears.

Sam looked at Andrea. "It was the same bastard who shot Trooper Phillips. He left through the middle room upstairs. I want to kill that bastard."

With a soft sigh, Juli whispered in agony. "I love you, Sam. Go get that fucking thug for me."

Andrea, also pissed, touched Sam's shoulder. "I'll stay with her, Sam. Get that bastard for her. Kill that fucking thug!"

Sam didn't want to leave her side, but Juli muffled, "Get him for me, Sam."

"I'll get him, but you have to promise me you'll fight this through."

"I promise, Sam."

Then, two EMTs entered the room, asking the team to give them space.

"Sam, go get him. She's in their hands now," urged Andrea.

Sam cleared his eyes, stood up, and watched the EMTs working on Juli.

"Please, guys, take good care of her. Please," Sam pleaded with the EMTs. He was in physical and emotional pain as his stomach stirred like he was about to vomit. But, he held it back as he moved toward the stairs watching Juli with deep concern.

"Don't give up, Juli. Fight!" Sam yelled as he approached the stairs.

The EMTs placed Juli on a stretcher and carried her out. Andrea turned to Sam. "Go, Sam. Get that bastard for Juli and me!"

Not wanting to leave Juli but enraged with the guy who shot her, Sam turned away and climbed the stairs. He continued using his shirt sleeve to clear his tear-filled eyes and tried fighting back the sick feeling that draped his whole body. When Sam reached the landing, he replaced his weapon's magazine. The sickness in his stomach overtook the pain Sam felt in his wounded arm and chest area. He cautiously moved into the middle room with his gun up and ready to fire. He peeked around the door before stepping into the empty room. Sam noticed three mattresses on the floor and the open closet door. He knew it wasn't only a closet but an escape route to the basement.

He moved to the door and quickly peeked to verify no shooter was at the bottom. He held his weapon aiming toward the basement as he began stepping down the ladder one rung at a time. He passed the first-floor open door and stopped to peer into the room. It was empty. He climbed down and took his last step onto the concrete basement floor. He felt chilled, not only from the cool basement but also from his body's cold and nervous feeling from seeing Juli injured. He moved toward the dim lights he saw in the tunnel in front of him.

He switched on the tactical flashlight attached to his weapon for additional light. He entered the tunnel, striding toward a curve in the passageway. He stopped for a moment feeling nauseous. He considered heading back to Juli's side, but his anger toward the suspect was too strong to let him escape. His head felt like it would split open. His head felt like someone hit it with a hammer and was about to split open. The pain didn't matter. He'd promised Juli he would find Al Madari. It became his mission. He took a quick look around the bend before he hastened his pace. His head pounded like a drummer beating on it, banging away at his skull. He didn't see anyone in the distance and moved faster until reaching another turn in the tunnel. As he rounded the bend, he caught sight of a woman's legs stepping up a ladder about thirty yards ahead. *I'm close. That bastard is going to pay.*

CHAPTER
31

Sam stepped up the ladder to a closed wooden cover. He lifted it a couple of inches but heard voices close by, so he quietly closed the lid for a moment. When he lifted the cover again, he saw three females walking away from him, maybe fifteen yards ahead. Two of the females were young girls wearing shorts. They looked to be American. They got pushed along by a woman dressed in typical combat attire, light green fatigue pants, and a darker long-sleeved black and green fatigue shirt.

Sam could see the girls were tied together at the wrists and ankles. The suspects tied their ankles with a rope about two feet long, forcing them to step together as one. Slightly ahead and to the right was Rashid Al Madari, who continually looked behind him as he moved with a limp.

Sam waited until there was more distance between them before exiting the tunnel. While waiting, he tapped his microphone to whisper, "Charlie One, this is Caviello. I'm coming out of an escape tunnel maybe forty yards north of your location. Al Madari and a female associate have two bound American girls as hostages moving north forty yards ahead of me. I need help, over."

"Read you loud and clear. Caviello. We're on our way."

Sam lifted the tunnel lid, climbed out, and left it open as a marker for the Charlie team. He moved north towards the suspects as quickly as permissible, maintaining cover behind trees on the way. Sam's arm ached but became muted by his splitting headache and the soreness on his left side. As he advanced, he observed the group in front of him stopping. Sam moved behind a tree for cover. Peeking around the tree, he noticed Al Madari was on his cell phone. Taking advantage of a positioned target, Sam aimed his weapon at the suspect with his MP-5 selector switch on single-shot. Still, his hands and arms were shaky, not from his pain but from his blurred eyesight. He was distraught but consumed with nailing her shooter. After quickly clearing his eyes, Sam steadied his arm and pulled the trigger, hitting Al Madari in his left arm, causing him to drop his weapon. Al Madari quickly bent over to pick it up while his female colleague, his wife, returned fire in Sam's direction, ripping the tree bark apart that he hid behind. Unexpectedly, Sam heard return fire that he assumed was from the Charlie team. Al Madari's wife was hit and fell to the ground. Al Madari started shooting at the Charlie team from behind a tree. He then moved behind the two American girls for cover. He retrieved a pistol and shoulder weapon from his wife's body and moved to the north, using the young Americans as his shield.

Sam heard footsteps behind him. He turned to see two Charlie One members coming to join him.

"His female colleague is down, and he's wounded," Sam called to them. "Let's get after him."

They momentarily lost sight of Al Madari as they approached his wife's body. Her eyes were open with blood dripping from her mouth while gasping for air. Their attention quickly moved to the sounds of rustling leaves up ahead and aimed their weapons in that direction. Sam held up his arm, signaling not to fire as he spotted the two American girls heading toward them.

Sam yelled out to the youngsters, "Where did the guy go?"

One girl answered, "He got a call and then ran towards the road."

"Keep these two girls safe and call it in. I'm going after him," said Sam, directing the officers.

"I'll go with you," yelled out one of them.

"Stay with them. I'll get this guy. He's mine."

Soon after, Sam saw Al Madari on the other side of the stone wall near the road. Al Madari waved his arm at someone and started limping across the street. Sam rushed and launched himself over the wall. He watched Al Madari head towards a white panel van parked in an old white colonial's driveway across the street. The van, mostly hidden behind a large bush at the end of the driveway, began moving onto the road. Sam quickly aimed his weapon and pulled the trigger, hitting one of Al Madari's assault rifles, causing it to fall to the ground. Al Madari turned and fired as Sam dropped to the pavement to avoid getting hit. He eyeballed Al Madari, picking up the weapon and climbing into the van's passenger side.

"Police, stop!" shouted Sam as he sprung up and ran across the road, aiming his weapon at the van. The van spun its wheels on Country Farm Road as Sam fired, hitting it four times. One round went through the open driver's side window and shattered the windshield, with the other three hitting the side of the van. Sam noted the logo on the van that read "Crescent Drive Plaza Wine and Liquors." *I know that place,* Sam said to himself.

Sam looked back and saw a state police cruiser heading toward him. He waved for it to stop as the cruiser braked hard and skid to a stop. The trooper driving recognized Sam from the briefings.

Sam climbed into the cruiser. "Floor it. Follow the van up ahead."

As the trooper sped down the road, he glanced at Sam, saying, "You've been hit."

"Yeah, my whole body aches, but right now, we need to get the bastard escaping in that van. He's the guy who shot Detective Ospino during the raid and shot Trooper Phillips a few weeks ago."

"Good to know. I think we need to teach this guy a lesson. By the way, I'm Jim Markham."

"The van is making a left turn at the intersection, Jim. I'm Sam Caviello from ATF. Thanks for the help."

"I know. I remember you at all the briefings."

At the intersection, Markham slowly rolled through it, turning left. A short way down the road was the Crescent Drive Plaza. Sam didn't see the van. "The van had the liquor store logo on it. Let's drive around the back of the plaza."

There were no vehicles in the back of the plaza either. The lower level of the plaza shops had two garage doors with a solid exit door next to each. There were no windows on any of the doors, only two small windows on the upper level of the stores.

"I'll check out the back doors," said Sam.

Sam exited the cruiser with his weapon pointed at the upper-level windows. He checked the doorknob on the first exit door and the garage door. Both were locked. He continued to the next doors below the convenience store, where he found both secured. However, while standing at the garage door, Sam's body felt the eerie sensations he had felt so many times before. He knew what it meant. He was at the right place.

CHAPTER
32

Sam trudged back to Markham's car. "They locked all the doors. I'm going to call ahead for backup."

"What? You plan on hitting the place? Do you have enough PC to do that?" questioned Markham.

"I have enough probable cause. I saw who was driving the van. We will walk into the liquor store and check if the driver is inside. If he is not there, we'll check the convenience store. I'm confident there is a relationship between the two store owners. If the driver is there, then the suspect is also there hiding. That's why we need backup. The suspect has fully automatic weapons, and he'll use them."

"That makes sense," said Markham.

Sam pulled out his cell phone and selected Major Burke's number in his address book.

"Jack Burke. How can I help you, Sam?"

"Jack, I'm at the Crescent Drive Plaza with Trooper Jim Markham. I believe Al Madari is hiding inside the plaza, most likely in the liquor store. We're going to need backup."

"What makes you think he is hiding in there, Sam?"

Sam brought him up to speed on following the van to the store.

"Okay, I'll get you a backup team, but it might take a few minutes."

"Roger that, thanks, Jack."

"Thanks, Jack?" You obviously must be friends with the Major if you're calling him by his first name," remarked Trooper Markham.

"I'm not, but I have had a good working relationship with him so far. He's going to send backup, but it might take a while."

"Well, I hope the bastard is in there."

"Oh, he's in there, alright."

"How can you be so sure? You couldn't have seen anything with locked doors and no windows."

"It's a long story, Jim, but trust me, he is in there."

*   *   *

Inside the back room of the convenience store, Radir Semnami and his sister, Parnia, who operated the convenience store, quickly assisted Al Madari. First, they helped remove his bloody clothing and provided medicinal aid before bandaging his wounds. Parnia then cut his long hair short and trimmed his beard. Next, she searched and found American-style attire for him. In addition, she gave him a pair of sunglasses and a baseball cap.

While Parnia finished disguising Al Madari, Radir called Shahrad Abedini to report the situation. "Parnia and I are bandaging Rashid and giving him new clothing, but he cannot stay here much longer. We need to get him moved elsewhere. The police saw my van when I picked him up outside the woods, and they'll arrive here soon."

Abedini instructed him on where to bring Al Madari. "I will arrange for him to stay for the night and move him elsewhere in the morning."

"I cannot drive him. I only have the van. Unfortunately, my sister does not have her car here today, but I can call my young employee and ask him to do it."

Radir ended the call and called Benji Pahlavi, his young employee who worked part-time on weekends.

"Hi, Radir, what's up?"

"I need a big favor. Can you give a ride to an important customer? I will pay you extra."

"Yeah. I can be there in twenty minutes."

"Thank you, Benji. When you get here, park in front of Parnia's store."

Concerned, Parnia asked, "What will we do with the van? The police must have seen the store name on it. They will be here soon."

"Let's get Rashid out of here, first. One thing at a time. The van is in your garage, not mine. Once Benji arrives, I will hide the van somewhere else and tell the police someone stole it."

Benji Pahlavi was on his way to the store. At the same time, four Massachusetts state police cruisers with emergency lights flashing raced to the Crescent Drive Plaza to provide backup to Sam and Trooper Markham.

Less than twenty minutes later, Benji arrived in front of the convenience store in his silver 2014 Mazda3.

Sam and Trooper Markham, still parked near the back of the store, were waiting for the arrival of the backup team when they heard Benji's vehicle with its loud exhaust enter the plaza parking lot. Both driver and passenger side windows on the cruiser were cracked open.

"I'm going to take a look. It may just be a customer, but you never know," said Sam.

Sam exited the cruiser, walked to the corner of the building, and glanced at the car that had arrived. He saw a young guy, maybe twenty years old, exit his vehicle and enter the convenience store.

Radir greeted Benji and introduced him to Rashid Al Madari only as Rash, a special customer. He gave Benji fifty dollars and the address where to take him.

"Parnia also provided a bag for you to take, Benji. It has your favorite snacks, a Coke, and two loaves of your mom's favorite bread. Drive careful."

Al Madari, wearing chino pants, a black polo shirt, and a tan jacket, put on the cap and sunglasses and followed Benji out of the store.

As the two walked out to Benji's car, four state police cruisers drove by and turned to the side of the building to meet up with Sam and Trooper

Markham. Still watching from the corner of the building, Sam glanced at the two men exiting the store, but his eyes shifted to the arriving state police vehicles. Unfortunately, his glimpse at the two entering the young driver's car wasn't long enough to distinguish if the guy wearing a baseball cap was Al Madari.

CHAPTER
33

The four state police cruisers pulled along Trooper Markham's cruiser. The four troopers, including Lieutenant Randell, met with Markham and Caviello. Sam gave them the background on why they were there and a brief plan on what to do when they entered the two stores.

"I believe the van is a garage in the basement of the building, and Al Madari is hiding inside. I suspect the store owners have a connection to him. With your vests on, I would like you three troopers to enter the convenience store and, for your safety, take a quick search, including the back room and basement area. Be cautious and ready for anything. Lieutenant, Jim and I will do the same in the liquor store. We injured Al Madari, so look for blood, bandages, weapons, and the white van with bullet holes. Have your weapons drawn when checking around the store, especially the basement and garage."

They split into two groups and entered the two stores. Sam was first to enter the liquor store with the two troopers close behind. When Radir Semnami saw them enter, he turned to run when Sam shouted for him not to move.

"Where is Rashid Al Madari," demanded Sam.

"There is no one here by that name," responded Radir.

"Where is the white van you used to pick Rashid up?"

"I didn't pick up anyone. Somebody stole my van."

"You're lying. I saw you driving the van when you picked up Rashid from the woods. I put several bullet holes in your van. Lieutenant, could you watch him? For our safety, Jim and I will do a cursory look around."

Radir followed Sam and Jim until the Lieutenant told him to stay put.

Jim followed Sam into the back room while Radir was mumbling something under his breath in a foreign language to the Lieutenant. The two backrooms were joined, separated only by a wall with an open doorway. Sam noticed a chair on the convenience store side. Two troopers entered the room from the convenience store, and Sam joined them. They immediately noticed blood spots on the chair and black hair clippings on the floor. In addition, a trash bag was on the floor behind the chair. A trooper opened the bag and found Rashid's clothes, bloodstained bandages, and hair clippings.

"Let's check the basement. Yell out if you find the van," instructed Sam.

The two teams descended the stairs to the basement, with Sam and Jim Markham turning right towards the garage under the liquor store. It contained no vehicle.

"The van is in here, bullet holes and all!" hollered one trooper in the garage on the convenience store side.

Sam and Jim joined the two troopers who were looking over the van. "Two automatic assault weapons and an automatic pistol are on the floor of the passenger side of the van," shouted one of the troopers.

"We're going to need search warrants. I'll call Major Burke to let him know what we found. Could you two remain here for the security of the van? Don't touch anything. Jim and I will go back up and try getting the store owners to cooperate," said Sam.

On the way back to the first floor, Sam called Major Burke to notify him they found the van hidden in the store's garage, but not Al Madari. "I saw a young kid arrive at the store and later leave with another male dressed in American-style clothes. I suspect the other guy was Al Madari, disguised as an American with his hair and beard cut much shorter. He wore chino pants, a tan casual jacket, a black baseball cap, and sunglasses. I'll try to find out where they are heading. In the meantime, we need to get a search warrant for the two stores, the van, and any security video and evidence showing the store personnel aided and abetted Al Madari."

"Okay. Hang on tight. I'll call you back momentarily so we can get the PC for the warrant."

Sam turned to Markham. "Jim, would you have the trooper watching the woman in the convenience store keep her under control and not allow any phone calls? Have him lock the front door and place the closed sign on it. Also, find out where security cameras are inside and outside, and then join me in the liquor store. Thanks, Jim."

Sam proceeded back to the liquor store but paused when he heard a conversation between two men in the store. Unfortunately, the conversation was not in English. He listened for a moment, thinking the Lieutenant had allowed someone to enter the store, but only Lieutenant Randell and Radir stood by each other whispering when Sam entered the room. When the lieutenant saw Sam, he looked compromised, like a kid getting caught with his fingers in the cookie jar.

"Agent. Did you find anything?" asked Randell.

"Yes. We found the van that this guy drove hidden in the basement garage. He picked up Al Madari and brought him here. I called Major Burke to fill him in. They'll be getting search warrants for both stores."

Trooper Jim Markham entered the room, informing Sam everything was under control on the convenience store side and that they'd found where the security system was stored.

Satisfied, Sam then got in Radir's face, saying, "You hid the van in the garage on the convenience store side. Who is the woman in the convenience store?"

"She is my sister."

"Well, you and your sister are going to be arrested. You both gave Rashid medical assistance, cut his hair, and gave him a change of clothes. You had a young kid drive him somewhere, so tell me where."

"I do not know what you ask."

That response pissed Sam off. "Turn around, Radir. I said, turn around and put your hands up high. Now!"

When Radir turned with his hands up, Sam saw Radir's cell phone sticking out of his rear pocket. That gave him an idea. He grabbed the phone from his pocket and checked if he could access it, but it was passcode secured. Sam took a moment to think how he would get the passcode, knowing Radir wouldn't just give it to him. It didn't take long to figure out what to do.

"Radir, is there anyone you would like to call to care for the store when we bring you and your sister to jail?"

"I would like to call my sister's husband."

Sam handed him the phone, watched him enter a passcode, and quickly grabbed the phone out of his hand. He then searched for recent calls, noting the most recent call was to Benji Pahlavi and someone listed as Shah a minute before.

"Who is Benji Pahlavi? Is he the kid you called to bring Rashid to a safe place?"

Radir did not respond.

"Is Benji Al Madari's friend and helping him to escape?"

"No, no. Benji is a good boy. He works here on weekends."

"If you want help from us, now is the time for you to tell us where Benji is taking Rashid. Otherwise, I will arrest you and your sister, close your stores and take you to jail in Boston. I will also arrest Benji, seize his car and your van."

"My sister did nothing. It was only me."

"The police found your van with the bullet holes and the weapons Rashid left behind in your sister's garage. I'll be able to show your sister cut Rashid's hair and bandaged his wounds. That is enough for the police to arrest you and your sister. If you want to help your sister, tell me where Benji is taking Rashid. If you do, I'll make sure your sister does not get arrested today."

Lieutenant Randell interrupted Sam. "You should not make promises you are not in a position to make, agent. The judge has not even issued search warrants yet. I will decide on arrests made in good time once I know the status of the judge's decision. I'm sure both Radir and his sister will want to call their attorney."

On cue, Radir said, "I want to call my attorney."

"No calls. After the police arrest you and bring you before the Boston judge, the police will allow you to call your attorney, but not until then.

Understand?" said Sam, facing Randell with a stern look. Sam still had possession of Radir's phone. He went to the contacts list, selected "Shah," and called the number. While it rang, Sam put the phone on speaker as a male voice answered.

"Radir, is he on the way to Lynn?"

"Bale," responded Sam, meaning yes, and then hung up.

"So, I guess Rashid is going to Lynn. Where in Lynn is Benji taking him?"

"I don't see why Radir couldn't call his attorney so he could be present during the questioning and the search," interrupted Randell.

Sam didn't like how Randell supported the suspect and gave him an unyielding look.

"Lieutenant, we need to speak in private?" said Sam.

"What about, agent?"

"In private, lieutenant," Sam said more sternly.

"I'm in command here, agent. I'll decide who talks to who."

Trooper Jim Markham thought the lieutenant was out of line for siding with the suspect but avoided speaking against him.

Sam's temper reached a boiling point, but he got saved by his cell phone ringing. It was Major Burke calling back.

"Hi, Major Burke," said Sam as he glared directly at the lieutenant. "Any progress on the warrants?"

"An FBI agent will take the phone from me and have you outline the probable cause for an affidavit. Everything going alright there?"

Sam paused to walk away from the lieutenant and into the backroom before answering in a soft tone. "We have a minor problem here, Major."

"What do you mean? Is this going to affect getting the warrants?"

"No, sir. The problem is Lieutenant Randell. I'm trying to get the guy who helped Al Madari escape to cooperate, and the lieutenant is acting as the guy's attorney."

"How so, Sam?"

"The lieutenant is pulling rank and making decisions that are not in the interests of our case, and the officers killed this morning. He wants the suspect to have his attorney present while we ask him questions. We haven't even arrested the guy yet. This guy and his sister helped the shooter escape. I'm pissed off at Randell."

"I'm going to turn you over to the FBI now. I'll deal with Randell momentarily."

"Before you do, I'm certain that Al Madari is being driven to Lynn by the young kid I mentioned. I learned the kid works here part-time. His name is Benji, with a j instead of a g, Pahlavi, spelled Provo, Alpha, Hotel, Alpha, Lima, Victor, India. He drives an older model silver Mazda. Have someone do a DMV registration check on his Mazda and follow it up with an APB on his car. Jack, I want to be there when the police stop that car, but I don't have a car. Can I get your permission to have Trooper Markham partner up with me for the rest of the day?"

"I'll take care of it, Sam. I'm going to turn over the call to the FBI agent."

"Agent Caviello, this is Dell Haskins with AUSA Donna Ranero on speakerphone. We need you to provide all the information you have to support an affidavit for a search of the Crescent Drive Plaza convenience and liquor stores."

For the next twenty minutes, Sam, with some legal guidance from AUSA Ranero, provided the probable cause that evidence of a crime existed at the stores. Sam specifically mentioned they conducted a cursory search for the safety of the officers when entering the stores and found the evidence in plain sight during the security search.

Sam summarized how Radir and his sister helped Al Madari and arranged for an employee to transport him to Lynn. He emphasized that the warrant should specify searching for the van, weapons, fingerprints, hair cutters, hair clippings, medical bandages, Rashid's bloody clothing, and all instruments used to aid Rashid's escape, including cell phones, security camera recordings, and the like. Finally, he added that they should arrest and incarcerate Radir Semnami and his sister, Parnia, for aiding and abetting.

"Thanks, Sam. You have been a great help. We'll get this over to the federal judge. We have six FBI agents and two state detectives heading to your location to execute the warrants once the judge signs it," Ranero said.

"Okay, Donna, but I'm not staying here once the agents arrive. Major Burke put out an APB on the vehicle Al Madari is in, and when it is spotted, I intend to be there. If needed, you can call me on my cell phone."

"Any idea where Al Madari might be going?" asked agent Haskins.

"I could only guess it could be the mosque in Lynn. One last thing: I observed Rashid get in the van with two assault rifles and two pistols. The van contained only two assault weapons and one pistol. So, I suspect Rashid is armed."

"Can I assume the store owners are not talking?"

"Radir is not cooperating yet, but I believe he'll talk if enough pressure is put on him, especially if we promise not to arrest his sister today. You can always indict her at a later time."

"Thanks for the info, and nice work, Sam," said agent Haskins as he hung up.

Sam walked back into the liquor store and noticed the lieutenant had received a call, presumably from Major Burke. The lieutenant didn't look too happy as the call ended. Sam overheard him tell Trooper Markham he had to return to the command post. The lieutenant glared at Sam with a disrespectful look before leaving the store. As he walked past the store's front windows, Sam noticed the lieutenant was on his cell phone again.

Trooper Markham was also ending a call. "The lieutenant said Major Burke asked me to call him. So that was Burke on the phone. He instructed me to assist you until you call it a day and then drive you home. The other troopers will maintain control here until the FBI and detectives arrive. Are you ready to leave now?"

"Yes, I just need to make a quick call first." Sam moved towards the backroom while searching for Detective Andrea Serrano's cell number. He wanted to find out how Juli was at the hospital.

Radir got Sam's attention. "If you let me talk to my sister and promise you will not arrest her, I'll tell you where Benji is taking him. Benji is a good boy who knows nothing about who Rashid is."

"I'll let you talk to your sister, but you have to speak English only. Understand?"

Radir nodded his head as he kept looking at his watch. He followed Sam and Trooper Markham into the convenience store. As they walked, Sam's thoughts were on Juli's medical condition. *I pray she is okay. Andrea should have called me by now.*

Radir informed his sister the police would search the stores and arrest him for helping Rash. "They will not arrest you if I tell them where Benji is taking him. So maybe your brother could run the liquor store for a while." Parnia nodded okay.

Radir glanced at his watch again. He wanted to give Benji enough time to get to Lynn before the police could track him down.

"Radir, I need the information now, right now, or your sister gets arrested along with you," demanded Sam.

Radir took a last look at his watch before saying. "Benji is taking him to the mosque in Lynn."

Sam quickly called Major Burke. "Jack, Benji Pahlavi is driving Rashid to the mosque in Lynn. Pahlavi doesn't know Rashid. He's an innocent kid helping his boss give the guy a ride. The troopers and local police should know that he's not part of this group."

"We'll get the word out. Thanks for the update, Sam."

Sam then pulled Trooper Markham aside. "Jim, I'm ready to leave. Let's join the chase for Rashid. Could you instruct the troopers that FBI and state detectives are on their way to search the premises? Also, have them secure Radir and his sister and lock down everything until they arrive with the warrant. Thanks."

While Jim instructed the other troopers, Sam received a call from Andrea. Sam hesitated with apprehension before answering the call. "Andrea, how is Juli doing?"

Andrea remained silent for a time before emitting sounds of sniffling. Trooper Markham waved to Sam, signaling he was ready to go. Sam followed Markham out of the store, still waiting for a response from Andrea.

"Andrea, are you still there?—Are you crying? What's going on?—Tell me."

"Yes, Sam. I'm crying. I don't know how to tell you." Andrea repeatedly sniffled until finally mumbling, "Juli didn't make it."

Sam stopped in his tracks. His hand began shaking while holding the phone like it suddenly was too heavy to carry. He immediately felt ill and couldn't speak. His emotions took complete control of him. He wobbled and held onto a support pole in front of the plaza building. Trooper Markham recognized the shattered look on Sam's face as he held himself up, leaning on the structure. Jim thought maybe Sam was about to faint from a loss of blood.

"Sam, are you okay? Should I call for an ambulance?"

Andrea was still on the phone, asking Sam if he was alright.

Sam held up his hand to Markham. "Give me a minute, Jim." His stomach was still upset, churning inside out. "Andrea, I can't talk." Sam then turned away from Jim and vomited.

"Sam, don't hang up. Are you still there, Sam?" There was no response. Andrea heard the call go dead. She knew Juli's death devastated Sam as much as it did her. She realized they both needed each other's support now.

Sam slowly recovered and moved toward Markham's cruiser while wiping his face and blowing his nose. "I just got bad news about the death of my partner, Detective Ospino. I can't talk about it right now. Sorry, Jim. I'm upset. Let's head to Lynn. I need to settle a score with her killer. I'll make that bastard pay, so put it in overdrive with your emergency lights on."

While driving, Sam turned his head away from Jim, needing fresh air from the open passenger window. He was in emotional pain and desperately trying to hold back his sobbing. *Why? Why did this have to happen to her? I promised I'd protect her. It's my fault.* He whimpered as softly as he could, but Jim knew he was really hurting.

Sam was more determined than ever now. *I'm going to find that bastard. I'm coming for you.*

CHAPTER
34

"6142 to base."

"Go ahead, 6142."

"I'm following behind the silver Mazda traveling on route 129 south in Saugus heading toward Lynn. I request backup and further instructions on the APB."

"Roger 6142. All units near Route 129 south in Saugus reroute and communicate with unit 6142 in backup support. The suspect passenger is wanted for murder. Proceed with caution. He is armed and dangerous, but the driver is an innocent bystander. All responding units report in."

Four state police units responded within seconds.

Sam wiped his eyes and blew his nose listening to the radio traffic regarding the sighting of the Mazda. Sam's stomach was rumbling, and tense pressure pounded the back of his head. He saw images of Juli smiling while staring at him with her dazzling hazel-blue eyes. Trooper Jim Markham sensed the burden Sam was experiencing. "You okay, Sam?"

Sam nodded, but his body was bursting with anger and guilt. Grief had taken hold of him. *If only I had stayed with her.*

With his gas pedal hugging the floorboard and the cruiser's lights and siren causing traffic to make room, Jim asked, "Is Al Madari the leader responsible for what happened this morning during the raid?"

"He is, and I'm not letting him escape again if I can help it. He's going to pay with his life for what he did."

"This is 6142, subject entering Lynn."

"6142, this is unit 5116. We have the mosque on Esson Hill Road covered. Don't give the suspect a reason to change course." Five responses from state police troopers indicated they were minutes from the mosque.

While taking instructions from Rash, Benji Pahlavi tried to get him in a conversation during the trip, but Rash was not interested in talking. As they entered Lynn, Al Madari's cell phone vibrated. He whispered when answering the call. He listened to instructions from the caller. After the call ended, Al Madari typed information onto his phone's navigation app. He then gave Benji new directions to follow. He checked the side-view mirror for cars following behind them. He detected what he believed was a police car surreptitiously following two cars behind them

"The subject vehicle has its directional signal on for Esson Hill Road," reported unit 6142. Two units were in position at the mosque. Other units were five minutes out.

Sam looked at his GPS that gave the estimated time of their arrival. "Shit. We're still six minutes out at best. Can you drive faster, Jim?"

"Too many intersections up ahead. We don't want to get into an accident now. We'll get there soon enough. The guy will be in cuffs or dead by the time we get there," responded Markham.

"I hope you're right, Jim, but I wouldn't count on it."

"This is 6142 to all units. The suspect drove right by Esson Hill Road and stepped on it. He's moving fast and went through a red traffic light. He's now turning left up ahead. I can't see the street sign—wait—stand by—there it is. He went left onto Hillside Avenue, but I don't see his car. He must have taken a right onto Freemont Street. Making the turn now—I still don't see the car—stand by one—I got it now. The Mazda pulled out from in front of a small market heading— stand by—his blinker is on for a right turn.

"Jim, ask if it was a Muslim market," said Sam.

"4458 to 6142, was it a Muslim market where he stopped?"

"It could have been, but I'm not sure. I had my eyes on the car. I still see a driver and a passenger in the vehicle. It appears they turned back toward Esson Hill Road."

"Jim, we have to get to that market. They stopped there for a reason. Head to Fremont Street," advised Sam.

"6142 to all units, subject Mazda has the directional signal for a left turn onto Esson Hill." A moment passed. "He's now approaching the mosque— he has his signal on for the mosque parking lot." Seconds later. "The subject is turning into the parking lot. It's a go for the takedown."

"Sam, should we head to the mosque?" asked Markham.

"No. Let's go to the store. I'd like you to cover the back. If Al Madari is still in the Mazda, we'll head there once we know they arrested him."

Trooper Markham pulled up in front of the market. Sam rushed out of the car and entered the market as Trooper Markham hustled to the rear.

When Sam entered, he surveyed the store first and spotted a woman at the counter. "Police. Where is Rashid Al Madari? He came in here a few minutes ago."

Stunned by his remarks, the Muslim woman claimed no one came into the store.

Upset, Sam yelled at her. "We were watching outside your store and saw him come in! Are you hiding him, or did you take him someplace else?"

The woman nervously answered that she was in the back room and didn't see anyone enter the store. Sam knew she was lying because a buzzer sounded off when he entered the store.

"Is he in your backroom?" asked Sam while moving toward the room.

As Sam approached it, Trooper Markham, who had entered from the back door, walked out of the room saying, "I just heard radio communication that they identified the two in the Mazda. Our guy was not one of them. They identified Benji Pahlavi and Arian Baraghani as the passenger."

Sam looked at the woman and asked, "Is Arian your husband?

She hesitated, shaking her head no, then muttered, "He is my son."

"The police arrested your son. He is in big trouble. If you help us, I will make sure your son will go free," said Sam.

The woman was afraid and on edge. She wasn't sure what to do, but she wanted to protect her son. "Someone called to take him someplace else. I do not know where."

"Take who someplace else? The guy who came into the store?"

The woman was silent, nodding her head yes.

"Who took him someplace else? Was it your husband? The police want the guy who came into the store. He killed people. He killed the police. We don't want your husband, only the guy who came here. Now help us, or the police will arrest your husband and send him and your son to jail!"

"I don't know where. My husband got a phone call. I did not hear where?"

"What car did your husband use?"

"A Toyota," she said.

"What color? Is it a car, a van, or an SUV?" asked Markham.

"A white SUV," she reluctantly revealed.

"Is the SUV registered to your husband or the store?" asked Markham.

She said she did not know. Markham asked to see the store's state permit to operate.

The woman took them to the back room, where Markham reviewed the permit and radioed for a motor vehicle registration check on a white Toyota SUV registered to Kazmi Baraghani or Baraghani's Market on Fremont Street in Lynn. In minutes, he received the license plate information and put out an APB request on the vehicle last seen leaving the vicinity of Fremont Street.

Before leaving the store, Sam asked the woman one last question. "Did the man leave anything in the store or take anything like a hat or a jacket?"

"My husband gave him a gray sweatshirt with a hood."

Sam and Jim left the store. While back in the cruiser, Jim radioed for a status check on Pahlavi and Baraghani and got an immediate response. "Pahlavi said his boss asked him to give Rash a ride to the mosque. When Rash got a phone call, he told Pahlavi to drive to the market. At the store,

Rash went inside, and Baraghani took his place in the car with instructions to drop him off at the mosque."

"Roger that. Hold both for further questioning." Markham turned to Sam. "Where to next, Sam?"

Sam used his cell phone to search for other mosques in the area. "There's another mosque on the North Shore, so let's head in that direction. Hopefully, a patrolling officer will spot the SUV. We need to find this killer before he disappears for good."

CHAPTER
35

Agents Jennifer Clarkson, Ziggy, and Pete, met with Assistant U.S. Attorney Brian Murphy regarding the undercover meeting with Sonny at Macky's Grill. State police Detective Sergeant Patrick Haywood joined them.

Pete showed Murphy the slip of paper he got from Sonny, identifying the target.

"Just as we figured. Did Sonny mention who put out the contract?" asked Murphy.

"No. He's not saying. Not yet, anyway. Once we bust him, he'll have plenty of incentive to cut a deal and talk," answered Pete.

"We now know who Sonny is, and he has a record. So let's find out from the local police and Dawkins the identity of any known associates of Sonny," said Murphy.

"I'll call my office for any intel on that," asserted Detective Haywood.

Clarkson spoke up. "We're already on that. We have three agents contacting police departments. Addison Hooks, aka Sonny, is a felon with convictions for assault twice, possession of stolen goods, and sale of cocaine. He was a person of interest in two murders, but there was insufficient evidence to charge him. He served prison time for assault and drug charges and is on parole after serving fourteen months for the second assault charge."

Ziggy interrupted them. "I think we all know who put out the contract. We've talked about this already. Forster Harrington has to be behind this whole thing. He threatened Sam to get even with him by getting at his son. So now we have this guy, Sonny Hooks, as the middleman on a contract to kill Sam's son. I put my money on Harrington."

"You're probably right, Zig. However, he's in prison, as is his fixer Tony Dellagatti. Let's find out who's been visiting Forster at the prison. Also, find out who Forster has called and who has called him. We have to find a link between Harrington and Hooks," said Murphy.

"We'll get on it. Do you think we should contact Sam and let him know?" asked Clarkson.

"You bet your ass we should let him know. He'll be pissed if we don't. I guarantee he'll want to be in on this," said Ziggy.

"I agree. We should let Sam know. I'm going to inform the U.S. Attorney, as well. She definitely will want to know if Forster Harrington is behind this, and if he is, she'll push for a longer prison term," added Murphy.

"Remember, Harrington's daughter, Rachel, also threatened Sam for revenge, and she never got charged and is not in jail. My bet is she's the go-between for her father and Sonny," said Ziggy.

"Alright. Let's work on finding the connection between Harrington, his daughter, Sonny, or anyone else involved. Contact Sam and let him know what's happening. I also recommend calling his son's boss at the State Department. Keep me informed on anything you find out," directed Murphy.

When back in her office, Clarkson called Sam to give him the update on the murder-for-hire investigation.

"Hi Jennifer, I'm in the middle of something here. I only have a minute."

"Pete, Ziggy, and I met with Brian Murphy to discuss how we should proceed with the murder-for-hire investigation. However, before I fill you in on the plan, I have to tell you we know who the target is in Boston."

"Boston, huh? You're not saying it's me, are you?"

"It's not you, Sam. It's your son, Drew."

"Drew? If that's the case, there's no doubt that Forster Harrington is the brains behind the hit. He threatened he would get even with me by getting at my son."

"That's who we figured too, but we have to prove it. Since Harrington's currently serving time, he has a perfect alibi, and the same goes for his enforcer, Dellagatti."

"So, what's your plan?"

"First, we contact Drew's boss to arrange a scheme with Drew's cooperation for a staged hit on him while we begin surveillance on Sonny. Then Pete will call Sonny that he finished the job and wants to get paid. Hopefully, Sonny will lead us to the person we believe is Harrington's money conduit for the payoff. Right now, we suspect it's his daughter."

"That sounds good, Jen. Just remember, I want to be there when you reach the point we nail Harrington."

"Of course, Sam. We already penciled you in for that. I'm going to call Drew's boss and meet with him tomorrow. If things go as planned, this could be over in three or four days."

"Thanks for the update, Jen. I'm going to call Drew and fill him in."

*   *   *

Trooper Markham and Sam headed toward Route 129 north when they heard a Lynn police officer report spotting the SUV. "This is Lynn unit 6812. I'm behind the white Toyota heading south on Drake Street, with only the driver inside."

"Tell them to pull him over and wait for our arrival," said Sam.

"This is state police unit 4468 to 6812. Request you pull over the SUV and hold the driver until my arrival."

"10-4, 4468. Pulling over the vehicle now."

Sam set his phone's GPS for Drake Street. "Looks like we're only minutes from Drake Street, Jim."

Ten minutes later, Trooper Markham pulled up behind two Lynn police cruisers and the white Toyota. Markham and Sam met with the two officers who had the driver up against the police vehicle hood. One officer handed Markham the guy's driver's license. Sam and Markham saw it was in the name of Kazmi Baraghani.

Sam took over the questioning. He pushed Kazmi's head down on the cruiser's hood and whispered close to his ear.

"You gave a ride to a terrorist who shot and killed police officers. We will arrest you, your son, and your wife for helping a murderer escape. You all will spend years in prison and then get deported. Your troubles could only go away if you tell me where you took Rashid right now."

"I don't know any person with that name."

"Kazmi, Rashid is the guy who entered your store. Your wife told us you gave him a sweatshirt with a hood. Your son Arian switched places with Rashid in a car that drove to the mosque, where the police arrested him. Your wife told me the guy went with you in your Toyota. The police followed you until they lost you. We know you gave him a ride. Tell me where you brought the man if you want me to help you and your family. Tell me now, or you go straight to jail from here."

"If I tell you, will you let me and my son go?"

"Yes, but you must tell me where he is now, and he'd better still be there."

"I got a call to drop him off on Bowen Court. It is a small street not far from the mosque. A guy was waiting there for him. That is all I know."

"Who called you?" asked Sam.

"I got a call from the Imam's friend telling me a guy would stop at my store, and I should take him to Delaware Drive. Later, I got a second call telling me to bring him to Bowen Court. I do not know who called me then."

"I want you to show me where you brought him. Did you see the guy waiting for Rashid and where he took him?"

"Yes, but I do not know the man. He wore a hat and sunglasses and turned away so I could not see his face. He did not move until I drove away."

CHAPTER
36

With Kazmi slouched down on the back seat, Sam and Trooper Jim Markham, utilizing an unmarked state detective's sedan, drove to where Kazmi dropped off Al Madari. Bowen Court was a short cul-de-sac street off Delaware Drive within a half-mile of the Mosque on Esson Hill Road, a parallel street. Sam reached into his pocket, ensuring he still had the necklace that Al Madari dropped. Jim stopped at the corner of Delaware and Bowen Court to survey the cul-de-sac before turning onto the short street. Sam counted six homes total, three on each side of the street considered part of Bowen Court. The end of the cul-de-sac had a wide circular area that allowed vehicles to turn around easily. Also, a line of woods at the end of the street, ranging between forty and fifty yards wide, ran between Bowen Court, Delaware Drive, and Esson Hill Road.

"Kazmi, where exactly did you drop off Rashid?" asked Sam.

Kazmi pointed in front of the last home on the left. Sam noticed a narrow path into the woods to the right of that house. While Markham slowly turned around in the cul-de-sac, Sam took a few photos and wondered if the path led to the mosque. At that moment, he began to experience the typical unexplained weird feelings that alerted him. Sam noted the address of the homes located on Bowen Court as Markham headed back to Delaware Drive. "Jim, let's take a right on Delaware Drive. Drive slow, so I can note the street address of the first three or four house numbers as we make the turn," said Sam.

While they rolled slowly by the first three houses, Sam again felt the eerie sensation he got when receiving a sign.

"Okay, Jim. Let's turn around so I could take note of the street address of the houses on Delaware on the other side of Bowen Court." As they drove slowly by those houses, Sam felt no sensations. "Jim, let's drop Kazmi at his store and take a statement from him."

Trooper Markham had noticed Sam's trembling before heading back to the market but didn't mention it while Kazmi was in the car.

It wasn't long before they had the statement in hand and left the store.

"Where to now, Sam?" asked Markham.

"Let me make a couple of calls, and then I can tell you where. It will only take a few minutes." Sam first called Major Burke's cell number. Burke answered the phone, asking if they'd located Rashid.

"Not yet. I'm still with Trooper Markham. We interviewed and took a statement from a guy who dropped Rashid off near the mosque on Bowen Court in Lynn. An unidentified guy was waiting there for him. I'm certain this unknown guy is hiding Rashid until they can move him elsewhere. I recommend we put a twenty-four-hour surveillance near Bowen Court and the mosque. We can't let this murderer escape."

"How many cars do you estimate we'll need?"

"Minimum four cars. I can explain in more detail where to position them. Where are you?"

"I'm at Mass General, where the injured troopers are under treatment. I'm here for the duration of the night."

"I'll meet you there. I'm about thirty minutes out. We could meet at the cafeteria if that works for you. I'm wounded and should see a doctor there, as well."

"That works. I hope your wounds are not serious."

"The pain has diminished, so I hope it's only minor. See you there shortly." Sam downplayed the physical pain that subsided, but the emotional pain remained high.

"Jim, drop me off at Mass General in Boston. I'm going to meet with Major Burke there. You're welcome to join me when I meet with him if you want."

"I'll stick with you, Sam. I'm on the clock. Plus, I could use a coffee and something to eat. I'm starving."

"That makes two of us. So let's put the pedal to the metal. Pretend you're an ambulance driver bringing an injured person to the hospital."

Jim switched on his emergency lights and siren and pressed the gas pedal. "Well, it's justified. You're injured and in need of a doctor."

During the drive to Boston, Sam called Andrea.

"Sam, where are you?" asked Andrea.

"I'm on my way to Mass General. I should be there in about thirty minutes."

"That's where I am. Major Burke and quite a few officers and family members are here."

"I just got off the phone with Burke. He's going to meet me at the cafeteria. Why don't I meet you there too?"

"I'll be here, Sam. I need to see you. We need each other's support now."

"Can you tell me the body count from the raid site?"

"Twelve dead, eight severely injured. It was a horrific scene. I've been in tears for hours. I'm brokenhearted and so emotional over what happened to Juli. I know you are too. We need each other now, Sam."

Hearing the hurt in Andrea's voice only caused Sam's sick feelings and emotions to elevate.

Twenty-five minutes later, Trooper Markham pulled up in front of Mass General with his emergency lights flashing. A trooper assisting in the parking for the high volume of state police cruisers directed Markham to an empty spot to park. Andrea waited by the entrance doors as Sam and Markham entered the hospital. She embraced Sam. Sam felt Andrea trembling as she burst into tears. He tried comforting her, but it didn't help. It took a couple of minutes before she released her tight grip on him.

"Sam, you have bloodstains on your shirt. Are you hurt? Do you need to see a doctor?"

"Yes, but it can wait a few more minutes. I need to meet with Burke first to establish surveillance in Lynn, where I believe Al Madari is hiding. Once that's done, I'll see the doctor."

Sam and Markham followed Andrea to the cafeteria where Burke was waiting. Sam asked for a sheet of paper and a pen. Once in hand, he diagramed Bowen Court between Delaware Drive and Esson Hill Road. Next, he placed an X to mark the positioning of the surveillance cars, including two vehicles near the mosque and two on Delaware Drive. Then, Sam recapped where Kazmi Baraghani dropped off Al Madari on Bowen Court and circled the three homes to focus on along Delaware Drive.

"Why those three houses, Sam?" asked Burke as Markham and Andrea looked on.

"I can't specifically explain the reason, but trust me on this, Jack, these three and the mosque are more relevant than the other homes. I need to be checked out by a doctor and then get some rest, so I'd appreciate it if you could let me know the officer in charge of the surveillance. I'll call him in the morning to let him know I will join them. I'm convinced Al Madari is hiding in that area."

"You have an uncanny sense of finding things, Sam, so I'll trust you on this. I hope you're right. My problem is we are down quite a few officers because of what happened during the raid. We still have a large contingent of officers at the raid site. I can get one team to head over there now until I can get additional detectives from other parts of the state. The earliest we can get four teams in position would be tomorrow morning. Now, go get checked by a doctor. I'll talk to you later."

"Thanks, Jack. Oh, by the way, where is Lieutenant Randell?"

"Like most of us, he worked long hours today. Plus, his wife is pregnant and wasn't feeling well, so he asked to go home and care for her. He'll be off duty for a couple of days."

"One other thing before I forget. Trooper Markham has been a tremendous help today, not just to me but for this whole operation. I need you to know he is one outstanding officer. It shouldn't go unnoticed."

"Well, thanks for saying that, Sam," said Burke, who turned to Trooper Markham with an appreciative nod of recognition.

Sam then followed Andrea to a doctor while Markham followed behind. He thanked Sam for the praise.

"It needed to be said, Jim. I appreciate all you did. I'm going to see a doctor, and then I'm done for tonight. There's no need for you to come with me. Detective Serrano offered to drive me home. You should get something to eat, then head home and get some rest. I hope we get a chance to work together again. Maybe you can volunteer for the surveillance."

"I'll go volunteer to the major right now. Maybe we'll see each other again tomorrow."

CHAPTER
37

Sam followed Andrea to the cadre of doctors caring for the injured officers. He didn't have to wait long before they took him into a private room for examination. Andrea accompanied him into the room. He took off his shirt and vest for the doctor's examination. The doctor entered shortly after that and examined the wound on his arm.

"Umm. You're lucky. The bullet didn't go through your arm, but it put a good-sized gash that I'll need to clean and stitch. I assume you were wearing that vest because it looks like a second bullet hit your vest here on your left side. It's bruised, and you may have fractured a rib. I'm sure you have pain in that area. I'll give you some pills to take for the pain because it's not going away soon. It will most likely become black and blue. I'll arrange to have someone take x-rays of your ribcage. Sit tight. I'll be right back to clean and stitch your arm.

Once the doctor sutured the arm, Sam and Andrea followed the doctor to the x-ray room, where a technician took pictures of Sam's chest. When finished, the technician had them wait in an adjoining room for the doctor to read the images.

While alone in the room and they had privacy, Sam gave Andrea a list of the addresses of the six homes, three on Delaware Drive and three on Bowen Court, and asked her to find out the names of the persons living in them.

"I need to know like yesterday, Andrea. No later than nine tomorrow morning. Can you do that?

"Is this connected with where you think Al Madari is hiding?"

"Yes, and I want to get to him before he gets moved elsewhere."

"I'll make the call right now. I'll put a rush on it. I'll be right back. They don't like you using cell phones here, plus the signal is weak."

Sam looked at his watch. He was hungry and exhausted and needed sleep. He wanted to call his son to let him know he was okay. He also had a hunch and wanted his son to do a background check on someone.

Several minutes later, Andrea returned. "I'll have the information by nine-thirty in the morning. I have the keys to Juli's place. Let's get a takeout dinner and go back to the apartment. You can spend the night. We're both emotionally drained and feel like zombies and could use the rest and each other's support right now. The apartment is close to the hospital and Lynn. My sister agreed to watch my daughter for a few days."

Before Sam could answer, the doctor entered the room. He placed the x-ray films on the lit screen and studied the images. "You were lucky. It looks like a minor fracture on one of the ribs. It will heal itself in time. So here are the samples I promised. Take one every six to eight hours, preferably with food, until the pain subsides. You could also take three 200 milligrams of ibuprofen if you prefer."

"Okay, thanks, doc. I'd like to get home, eat, and get some rest. I haven't eaten all day and have been up since three in the morning."

"I understand. I've heard about what happened. I'm sorry for the loss and pain you're experiencing. I'll have you sign a release form, and you can be on your way. I'll write my name and telephone number on your copy should you need to see me again."

"Will do, doc. Thanks for looking me over. I needed to know I was still alive," Sam said jokingly.

On the drive to her apartment, Andrea called for a take-out order at a restaurant not far from the apartment. Sam said he had to make a call when they arrived at the restaurant. He gave her a fifty-dollar bill to pay for the order. While she went into the restaurant to pick up the dinner, Sam called his son, Drew. He was still at work in his office.

"Dad, I heard about the raid this morning. Are you alright? I've left messages with you all day."

"I'm fine, but so many officers are not. Sorry about not calling sooner, but I've been on the go all day. I got winged and bandaged up at Mass General, so I'm fine. But, unfortunately,"—Sam's lips began quivering, and his eyes teared—"I, uh,—uh—Juli was hit severely and—and, uh, she didn't make it," whimpered Sam, as he covered his mouth to silence his sobbing.

"Shit. I'm so sorry, dad. You must be hurting pretty bad. Is there anything I can do?"

Sam paused to get control of himself. "Yeah, I'm hurting. I need sleep, but I don't know if I'll get any tonight. I'm an emotional mess right now. The guy who shot her is the same guy who shot the state trooper you, and I witnessed. I have to get the bastard, but I need sleep right now. Andrea is also emotionally under the weather. I'm with her now. Anyway, I'm okay." Sam paused, wiping his tears and trying to get a grip on himself. "How did the meeting go with the Hartford agents?"

"Good. Agent Clarkson called and said they wouldn't be here until tomorrow mid-afternoon. They decided it would be more convincing if we staged the hit when it was nighttime while I pretended to be sleeping in bed. We'll discuss the plan in detail when they arrive. We plan on having dinner together before executing the plan at my apartment."

"Sounds good. I need you to run an immigration check on someone. It's critically important I get the results soon." Sam gave him the name, approximate age, and all the information he had on the person. He ended the call when Andrea returned with the food. She saw him with the phone in his hand. "Is everything alright, Sam?"

"Someone hired a hit on my son as payback to me. I had arrested an influential businessman's son, who kidnapped and murdered young boys. His son subsequently committed suicide in jail, so he's seeking revenge. We convicted the father for trying to obstruct our investigation, resulting in him threatening me."

"Jesus, not only do you have to deal with all the hurt over Juli's death, but now you have to deal with threats against your son too."

"I don't want to talk. I need to eat, have a drink and get some sleep."

It only took a few minutes before they entered Juli's apartment. They relaxed on the stools at the kitchen counter, where Juli and Sam often ate and drank wine. While Sam unwrapped the dinner, Andrea opened a half-full bottle of red wine and poured them a glass. They both stared at each other when she put the bottle on the counter. Within seconds, tears began falling from their cheeks, causing them to embrace each other.

Andrea tried speaking, but her words were hard to understand. Finally, when she calmed herself, Sam got the drift of what she tried to say.

Sniffling, Andrea repeated that Juli was like a sister to her. "I still can't believe she's gone. I miss her—terribly. I don't know if I will ever get over her death. We did everything together." Andrea sniffled again and wiped her eyes. "I know you loved her, Sam, but I loved her too. What am I going to do without her?"

Sam sniffled and wiped his eyes and runny nose. He could hardly speak himself. He was heartbroken and slurred his words. Their emotions got the best of them for several minutes before Andrea put her arms around Sam, whispered she needed him, and then kissed him. Sam was not expecting it and pushed back from her.

"Sorry, Sam, but I'm an emotional wreck. I lost a part of me when Juli died, and I need someone to lean on. I've been crying all day and can't stop. I'll never be able to sleep. I don't have anyone that understands how close Juli and I were."

Sam understood the hurt she was dealing with since he felt the same pain.

"Andrea, you can lean on me, and we can support each other. However, our need for emotional support can't extend to the bedroom. I liked Juli a lot, and she's the only one that I can think of in that way right now. It's going to take me a long time to get over her. Please understand that."

Andrea released her tight grip on him. Tears rolled down her cheeks. Sam knew she was suffering and needed someone—anyone—to comfort her. "Listen, Andrea, I'm starving and exhausted. I know you are too. So let's eat a little and get some sleep. I'm emotionally uptight, so I don't even know if I could get any sleep. Maybe we can talk until we pass out on the couch."

"Okay, I understand, Sam. Thanks for staying here for me. Hopefully, with you here, maybe I'll be able to fall asleep. I don't want to be alone."

"After we eat, I'm going to take a shower. I'm sure you do too, so you can go first. I'll shower after you."

After eating and having more than one glass of wine, Sam showered, walked into the bedroom, and saw Andrea was in bed. She told Sam they would have a better chance of restful sleep in a bed rather than the couch. Sam felt she probably was right but only agreed to get into bed until she fell asleep. Then, he'd move to the sofa.

Once both were in bed, they talked for nearly an hour, mainly about Juli. Andrea didn't take long to close her eyes and fall asleep, but she put her arm around him before she did.

Sam waited until he was sure she was sound asleep before slowly moving away from her and getting out of bed. He brought a pillow with him and tip-toed to the couch. There, Sam's only thoughts were to find Al Madari. But as exhaustion set in, Juli's image filled his mind. He remembered the good times they'd spent together talking, laughing, and making love. The image of her beautiful eyes sparkling seemed to light up the darkness in his thoughts. The vision of her remained until he faded into sleep.

As the sun shined into the living room window, a cell phone rang that awakened Sam. He saw the time was nearly ten in the morning. It was time to get up and help with the surveillance. He returned the pillow to the bedroom, where Andrea was still sleeping. Sam softly asked Andrea to wake up but to no avail. After repeating it three more times, Andrea moaned and said, "I'm too tired."

"I have to go to work and find Al Madari."

Andrea opened her eyes and whispered, "We can go later, Sam."

"Your phone rang. It might be important," Sam responded.

"I'll get it later."

"I have to go now, Andrea. Sam scrambled three large eggs and toasted two English muffins while brewing coffee. When doing so, Sam heard Andrea talking on the phone. When the call ended, Andrea finally joined Sam at the counter. She thanked him for making breakfast.

"I agreed to help Juli's uncle with the funeral arrangements. That was him who called. I know Juli wanted you to meet him. He was like a father to her. Juli told me he also wanted to meet you. So I thought you might want to meet him and help with the arrangements."

"Of course, I will. Let's eat so I can get out of here. I could come back here after I finish the surveillance, and we can talk more about meeting with him. Okay?"

"Great, but we'll be coming back together because I'm coming with you. I called Major Burke and asked if I could help with the surveillance. He said it was okay. Also, I got the names of the residents living in the houses you wanted."

Although Sam had a mouth filled with food, he managed to ask if any foreign names were on the list.

"Just one," she said while handing him the list.

Sam read all the names to himself and remembered only one of them—Sara Naceri Rahmani. He immediately called his son and asked him to add her name to the one he gave him the evening before for a background check. When he finished breakfast, he called the trooper in charge of the surveillance to let him know Andrea and he would join the crew. Sam was eager to get back to Lynn. He felt he was close to finding Al Madari.

CHAPTER
38

A gent Clarkson, Macheski, and Ziglar arrived at the Boston federal building shortly after three o'clock. At the Diplomatic Security Service Office, they meet with Drew, his training partner Eric Mills, and their boss, the agent in charge, Pat O'Shae. They discussed their plan for staging the hit on Drew after dark at his apartment. Once all in agreement, they met the staff at the office before breaking for dinner. Then, as it became nighttime, they put their plan in motion.

Pete Macheski took photos of Drew's apartment building entrance, showing the address on the glass door. Inside his apartment, they shut the bedroom shades to create total darkness in the room. The agents had Drew lay in bed with fake blood all over his white t-shirt. Agent Macheski, holding a fake theatrical gun with a silencer, videoed him shooting four times at Drew and then pulling back the bloody bed cover showing fake blood covering Drew's body.

After helping clean up the bed, the ATF agents headed back to Connecticut. With surveillance on Sonny and Harrington's daughter, Rachel, Pete would contact Sonny in the morning, letting him know he had finished the job.

*   *   *

Sergeant Corey James had told Sam where to meet. Thirty minutes later, Andrea and Sam met with Sergeant James in a strip mall parking lot a short distance from the surveillance vehicles covering Delaware Drive and Bowen Court.

"Why are we watching those particular homes on Delaware Drive? Do we have information that Al Madari may be hiding in one of them?" asked James.

"I can't say with certainty Al Madari is in one of those six houses. However, we ran a check to determine the names of all the residences, three on Bowen and three on Delaware. One returned with a Middle Eastern name, Sara Naceri Rahmani, who hadn't lived there for a long time. The others came back to older residents who have lived there for decades. So, it's just a hunch that we should focus on that particular house but still be aware of the others, just in case." said Sam.

The sergeant showed Sam a photo taken from the security camera at the Crescent Drive Plaza convenience store during the search warrant. "Al Madari looks more like an American now with his hair and beard cut way back and wearing American clothing."

Andrea checked her email. "I received the photo too. I'll send you a copy, Sam."

Sam and Andrea relieved the officers covering the homes on Delaware Drive. They sat there for two hours before Sam received a call from Drew.

"How did the staged event go last night?" asked Sam.

"It went as planned. This morning, Pete was supposed to contact Sonny letting him know the job was done and demanding the final payment. ATF has a wire on Sonny's phone to listen in on his calls and a tail to see where he goes. They figure he will call and meet with whoever has the money and hopefully identify that person, most likely Harrington's daughter. I haven't heard anything from Agent Clarkson yet, but assume she won't report anything until something significant happens today."

"Okay. I'm glad to hear everything went well last night. I'll probably hear from her later today too."

"I called to tell you I received some preliminary information on Sara Naceri. She is Iranian and legally entered the country from the UK under a student visa in 2004. She graduated from a college in Ohio, earning a

Bachelor's and Master's Degree in Computer Hardware Engineering in 2010. She is five feet six in height, with black hair and brown eyes. In 2012, she married Mateen Rahmani, an Iranian who also attended the same college in Ohio. She worked in Ohio for a while before landing a job at a computer software company near Boston and took residence in Lynn. Headquarters is still working on completing Mateen Rahmani's entire background. He came to the U.S. as a child, lived with his aunt until she died, then got placed with multiple foster parents. They need another day to complete the background on him. I'll get back to you when I get it. Regarding the other person you wanted me to get information on, it's in the works, but nothing yet."

"Thanks for the quick response. I appreciate it. This information could lead us to the killer I'm trying to find. Let me know as soon as you get the information on her husband."

"I will, dad. How are you handling everything? Is there anything I can do to help?"

"You are helping. I'm still hurting, but hopefully, time will heal the pain. Thanks, son. I have to run." They ended the call.

"Everything okay, Sam?" asked Andrea.

"Yeah. Drew provided some background on Sara Naceri. She is Iranian and legally entered the country from England as a student in 2004. After graduating from college in Ohio in 2010, she married an Iranian, Mateen Rahmani. Some years later, she got a job near Boston and moved to Lynn. Drew is checking to get additional information on her husband and another guy I'm checking on.

"You think there is a connection between Rahmani and Al Madari?"

"There could be. We have to find out who Al Madari met on Bowen Court. I'm betting that whoever he met is either hiding him or knows where he is hiding. If it was Rahmani, she or her husband might be hiding him in that house. We need to find out if he is in there now."

Later, Sam and Andrea got relieved for a lunch break. They went to a local café recommended by Sergeant James near the surveillance site. After lunch, they rotated to a position watching Bowen Court from a bank parking lot diagonally across from the entrance to Bowen Court. After three hours, they rotated to watch the mosque before the next team arrived to replace them. Then, Sam requested they get positioned to surveil the homes on Delaware Drive during the last two hours. While on surveillance there, Sam got a call from Agent Jennifer Clarkson.

"Hi, Jen. Tell me some good news."

"Everything went good until Pete picked up a tail after Sonny paid him six grand. We figured Sonny ordered the tail, and when it didn't work, we felt he probably wouldn't meet with Pete again. But when Pete called to tell him the job got done, Sonny answered. Pete filled him in on the successful hit and wanted to get paid. Sonny asked a lot of questions about how, when, and where the job got done. Pete answered his questions, but Sonny wanted proof before making any payment. Pete told Sonny he videoed the hit and would show him when they met, but Sonny insisted Pete text him a copy of the video. Pete did what he could to convince Sonny to meet in person, but Sonny insisted on seeing the video first before meeting with Pete. Long story short, Pete texted him the video and waited until he heard Sonny's phone ding when he received the text. Pete gave him time to view the video before demanding to meet to get paid. That's when Sonny hung up. Pete called him back twice, but Sonny never answered."

"So what's the plan now?" asked Sam.

"We have surveillance on Sonny and Rachel Harrington and have his cell and Forster's private cell tapped. We expect Sonny to turn over the video in return for the money, and we'll be there to film it all. We'll take down Sonny and whoever is involved when that happens."

"Okay. I think Sonny planned on ripping off Pete from the start. Thanks for the update. You guys are doing great. Tell the crew the same for me."

Sam was less than pleased, but he knew investigations have setbacks. Nevertheless, Sam remained optimistic that the Hartford agents' plan would work and result in the arrests of all those involved. Moreover, he felt the arrests would lead them to Dellagatti and Forster Harrington.

CHAPTER
39

"**O**ur shift is almost over, Sam. We still have some of last night's takeout orders in the refrigerator. There's a liquor store on the way to the apartment where we can get a bottle of wine."

Sam's first thought was to call Alli Gaynor to tell her when he could meet for dinner. "I promised to have dinner with a friend I worked with in Harford, but I'll put it off until tomorrow night."

Twenty minutes later, Andrea was driving back to Juli's apartment after being relieved by the night surveillance team. They stopped at a liquor store on the way. While Sam searched for the wine, he called Alli's cell number. It took five rings before she answered.

"Sam, I hope you're calling to tell me you can meet for dinner."

"I am. Can we meet tomorrow night? I'm still on the job and tired. I hope that works for you."

"That's fine. I've been covering the story of the FBI raid in the Haverhill area. I heard an ATF agent was involved with the raid. Was that you, Sam?"

"It was, and I'm okay if that's what you were going to ask."

"No, I have the names of those injured. It had to be a horrific scene. What happened there, Sam? This tragedy for law enforcement is unprecedented. I have a thousand questions to ask you."

"You know it's an ongoing thing. I'm limited in what I can tell you."

"I know, Sam, but I would like to get an insight that no other reporter will have. So I'm counting on you to be an unnamed source for something that will make my story stand out from the others."

"I'll think of something, but where it came from has to stay strictly between you and me."

"I knew I could count on you. I need to see you. I have so much to tell you. Could you spend the night, Sam?"

Sam was surprised by that request. He didn't think he should. He had to think fast for his answer. "I won't know until I see you. I don't know what the day will bring tomorrow. I have to run, Alli. I'll call you tomorrow. I'm looking forward to seeing you."

"I can't wait either. Please try to stay the night, Sam. I miss those nights we had together."

Sam ended the call, picked up a bottle of wine he was familiar with and climbed into Andrea's car. Once at the apartment, Sam chilled the wine and warmed up the rest of the previous night's takeout dinner while Andrea showered. When Andrea returned to the kitchen, she wore only a long white T-shirt that left little to the imagination.

"Wow, I think I know what you are trying to do, Andrea, and it's working. But, if you want me to stay the night, it's for talking only. I'm not sleeping with Juli's best friend. Please understand."

Andrea sighed with a frown on her face. "Juli talked about you so much that I became a little envious. I began liking and trusting you as much as Juli did. I shouldn't tell you this, but when I drove in the ambulance to the hospital with Juli, she held my hand and told me to take care of you. She said you were her dream come true, and I should see that you are happy and loved. I took that to mean Juli wanted us to be together. I think she'd want us to move on and live our lives to the fullest." Tears ran down Andrea's eyes as she spoke.

Sam wiped her tears with his fingers and cupped her cheek. "Andrea, you are a beautiful woman. But you have to understand it's not right for me to be with Juli's best friend soon after her death. It will take a lot of time before I'm ready for a relationship right now. But, I'll be here for you as a close friend and try to comfort you the best I can. This is how it has to be right now."

"Alright, Sam. I understand." Her eyes started to fill with tears again. She used a nearby towel to clear her tears. "Before I forget, I was on the phone with Juli's uncle, Luis Costillo. Major Burke contacted him regarding plans for the procession following the funeral service. Luis wants to meet and have both of us speak at her funeral."

"Oh, God. I don't know if I could speak without crying like a baby. I mean it. I know I'll get very emotional. I may not be able to finish what I would say."

"I know. I'll cry like a baby, too, but we have to do it for Juli."

Sam held up his glass of wine. "A toast to a beautiful and dedicated woman. I miss her and will never forget her."

"I loved her, and she will always be with me." Andrea's words became indistinguishable as her emotions got the best of her again. She put her glass down and wrapped her arms around Sam as her tears rolled onto his shoulder. Sam rubbed her back and softly whispered comforting words to her.

Andrea pushed back away from him. "I feel guilty asking you to be with me like this, but I need to take my mind off the constant feeling of hopelessness, especially when alone. I can't seem to get a grip on myself."

"Andrea, let's not talk about Juli for the rest of the night. It only hurts more thinking about her constantly. Instead, let's eat and enjoy the rest of the wine." They ate and finished the wine, most of it by Andrea. Soon, she felt a buzz that helped settle down her emotions. Sam took a shower, put on a pair of gym pants and a t-shirt, and checked for messages on his phone before returning to the living room.

Andrea was sitting on the couch, looking a little exhausted. Sam sat with her as they talked and laughed for nearly two hours, mainly about Andrea's time in the military, how she and Juli met, and the times they had together during state police training. With the amount of wine Andrea drank, it didn't long for her to doze off. Sam quietly left the couch, covered Andrea with a blanket, dressed, and left the apartment. The walk to Drew's apartment was only fifteen minutes. He had his own key to the apartment and went straight to bed.

Sam's eyes opened as the morning sunlight lit up the room. He shut off the alarm that was about to go off in a few minutes. He got dressed and called Andrea. Her phone rang six times before she answered. "Sam, what happened? Where are you?"

"After you fell asleep, I got a text from Drew. He needed something I had locked in my SUV. He lives only fifteen minutes away, so I went to his place. I decided to stay there. I'm on my way back to your apartment. We can have breakfast there and then head out to Lynn."

Sam felt guilty about leaving Andrea on the couch and making up a story about why he left, but he had no choice. The situation was getting out of hand. Once at her apartment, they had a quiet breakfast together as both felt awkward about the previous night. Following breakfast, they drove to Lynn and met with Sergeant James later than Sam wanted. Andrea apologized to the sergeant for being late.

"Sorry, Sergeant, we'll work until eight tonight to make up for it. That will allow the night shift guys to take a longer dinner break."

"No problem. I planned to take the first couple of hours for one of our guys, who called in saying he would be late for the night shift. So now I don't have to," said James.

Sam and Andrea's first post was watching the mosque on Esson Hill Road. It wasn't the assignment Sam wanted, but later they got rotated to Delaware Drive, closer to where he believed Al Madari took refuge.

"Sitting for hours on surveillance watching and waiting is tedious and not productive," Sam said restlessly. "I prefer searching for this guy, not observing." While sitting there bored, Sam got a call from his son.

"Hi, Drew."

"Hey, dad. I knew you wanted the information on Rahmani as soon as I got it. I just received it." Drew reported what he learned from his inquiry and asked, "Does that help?"

"Son of a bitch. The pieces are falling into place."

"So it does help?" replied Drew.

"Yes, it helps a ton. Thanks, but I have to go. I've got a promise to keep."

CHAPTER
40

"That sounded like good news," mentioned Andrea.

"Yes, it solved the puzzle. As I mentioned, Sara Rahmani, who lives in the house we're watching, married Marteen Rahmani, an Iranian. He came to the U.S. as a youngster and lived with an aunt until she died. Then, the state shifted him from one set of foster parents to another. His last foster father, a professor at the local college, had Marteen enrolled there at no cost while awaiting approval for adopting him. It was the same college in Ohio that Sara attended. They met there and shortly afterward were married. Unfortunately, the adoption didn't officially get completed until after they married. That's when Marteen assumed the name of his foster parents. His adopted parents' last name is Randell."

Andrea's eyebrows elevated while her jaw dropped, stunned by Sam's implication. "You don't mean Lieutenant Randell is this Rahmani guy?

"Yes, I do!" Sam said with emphasis.

"Holy shit. You're saying the lieutenant is harboring Al Madari. That can't be. He's one of us."

"Radir Semnami helped Al Madari escape from the farmhouse raid driving him to the Crescent Drive Plaza. A state trooper and I watched the plaza stores until help arrived. Randell showed up with a crew of officers to assist us. I left Randell with Radir to watch him while we searched the store's basement. I overheard Randell and Radir talking in some foreign language when returning to where they were. When I entered the room, Randell looked incensed that I walked in on their conversation. Then, when I started pressing Radir for information, Randell pulled rank, telling me he was in charge. He acted like Radir's attorney. I called Major Burke about it, and moments later, Randell got called back to the command center, and he wasn't happy."

"I don't know what to say. Are you sure it's the same person?"

"I'm ninety-eight percent sure. But based on Randell's actions and the fact that he lives right where Al Madari got dropped off, my gut tells me they're one and the same person."

"Jesus, Sam, what are you going to do? You have to be careful here. Randell is Burke's personal aide."

"I know. I'm in a quandary. If I call Burke and tell him what I've learned and suspect, he may order me to do nothing and let him handle it. That doesn't work for me. If Burke contacts Randell, he'll only deny it, and if he is hiding Al Madari in his home, he'll quickly have him moved to another location. The only way to be certain is to sneak up to the house when it's dark and see if I can see Al Madari inside. If I see any signs of him, I'm going in."

"What if you don't see Al Madari in there, or Randell or his wife sees you? It could end your relationship with the state police or your career."

"I have my way of finding out if he is hiding in the lieutenant's home." *Shit, I shouldn't have said that,* Sam thought.

"You do? How? Do you have a source?"

"Uh, yeah, yeah. I have, uh, an anonymous source." Sam didn't but had to satisfy her concern, somehow. "But listen, whatever I decide to do, it would be better if you don't take part in it."

"No way, Sam. We're partners now. I'm with you whatever you decide."

Sam thought back to the morning of the raid. *Andrea is acting like Juli did that morning. I need to keep her from taking any blame if my plan goes wrong.* Torn between going solo and checking with Burke first, Sam decided he couldn't chance it with Burke. Burke picked this guy as his aide and could stall any immediate action against him. *I have a promise to keep, and I'm going to keep it.*

"Since we told the sergeant we'd work until eight o'clock, it will be dark by then. So, when our shift ends, let's drive back up to Esson Hill Road, which parallels the one we're on. Let's drive approximately the same distance on Esson to about where Randell's house is on Delaware Drive. I'll go on foot into the woods behind Randell's place and get a closer look from the backside to see if I can spot Al Madari. I'll have my phone's earbud on so we can communicate. Burke said Lieutenant Randell is taking a few days off, so he's probably home."

"Sam, that's too risky. What if someone sees you and calls the cops?"

"I have a black hoodie in my tactical bag. I'll wear it over my ATF jacket. If anyone spots me, I'll run like hell. I'm convinced he's hiding in there. If I confirm it, I want you to contact Sergeant James and tell him I saw Al Madari inside the house from the backwoods. Tell him to have the team surround the house because I'm going inside to arrest the bastard."

Andrea shook her head no. "That's not a good plan. The sergeant might wonder if it's legit. We're not giving him a head's up on your plan, so he'll question what authority you or I have to order them to take part in hitting the house without instructions from someone in command. You could end up alone with no backup. We should contact Major Burke first and have him order the team to help."

Sam thought about what Andrea suggested. "You make a good point, Andrea." Sam reassessed his strategy. "Okay, let's do this instead. If I see Al Madari inside, I'll let you know. Call Burke and tell him you found the listing of the house we're watching in the name of Sara Rahmani, an Iranian who got married to Marteen Rahmani. Tell him we found out Rahmani changed his name to Martin Randell. Let him know I conducted surveillance on their house from the backwoods and, using binoculars, spotted Al Madari inside. Request immediate backup from the surveillance team because I'm entering the home on the grounds of exigent circumstances to arrest him. If he demands I don't go in, tell him you tried reaching me but got no response."

"God, Sam. You can't go in alone. You need backup. Randell will not be on your side. It'll be two against one."

"Probably not, but if he takes Madari's side, he goes down with him. I promised Juli I would get that guy, and that's exactly what I'm going to do. Tell me if Burke agrees to order the teams to back me up. If he does, listen to the radio chatter from the team and then request they surround the house. I'll have my vest and ATF raid jacket on when I enter the house. I have all the ammo I need if the worse happens. Wish me luck."

"Of course, but wait for me after I talk to Burke. I'll come in with you, Sam. I can cover Randell while you get Madari."

"I don't want you in harm's way. I couldn't convince Juli of that, and you know the outcome. I don't want the same to happen to you. You have a daughter who needs you. You could join the team for backup."

Andrea heard his plan, but once Sam left the car, she put her vest on and ensured she had additional ammo magazines.

Sam covertly walked between two apartment buildings and into the band of trees separating the residential homes on the parallel streets. He didn't have to move too far to align himself with the back of Randell's house. Lights were on in the raised ranch, both in the upper main living area and the basement. Sam guessed the house might have a finished basement separate from the two-car garage like many raised ranches.

As he got closer to the house, Sam could see no one through the kitchen's patio glass doors. Lights were on in the basement level, but he couldn't see anyone below the small basement windows. He first reached into his pocket and felt the necklace Al Madari dropped when he pumped gas into the van. For some reason, Sam thought it helped to find who or what he sought. From his position, Sam saw that the curtains on the two low-level windows were not fully closed. He had to get close to a basement window to see who was in the basement. Sam looked left and right to ensure it was clear before scrambling across the back lawn. He dashed swiftly but quietly across the yard and up against the house. Sam took a few deep breaths before slowly stepping toward the windows. Then, unexpectedly, an outside light lit up the backyard. Sam was sure someone saw him in the backyard. Startled and motionless for a second, he took slow steps to the corner of the house. As he passed the basement window, his body shuddered, causing his legs to wobble before reaching the corner. That's when he heard a woman's voice.

"Come on, Winnie, out you go! Come on! Out!" A small dog raced out the kitchen slider and zig-zagged around the lawn, looking for a spot to do its business. Sam soft-stepped to the corner and stepped around it to hide. The dog must have sensed his movement and began barking like crazy. Taking another half-step back, Sam nearly fell backward and had to catch hold of the gutter that made a creaking sound. That caused the dog to yelp even more. Sam realized he stood on a container wall between the backyard and the driveway four feet below near the two-car basement garage doors. Sam heard the dog's bark getting closer as it trotted toward Sam.

Sam's heart was pounding against his chest. All the time he hid, he sensed the familiar spine-chilling sensation that ran through his body, causing his body to shake as if drenched in ice-cold water. He wondered whether the feeling was a sign he had found his prey or just his nerves from being trapped and nearly discovered. Sweat rolled down his armpits.

"Quiet, Winnie. Come. Come on, girl," shouted a female voice. Sam peeked around the corner as the dog trotted back into the house. As soon as the porch light went off, his anxiety settled down. He wiped the sweat from his forehead. Then, as his quivering subsided, he cautiously moved toward the basement window with his eyes peeled on the patio porch. He knelt on one knee and was about to peek through the open portion of the curtains when he jerked up suddenly, alarmed by a call sounding in his earbud. It scared the hell out of him. Sam backed away from the window, pressed the earpiece to answer Andrea's call, then whispered, "I'll call back in a minute," and hung up.

Sam wondered if anything else was going to disrupt him from finding the killer. He shook his head, shrugging off the interruptions. He then cautiously moved forward once again. Sam leaned over and peeked in the window. What he saw brought instant rage.

CHAPTER
41

S am stared into the basement window with deep disgusting thoughts. *There's that fucking thug dining and laughing it up with the traitor, Randell. Get ready. I'm coming for both of you.*

Sam guardedly moved back into the tree line, taking cover. His pulse and heart rate were racing near top speed. He leaned against a tree and wiped his face, wet from perspiring. Sam took the time to settle his anger before realizing he needed to explain how he saw Al Madari inside the basement without crossing the private curtilage of Randell's property. Sam scanned the area for ideas when he noticed a large boulder that appeared to be in line with one of the basement windows. He mounted the boulder with one hand on an adjacent tree for balance. Sam looked through the window with his binoculars and could see the top of Madari's head sitting at a table with Randell. He had time to wait for Al Madari to move around the room, so he waited. In the meantime, Sam set his phone's camera to focus on Madari's head. He used his two fingers to spread the phone's screen to bring the view closer before selecting the video on the phone's screen. As Sam steadied the camera on Madari, his phone rang in his earbuds again, causing him to lose his balance for a second. Still pointing the phone at the window, he pressed the earbud to answer the call.

"Sam, what's going on? I'm worried. Are you okay?" asked Andrea.

"Yes, I'm fine. I'll call you back in a few minutes."

It took several minutes before Sam saw movement. The video captured Randell's face walking from the window's left side to the right side. Then Al Madari stood and moved toward Randell. The video footage captured Al Madari's face as he stepped in Randell's direction. Sam's face blossomed with satisfaction, thinking, *The heavens are finally with me tonight. I got what I need now.*

Sam carefully stepped down from the boulder, pocketed his phone, and moved behind a large tree for cover. His breathing was heavy, and his anxiety elevated. He could hear his heart thumping in his ears and chest. "Calm down, Sam. That was the easy part. Now, the hard part is about to begin," he murmured.

He called his partner. "He's in there, Andrea. I saw him with Randell. Call Burke. Tell him exactly what I told you. I saw him in the house, and I'm going in to arrest him. Call me back as soon as you hang up with him and tell me his reaction." Andrea was about to say something, but Sam stopped her. "Andrea, do it now, please."

Dreading the call, Andrea selected Major Burke's cell number on her phone and nervously waited for him to answer. When he answered, she repeated what Sam had told her to say. Burke was upset and seemingly did not believe, or did not want to believe, that the lieutenant was harboring a fugitive who killed state police officers.

"Let me speak to Sam, Andrea!" he demanded.

Andrea befittingly resisted, "Major, Sam is in a tenuous position. He saw Al Madari in the lieutenant's house, near where Al Madari got dropped off on Bowen Court. Al Madari is responsible for killing many of our officers, and we have exigent circumstances to enter the house and arrest him without delay. Sam said he was going in for the arrest and needed backup now. Please, Major, Sam is determined to go in alone if necessary. Don't let him go in without help. You owe him that much."

There was a long pause. "I want to be there. Tell Sam to wait."

"Major, time is of the essence. It's the urgency that allows Sam to enter without a warrant. You can't expect Sam to sit back and wait. Exigent means immediate and compelling. I respectfully request you order your teams to move in to assist now!"

Burke realized she was right but paused, thinking how this would look for the department in the press. His hesitation didn't last long, however. "I'll give the order, and I'll see you there within thirty minutes." He hung up.

Andrea waited until she heard Sergeant James ordering his teams to immediately move to the second house on Delaware, where he'd meet them at the foot of the driveway.

Once she heard the order, Andrea called Sam. "Burke just gave the order. The teams are on their way." Andrea was already jogging towards the tree line to assist Sam on the entry. "Give the teams a few minutes to get here."

While maintaining an eye on the house, Sam noticed Randell's wife was now in the kitchen. He leaned against a tree, trying to calm himself as he waited a few minutes for the team to get in position before approaching the kitchen patio doors.

Sergeant James waited patiently for all eight officers to arrive at the foot of Randell's driveway, where he would explain the situation and give them instructions. Sam was about to walk toward the house but stopped when hearing a rustle of leaves coming from his backside. He moved back behind a tree for cover, thinking, *Now, someone takes a stroll through the woods?* Sam hoped the intruder wouldn't see him. Unfortunately, he couldn't see who it was moving his way. Sam felt anxiety building back inside him. He became suspicious that someone would approach him at this point. *Could an associate of Al Madari or Randell be tailing me?* He thought. Remaining motionless, Sam took another peek at the intruder.

"Sam, where are you?" a woman's voice whispered.

As the person moved close enough, Sam saw it was Andrea. Sam emitted the breath he held as the tightness in his body relaxed.

"You scared me, Andrea. What are you doing here? I told you to join the team for backup."

She caught her breath first before speaking. "I'm backing you up when 'we' enter the house. I'm not going to let you go in alone."

"I don't like it." Sam felt uncomfortable putting her in danger, but she was there now, so he had to revise his plan. "Well, now that you're here, maybe the entry might work better. Randell's wife is in the kitchen now. You can see her through the patio door window. It probably would be better if you, as a female state police detective, would knock on the patio door while showing your badge. I'll stay hidden up against the house on your right. When she comes to the door, tell her it's a state police emergency, and you need to talk to the lieutenant. When she slides open the door, I'll move up, and we'll enter. Once inside, you follow behind me. Al Madari and the lieutenant are in the finished basement."

"Okay, Sam, I'm ready. Let's do it."

Andrea and Sam moved swiftly toward the patio door. Andrea moved to the door while Sam stayed hidden with his back against the house. Andrea knocked quietly on the door window. It startled Sara as she turned to see Andrea holding up a badge at the door's window. Sara cautiously moved toward the door with the dog barking as it followed behind. Sara hesitated, wondering why Andrea was in the back of the house rather than knocking on the front door. Andrea spoke quietly. "State police. I need to speak to the lieutenant. It's an emergency." Finally, Sara reluctantly unlocked and slid open the door only partway.

"Wait here. I'll get him," said Sara with a concerned look. Andrea placed her foot so the door couldn't close. Sam moved up to the door, slid it wide open, entered, and rushed past Sara, with Andrea directly behind him. The dog barked relentlessly as they dashed toward what Sam assumed was the basement door. When he opened it, Sara yelled out, "Mateen, it's the police!"

With his gun drawn, Sam swiftly moved down the stairs, shouting, "Police." Hearing that, Al Madari dashed towards a nearby cabinet, where he grabbed his pistol and fled through the door leading into the garage. Enraged, Lieutenant Randell demanded Sam stop and tried to block Sam's movement. He grabbed at Sam, and they struggled only for seconds before Sam shoved him into a chair that tripped him to the floor. In the meantime, Andrea ran past them and into the garage as the garage door was lifting.

Sam heard the garage opening and ran to it. The lieutenant managed to get up and followed a distance behind Sam.

Al Madari limped out of the garage and saw several men running up the driveway toward him. He hobbled as fast as he could toward the tree line, still hurting from his thigh wound. With Sam following behind her, Andrea was closing within several feet behind Al Madari.

As Al Madari approached the tree line, he sensed the police were gaining on him. He knew he couldn't outrun them but was determined not to surrender to the infidels. Choosing to be a martyr, he suddenly turned and quickly fired his gun in Andrea's direction, missing her but hitting one of the officers chasing behind.

Andrea nervously returned fire from about fifteen feet away, hitting Al Madari in the left arm and the left side of his chest. Sam quickly moved up alongside Andrea with his gun aimed at Al Madari. Wounded, Al Madari leaned up against the nearby tree for support. Sam slowly walked within six feet of him with his gun still aimed at him.

Al Madari recognized Sam as the officer who had been relentlessly pursuing him. He considered it shameful and cowardly to be caught by his enemy. He would not allow it. *It is time*, he thought. He whispered, "Allah Akbar," and raised his gun towards Sam.

Sam, totally at ease, with a steady gun hand pointing at Al Madari, pulled the trigger while whispering, "This is for Juli, you fucking thug."

The bullet punched a hole in the center of Al Madari's forehead and ostensibly "nailed" him dead against the tree. His body became motionless but remained upright, with his gun hanging from his trigger finger by his side. Likewise, Sam just stood motionless, staring at his target with his gun still pointing at him. Andrea moved up to Sam's side. "You nailed him, Sam," Andrea proudly proclaimed. "You kept your promise to Juli."

Randell saw Sam pin the fugitive to the tree with his wife at his side as the backup officers took control of them.

Sam said nothing as Sergeant James came to Sam's side. "I saw him raise his gun at you. I'm your witness."

"I saw it too," said Trooper Jim Markham, approaching behind the sergeant. "You got him, Sam. You said you would, and you did. I'm glad I was here to witness it."

"Anyone hurt?" asked Sam.

"One of the officers following behind got it in the vest. It hurt, but he's okay," replied the sergeant.

"What about Randell and his wife?"

"I just got a message from Major Burke. He's ten minutes out. I'll leave that up to him. We have them secured for now," said the sergeant.

"They harbored a fugitive who killed countless troopers. They both should spend the rest of their lives in prison," remarked Sam.

"I'm with you on that," said the sergeant and Andrea in unison.

Fifteen minutes later, Major Burke arrived. As he walked up the driveway, he gave Randell a repulsed look. Burke immediately moved toward Andrea, Sam, and Sergeant James. Before saying a word, he spotted Al Madari dead against the tree with his gun dangling by his side.

Burke rubbed his brow, thankful that what Andrea told him was true, that Randell had harbored the killer. "First and foremost, I want to thank the two of you and the surveillance team for a hell of a job. I still can't wrap my head around the fact that Lieutenant Randell was harboring this guy in his home. I'm so pissed that a red flag didn't pop up when we did a background on him. It's not good for our department, for me either, that we hired and fast-tracked his promotion. It will not look good in the eyes of the public when it breaks out in the news."

The sergeant asked Burke what they should do with the lieutenant and his wife.

"Separate them and bring them to the Revere station. I'll send a team of detectives to interview them. Secure the area and contact the coroner. We'll need to get a search warrant for the house and have forensics go over the scene. Andrea and Sam, I need you two to meet with me privately and brief me on how this went down. I want to know everything you both knew that led you to the point of entering the lieutenant's home and the death of this scumbag. Let's sit in my car for privacy so I can take some notes."

As they walked to Burke's car, a trooper approached Burke. "Major, the Lynn police are here and want to know if we need assistance."

"I'll deal with them, but, first, make sure the scene and house are secure."

Burke led Sam and Andrea to his car at the end of the driveway. He stopped to identify himself to the local officers. "I'll contact your chief of detectives and have him send detectives to assist. It would be appreciated if you could standby and help secure the area from the public and any press that might show up."

For the next thirty minutes, Sam and Andrea provided details on what led them to suspect Lieutenant Randell of harboring Al Madari. They answered many questions from Burke that convinced him that what they did was legal and good police work. When satisfied, Burke said, "I need both your firearms. It's protocol in all shootings. Also, you both need to give statements, so take your time to get yourselves on the same page."

After safely handing their unloaded firearms to Burke, Sam said, "Major, it's been a long tiring day. We're hungry and exhausted. We've been through a very hectic situation here. Andrea and I should get something to eat while we talk this over and then get some sleep. We need to be well-rested before giving our statements. So, if okay with you, we'll rest up and meet you in the morning at headquarters."

Burke slowly shook his head in agreement. "Yeah, that's fine with me. You both must be exhausted, so rest up, and I'll see you both in the morning."

Leaving Burke's car, Andrea suggested they order dinner to take back to the apartment, so they could celebrate with champagne in honor of fulfilling the promise to Juli.

"That's fine, Andrea, but once we eat and get our story straight for our statements, we'll need to get some sleep, if you know what I'm getting at."

"I'm tired too, Sam. I'm wired and need to calm down from it all. We both do, especially you."

"We eat, get our story straight, and take the time to come back down to earth. Then, we sleep, and no negligee, okay?"

Andrea giggled and responded with a joke. "I got it, Sam. You don't want me to wear anything tonight."

It brought laughter to both of them. "Wow, Andrea, you're becoming a comic like Juli."

"I promise not to tease you, but I'd don't want to be alone tonight."

"On a more serious note, Andrea, I want to thank you for backing me up at the house. Although I didn't want you to get involved, you came to my rescue. I appreciate it. Thank you."

"I'm here for you, Sam. Always."

"I have to take a few minutes to, once again, call and cancel my dinner appointment with my friend. I'll be back in a few minutes. Maybe you can get an officer to give us a ride back to your car."

Alli's phone rang only twice before she answered, "Hi Sam. Are you on your way?"

Sam walked further away from the possibility that Andrea could overhear him. "I hate to disappoint you again, Alli. I apologize. I'm working in Lynn, north of Boston, and need to finish up here, and it will take quite a while."

"Oh, Sam, you keep canceling on me. Am I ever going to see you, or will you continue breaking our date at the last minute?"

"I don't want to break our date. I'll make it up to you. Right now, I'm going to be an anonymous source. Don't repeat to anyone what I'm about to tell you. We have killed the fugitive responsible for killing state police officers and FBI agents during the raid. The police are now waiting for a warrant to search the home where he was hiding. The home is on Delaware Drive near Bowen Court in Lynn. You'll see all the police at the scene when you get here. You can say people heard shots fired in the area, and you came to investigate. I'll tell you more when I see you, hopefully tomorrow night. I'm at the scene now. Be sure to inquire whose house the killer was hiding in."

He ended the call, and before putting the phone away, he got a call from Agent Clarkson.

"Hi, Jennifer. Give me some good news."

"It is good news. We listened to Sonny's call to Rachel regarding the video and payment. Rachel told him to meet with Leo at the same location for an exchange. If satisfied with the video, Leo would pay him. We had set up surveillance across the road and videoed the conversation. Once Sonny left with the money, Leo walked up the hill to Rachel's office. We had the state police and our agents pull over Sonny and arrest him. We seized the money he had on him. We also had two agents and a state police detective follow Leo. When Leo handed Rachel the video copy, we arrested both of them

"You identify Leo? What's his connection to Forster?"

"His name is Agustus Walker, Forster's second in command and confidant. He only used the name Leo when dealing with Sonny. We interviewed Rachel Peterson and Walker separately at our office. Peterson initially claimed not to know anything, but when we told her we arrested Sonny, and he and Walker, agreed to cooperate, she changed her tune. She then wanted a guarantee she wouldn't serve any time in jail before cooperating. Murphy said he would go along with it if Rachel testified against her father. She agreed."

"Great work, Jennifer. I can't thank you and all the guys enough." Sam thought ahead for a moment before giving Jennifer instructions. "First, when you inform the boss, please boast about the significance of the arrests and give credit to your staff and the state police. Second, let me know when the indictments come down. I want to be a part of any arrest of Forster Harrington. Third, contact our usual reporters, have them show up at the federal building, and ensure you and the state police give statements together, with the US Attorney. Talk to you soon." Sam walked back toward Andrea.

"That was a long phone call, Sam. Everything alright?" asked Andrea.

"Yes. I got a call from the Hartford office filling me in on the progress of the murder-for-hire investigation. They had some obstacles to overcome, but everything worked out, so we can celebrate with champagne for the capture and demise of Al Madari and the outstanding job by the Hartford agents."

"Great, we'll celebrate both," responded Andrea.

Later, Sam and Andrea enjoyed dinner and champagne at Andrea's apartment while prepping for their statements the following day. They talked and joked around before tiring from the day's frantic activity and too much champagne. Finally, they faded to sleep, first Andrea and then Sam, both on the couch.

CHAPTER
42

On the way to state police headquarters the following day, Andrea reminded Sam of the meeting with Juli's uncle after providing their statements. At headquarters, they gave statements that took nearly two hours. Their statements got recorded, typed, and signed. Andrea finished minutes before Sam, so she contacted Juli's uncle, who invited her and Sam to his home for lunch in Southborough at one o'clock.

After Sam completed his statement, he saw Andrea on the phone, so he called Alli Gaynor while he had the time. When Alli answered the phone, she seemed hurried.

"Everything alright, Alli? You sound like you're out of breath."

"I've been rushing between the phone, the fax machine, and the laptop trying to meet a deadline for the story on Al Madari's death. After all the interviews and photos taken at the scene, I'm trying to finish the storyline before heading to state police headquarters for a more in-depth interview with Major Burke. Anyway, I hope you are not calling to cancel dinner for tonight."

"No, I am not, but I have my fingers crossed, hoping nothing prevents me from being there. Tell me where and what time."

"They have a great restaurant at the hotel I'm staying at, so I thought this would be a great place for dinner, hoping you'll be able to spend the night."

Sam didn't respond to spending the night. He only asked for the address and time.

"I'm excited. I can't wait to see you. And much thanks for the heads up on the Al Madari matter. No one else had the story. So I owe you big time. I have a hundred questions to ask you."

"Just remember, I'm limited on what I can say."

Alli understood but knew she'd be able to extract bits of information from him that no other reporter would get for their story.

Andrea approached Sam as he ended his call. "Juli's uncle invited us for lunch at his home in Southborough at one o'clock. It's twelve-twenty now, so let's head to his place."

"Before we go, I want to stop by to see Major Burke. He requested I see him before I leave." Burke saw them at his office door and waved them in.

"I wanted to fill you both in on some developments before leaving. First, the FBI will schedule a federal grand jury to indict all those involved in Trooper Phillips's shooting and the farm incident. Sam, of course, you know that you will be a key witness to give testimony before the grand jury. Furthermore, I wanted to thank both of you again. I can't say enough about the tremendous help you both have given to the department during this investigation. Sam, our department will formally honor you for your contributions when this case is over. Also, I know both of you were close to Detective Ospino. I had conversations with Colonel Luis Costillo, my mentor, who recommended, and so do I, Andrea, and Juli for promotion to Detective Sergeant, Juli, of course, posthumously. The three of you have done an outstanding service to the state police and the citizens of Massachusetts."

Humbled by Burke's recommendation, Sam and Andrea responded with appreciation and great pride. When they left headquarters and drove to Juli's uncle's home, Andrea couldn't stop giving Sam credit for the honor she and Juli would receive from the department.

"I'm not taking any credit for the great work both of you did. Don't short-change what you both contributed. You both impacted the investigation more than any other state police officer. So pat yourself on the back, not me. You deserve the promotion, and the extra pay helps."

Andrea didn't answer, knowing Sam wouldn't take any credit. She appreciated what he said but felt she probably wouldn't have gotten recognized with a promotion if it weren't for him.

Luis Costillo's home was a mid-size ranch with an attached two-car garage, a beautifully landscaped front yard with flowering shrubs, and a white dogwood tree. In addition, their lawn was plush and green. As Andrea and Sam exited their car, Luis waited by the front door to welcome them to his home. Andrea has known Luis and his wife for several years since she and Juli often visited and socialized with them. Luis was a handsome guy and in great shape for a sixty-two-year-old man. He stood five feet, ten inches tall, weighing about a hundred and sixty-five pounds, and still had most of his hair, although mostly grey. He introduced Sam to his wife, Daniela, or Dani, as Luis called her.

Dani immediately hugged Sam. "It's a pleasure to meet you finally. Juli and Andrea always said such nice things about you. I wouldn't say this if Juli were present, but she was crazy about you. She told me in confidence that she had found her soulmate. Luis and I know you saved her life, and we are grateful you cared so much for her. We miss her terribly. She was like a daughter we never had. When her dad died, we became parents to her. We loved her very much." Dani's eyes began to swell with tears as Luis comforted her.

Dani's words triggered an emotional response from Sam. "I miss her terribly, as well. Juli was very special to me. I wish she were here with us right now. She was a beautiful woman and a dedicated detective who was a shining star and a credit to the state police. Juli told me Luis encouraged her to join the state police, and she became an exceptional trooper once on the job. I believe it was in the DNA she inherited from her dad and Luis."

"Thank you for saying that, Sam. At first, she didn't think the state police would be a good fit for reasons you probably know, but once she applied, she finished near the top of her class at the academy and quickly advanced to the rank of detective. I was so proud of her—and Andrea, who was like a sister to her."

Dani beautifully designed the interior of their home with traditional furniture, custom-made draperies, and fine art pieces on the walls. She also served perfectly cooked ribeye steaks, mashed potatoes, and buttered steamed carrots. She accompanied the meal with a freshly made Caesar salad of romaine lettuce, topped with croutons and shaved parmesan cheese, mustard, salt, pepper, and a drizzle of her own creamy Caesar dressing. The red merlot wine was a superb match, with flavors of black cherry, plum, and chocolate layered with notes of vanilla and cedar. Dessert followed, with a delicious New York-style creamy cheesecake topped with blueberries. They spent nearly three hours telling ancient stories about Juli from birth until she joined the state police. All four of them experienced emotional moments during their time together. The conversation ended with thoughts about the state police funeral protocol for fallen officers and Luis and Dani's wishes for a private ceremonial burial service for Juli.

It was after four o'clock when Andrea and Sam left the Costillo's home. Andrea and Sam exchanged hugs with Dani and Luis as they departed to drive to Boston. Sam had earlier informed Andrea he had to see his son before dining with his friend that night. Knowing Sam was heading back to Hartford once the funerals were over, Andrea asked if he was planning on spending additional time with her.

"Of course, I will spend time with you and Micaela. Just about all the time I have left before heading back to Hartford. As a reminder, Hartford is not that far from here. We can visit each other on weekends, but you have to understand, Andrea, I'm still grieving the loss of Juli and not in a hurry to commit to a relationship, especially with her best friend or, should I say, with her sister."

Sam saw tears rolling down Andrea's cheeks. He used his hanky to wipe her tears as she drove. "Let's take some time and see where it goes, okay?"

Andrea nodded affirmatively, saying, "I understand." She glanced at Sam and smiled, but it was more of a sad than a cheerful smile. "Do you want me to drop you off at your son's place?"

"Yes, thanks, Andrea. I need to relax, shower, and spend time with Drew before meeting my friend for dinner."

"You don't have to answer this if you don't want to. Is your friend male or female?"

"A female. I told you I got falsely arrested while working the kidnapping case in Connecticut. Alli was the only reporter who wrote columns that didn't contain innuendo, second-guessing, and downright lies about me. Instead, her columns reported the words of colleagues who supported me and claimed the arrest was a scam. When the case was over, major news networks recognized her exceptional insight in reporting the story, resulting in her being offered a position with a national television news station in DC. She accepted the job with a nice bump in her salary. Recently, she called to tell me she got assigned to do a story in Boston and wanted to meet, probably to brag about her new job and gather what she could get from me on this case we all worked on together. It's no secret I was working with the state police on this case."

"Did you guys date?" asked Andrea.

"We had dinner to celebrate after the Connecticut investigation was over. We celebrated my success with the case and her new job. That's all there is to know, Andrea."

Andrea remained quiet for the short drive to Drew's apartment. Then, before exiting her car, Sam said, "I'll call you tomorrow, and hopefully, we can have dinner someplace special. You can bring Micaela with you."

"I would love that, Sam," Andrea said with a receptive smile.

CHAPTER

43

A t seven twenty, Sam arrived twenty minutes late at the upscale hotel restaurant and mentioned to the maître d, "Gaynor, party of two." "Right this way, sir. Ms. Gaynor has already been seated."

Sam followed him to a private semi-circular booth somewhat secluded from the surrounding tables. Alli greeted him with a smile as he was seated. Sam moved closer to Alli, who sat in the middle of the booth. He leaned to kiss her while her hand softly pulled his head to her lips for a long passionate kiss.

"I'm so happy you showed up. I had thoughts of you calling again to cancel."

"Sorry, I'm late. Just so you know, I never wanted to cancel, but I was knee-deep in the state investigation and couldn't even find time to get enough sleep." Sam filled her in on everything that had happened, starting with Al Madari shooting a state trooper, the raid at the farmhouse, and Al Madari's escape after killing his partner. "I found the bastard and killed him."

"Wow, Sam. We haven't seen each other in quite a while, and this is how our conversation gets underway. Seeing many of your colleagues and your partner killed must have been terrible. I'm so sorry. It had to be a battlefield that morning. According to people I've interviewed in the area near Haverhill, they heard explosions and ongoing loud sounds of gunfire."

"That's exactly how it was, Alli. It was a battlefield. I'm not going to relive that battle for you only to say it was like nothing I've ever experienced, and I hope I never have to again. But, unfortunately, we were not fully prepared for it."

Alli sat there, astonished at what Sam asserted. She wasn't sure if she should seize the moment when Sam openly told her they were unprepared for the raid. But, on the other hand, she knew she had to tread lightly for fear of getting Sam ostracized in the eyes of his fellow officers if he said too much.

"Sam, let's not talk about the case right now. Instead, I'm going to bore you with how my life changed over the past couple of years."

"You can never bore me, Alli. I enjoy listening to you."

The waiter approached and took Sam's order for a fine bottle of champagne. Alli then spent nearly thirty minutes telling Sam about her new job. Alli detailed her successes and was pleased that the broadcast company offered her the primetime weekend television anchor job just this morning.

"Yikes, that is big-time, girl! I'm so happy for you. Congratulations. I knew you were destined for it. I'm proud of you. Can I get your autograph to brag to all my friends that I know you?"

"You don't need my autograph. You already have as much of me as anyone has ever had. If you want all of me, you can have that too."

Hearing that, Sam was speechless. They'd dated and made love, but he never realized she felt that way. "Alli, I don't know what to say. When you accepted the job in DC, I assumed we would only become long-distance friends. I expected you to become a celebrity, with every guy you met instantly asking for your hand in marriage. Instead, I'm just an average guy doing my best as a public servant."

"Sam, you are far from being an average guy, and your service to the public is exceptional. Everyone I've talked to about you say you are a gifted investigator, including, I might add, Connecticut's U.S. Attorney, Debra Durrell."

Just about that time, the server appeared for the third time to take their order. Alli and Sam both ordered the fish special, a sautéed Halibut with fresh herbs and a special sauce with a side of mixed vegetables. They continued to talk about their jobs, people they'd met, and life in general. Alli admitted to dating a few guys short-term, but they didn't come close to being a soulmate. Nevertheless, she told Sam she always thought back to their times together. "Although the times we had were short-lived, they were very special for me."

After they finished dinner, they decided against dessert and continued talking until they finished their champagne.

"Sam, I sense the investigation you worked on has left a scar that is still healing. I didn't want to begin our time together talking shop, but to get to know each other better and how life is treating us. However, you know me well enough that I'd like to get insight into the horrific investigation you worked on with the state and FBI. You also know I'd never reveal where I got the information. Can you come to my room so we can talk privately about it?" Alli paused, giving Sam a sensual smile. "I confess I have an ulterior motive for wanting to be alone with you in my bedroom."

Sam had decided earlier that he would not pursue what Alli had in mind, not while still grieving the death of Juli. But he never knew Alli had harbored such strong feelings for him. He had fallen in love with her in Hartford but assumed it was just a fling once she left for DC. After all, she was a young rising star destined to obtain her journalist's dream as a celebrity news anchor on television.

He replied, "I'll keep my promise to give you whatever you need for your report, but I'm not staying the night. I think I know, but not sure what you mean by the ulterior motives you have in store for us."

Alli's face glowed with a wide smile. "Well then, when we get to the room, I can demonstrate what ulterior motives I'm referring to."

Although Sam presumed ulterior motives included sex, he felt he might end up in a no-win predicament if he didn't say something before going to her room. So, he held her hand and told her about his relationship with Juli.

"Juli's death haunts me, Alli. I promised I wouldn't let anything happen to her. I feel that I let her down, let myself down in failing to keep her safe, and I can't get over it. In the coming days, the state police will honor her with an end-of-watch funeral service given to fallen officers. Regrettably, I'm not in the right frame of mind to make love to you. I'm sorry."

"Oh, Sam, I'm so sorry for your loss. I understand. We'll keep this strictly professional."

"Thanks. I promise I'll visit you in DC when I get over this grief I feel. I hope you do understand. I promise we'll act on those ulterior motives when I visit you."

"Hmm, I like that idea, Sam. I'll hold you to that." She then changed her thought. "I want to thank you for being upfront and honest about your relationship with Juli. I appreciate it. Also, please let me know when they schedule her funeral service. I want to be there for you. Now that that's settled, let's talk shop."

"I'll suggest the questions you should ask the U.S. Attorney, the FBI, Major Burke, and anyone within the agencies who might talk to you," said Sam. "First, you should ask them if the terrorists were prepared and ready for them that fateful morning. Their answer should lead you to ask if they had a mole, someone with inside information that led them to prepare for the raid against the police."

"Sam, are you telling me there was a mole within one of the agencies?"

"Two plus two must equal four. If the terrorists were ready and waiting, they had to know in advance about the raid. Also, ask all three agency spokespersons if they had a plan for all contingencies. For example, did they know how many adversaries were inside the house and barn? Ask if the police were surprised the suspects used the barn as their stronghold and booby-trapped the farmhouse? Also, ask if there were any hostages to use as bait? Finally, did any suspects escape, and if so, how was that possible?"

"There were hostages, Sam? How many and who were they?"

"Get the answers from them, not me."

Alli took pages of notes while asking Sam for particulars but did not get specific answers. After nearly an hour of picking Sam's brain, she finally was satisfied with what she had. Alli didn't want the questioning to go on late into the morning since she had an early wake-up call.

"I was hoping you would stay the night and have breakfast with me in the room."

"I'd love to have breakfast with you in the morning, whether in the restaurant or in your room. But I can't stay the night, so let me know when to be here in the morning, and I'll be here."

"My tech and camera guys are meeting me at seven. We have to be on the road by eight. It's already late, and I'm sure you have a busy day tomorrow. So, get back to your son's apartment and get a good night's sleep. You wouldn't have gotten much sleep if you stayed here tonight."

"You're right about that, Alli. Thank you for understanding. Have a good night's sleep, and good luck with your interviews tomorrow. I'll catch up with you soon."

They hugged before Sam left the room. Alli was disappointed and hoped she hadn't lost him.

* * *

Sam was back at his son's apartment by midnight. Drew was already sleeping. Sam went straight to bed but tossed and turned, thinking about Juli, her funeral, and Alli's feelings about him. Hours passed before he fell asleep. He woke up when he heard Drew's alarm go off. Sam dragged himself out of bed, showered, dressed for work, and joined Drew for coffee. For the third time, Drew expressed his condolences and asked his dad if he could do anything for him.

"You and Juli seemed so happy together. I saw firsthand how you both looked at each other the night I joined you guys for dinner."

"Well, I feel guilty about what happened. I tried to keep Juli away from the gunfire, but she had a mind of her own to help her colleagues takedown the suspects. I still blame myself for not staying close to her and keeping her out of harm's way. Juli had tremendous courage and dedication to her job. I miss her, but I know, in time, I'd have to move on."

"She made her choice, Dad. You did all that you could. It was just unfortunate she was in the wrong spot at the wrong time. It just as easily could have been you. I'm glad it wasn't. Anyway, I have to get to work. Let me know what I can do for the upcoming funeral. If there is anything you need, just ask. I'll be there for you. But, hey, what happened during the raid is not your fault, and I agree that you have to move on."

Sam was finishing his coffee when he received a call from Andrea.

"Good morning, Andrea. How are you this morning?"

"I'm fine, Sam. How did things go last night with your friend?"

"It went well, as expected. We had a nice dinner and got acquainted with our lives over the past years before switching to talking shop for a couple of hours." Then, Sam changed the subject, "I'm at Drew's apartment. Would you like to meet for breakfast?"

"Can you come to the apartment? I'll prepare breakfast here."

"Yeah, I can be there in about twenty minutes, but I'd be happy to treat you to breakfast at a restaurant."

"Thank you, Sam, but I just got up and about to make breakfast here. I'll make something special for you."

"I didn't sleep well last night. I couldn't stop thinking about the funeral."

"I've been thinking about it too. I know I'm going to break down crying. I'll be counting on your support."

"I'll be crying along with you. We'll lean on each other for support."

"Thanks, Sam. I knew I could count on you."

"How about you, Micaela, and I have dinner together tonight, someplace nice."

"I'd love that, and so will Micaela. She always asks about you."

CHAPTER
44

Ablack van with a stick-on magnetic logo for Anderson Fine Wines and Liquors Warehouse, Taunton, MA, drove into the open garage door at the Crescent Drive Plaza. As the garage door closed, four men and two women exited the van and were escorted to a basement office by Parnia Semnami. The six from the van included the Imam, Shahrad Abedini, his sister, Tsarina, Ameen Nazari, Abedini's assistant, Parnia's husband Kasra Jahanbani, and Armita Shahidi Nazari, Ameen's wife. Armita, a clerk at the plaza's convenience store, and Tsarina are cousins.

The gathering was called together by the Imam and Shahrad Abedini to ascertain the name of the man who pursued and killed Al Madari, their most trusted and effective field leader. The Imam mentioned Marteen Rahmani had been arrested and not yet released on bail. "I have been in touch with his wife, Sara, who will be allowed to visit her husband before his bail hearing this afternoon. I asked her to obtain the officer's name and his woman partner who killed Al Madari."

Abedini also spoke. "We must take revenge against this man and woman responsible for the death of our comrade. We will cut off their heads for all Americans to see."

The government held Marteen over the weekend. His bail hearing got rescheduled until today. His wife Sara, not charged yet, visited him with his attorney at the courthouse to prepare for the hearing. During their visit, Marteen gave Sara the officers' names and said that the woman officer has a young daughter. The Imam didn't know that the judge denied bail for Marteen.

*   *   *

Andrea, Micaela, and Sam enjoyed dinner at the Mystic River Cafe overlooking the Boston skyline. Andrea and Sam joined Micaela in ordering pizza for dinner and ice cream sundaes for dessert. Sam enjoyed chatting with Micaela and telling her funny stories from children's books he remembered. After dinner, they watched the SpongeBob movie at Andrea's apartment before Andrea put Micaela to bed.

"I didn't get much sleep and need to get to bed early. It will be an emotional few days attending Juli's funeral, so I'm heading to Drew's place to prepare my message and rest. I'll call you tomorrow," said Sam. He then left Andrea's apartment, leaving her disappointed that he couldn't stay longer.

The following two days began the services for Juli and other officers who died protecting the public. Family members, the FBI, and state police officials agreed to hold the funeral processions on two consecutive days in Boston. They would schedule the services for the three FBI agents assigned to the New England area in Boston. The four agents assigned to Washington, DC, would hold their services in DC, and the funerals for the three remaining agents were held in their hometowns as requested by their families. The three local FBI agents had their church and funeral services held in Boston on the first day. Following their church ceremonial, a law enforcement procession of federal, state, and local police officers from around the country stood tall and saluted their fallen colleagues as their caskets passed by them. Family, friends, and the general public were among those honoring the fallen heroes. Bells rang from several churches as the caskets were placed in the hearse and driven past the FBI office, the city streets, the residences of the deceased, and then to the designated burial sites for each agent.

On the second day, the state police arranged church services two hours apart for the three state police officers, including Juli. Several dignitaries and family members participated in a eulogy for the honored officers during the church service. A U.S. Army Honor Guard served as pallbearers at Juli's funeral. During the church services, the dignitaries who briefly spoke included the governor, the Boston Mayor, the State Police Commissioner, and Major Burke. Juli's uncle, Luis Costillo, Andrea, and Sam, followed them with personal tributes.

With a quivering voice, Juli's uncle spoke of patriotism, honor, and dedication to describe Juli. But he was relaxed when telling his memories of Juli's childhood, love of school, and country. He proudly boasted she was one of only two women, including her best friend Andrea, to make it through the Army's grueling Special Forces training and serve in Afghanistan. Next, he told how proud he was when she joined the state police and completed her training near the top of her class. He finished his eulogy with funny stories about Juli as a teenager and how she grew up to be a model young woman dedicated to her country, the state, family, and friends. Andrea spoke of sorrow, love, and friendship, followed by Sam's inspirational depiction of his feelings and remorse about Juli's death, the pain and guilt about losing his partner, and his lasting commitment to her memory.

At the burial site, the priest led the service with prayers while Andrea and Sam held hands by the side of Juli's uncle and his wife. Alli was in attendance from a distance, covering the two-day memorials as a reporter. She had deep feelings for Sam and witnessed the heartache and guilt he endured.

Following the prayers and memorable words, the Army Honor Guard fired a three-volley gun salute followed by the bugle call, Taps, in honor of Juli's military service. Finally, the Army soldiers folded the American flag draped over her coffin and presented it to her uncle, ending the gravesite ceremony. At that moment, a state police headquarters dispatcher made the end of watch final radio call to Juli heard over the police radios carried by some at the cemetery. Then there was silence.

Luis Costillo invited those in attendance to his home for a small reception to share memories of Juli. Andrea and Sam stayed close and mingled with Juli's uncle and wife. In addition, Major Burke, Juli's close colleagues, Drew Caviello, and his boss Pat O'Shae were there. Alli Gaynor decided not to attend since she felt the reception was for family and friends. Before leaving the reception, Luis took Andrea aside and told her he had arranged for her to take over Juli's apartment at the same rent-controlled fee Juli enjoyed. Andrea thanked him but wasn't sure she would accept the offer. She felt the apartment would remind her of losing her best friend and cause too much discomfort and heartache. He told her to take her time before deciding.

Before leaving the reception, Andrea asked Sam to spend the night. "I don't think I can be alone without falling apart after this horrible day. I'll need a shoulder to cry on."

Before responding, Sam got interrupted by the vibration of his cell in his pocket. He excused himself to a quiet area to answer the call from Jennifer Clarkson.

"Sam, Brian Murphy just informed me that a new grand jury would start tomorrow in Hartford. Brian has the afternoon session and plans on indicting Forster Harrington, Tony Dellagatti, Sonny, Rachel, and Gus Walker. The indictments against Harrington's daughter, Rachel, and Walker were to ensure their testimony. The government has agreed to reduce their charges to misdemeanors with no jail time if they fully cooperate and testify against Forster. In addition, Murphy wants you to testify about the threats Forster made to you and would like you here to give testimony at two tomorrow afternoon."

"When will they bring Harrington and Dellagatti to Hartford?" asked Sam.

"Once the grand jury returns a true bill of indictment, the judge will sign the order to have them brought to Hartford by the U.S. Marshals for arraignment and processing. I'm not sure when that will occur, but when I know, you will know."

"Thanks, Jen. I'll be there tomorrow by one."

When the reception for Juli ended, Andrea and Sam drove back to Boston. During the drive, Sam informed Andrea he had to return to Hartford in the morning to testify in a grand jury.

"I understand, Sam. After you testify, will you be coming back to Boston?"

"I'll spend the night at my place and return here the next morning. I'll probably be here for several more days. I'll spend time with my son and with you."

Andrea only half-listened to what Sam was saying. She felt anxiety and emotional loss of not having Sam permanently close by. She was in love with him, and he was leaving her. It was an empty feeling. Andrea's eyes swelled with tears when they arrived at the apartment, emotionally saying, "I don't want you to go, Sam. I'll miss you."

"We talked about this, Andrea. I still feel some responsibility for Juli's death and need to get away for a while. I can't do that here where she died. I know it's difficult for you without her, but you have Micaela and your sister. You will be fine. I'll be back to visit with you and Micaela, and you could visit me in Connecticut."

"You promise you'll come back and visit, Sam?"

"I promise." Sam wiped away her tears.

"Micaela is spending the night with my sister. Can you spend the night with me, please, Sam? I won't tease you, I promise. I don't want to be alone."

"Okay, we can cry on each other's shoulder until we fall asleep." Once again, after comforting each other and drinking wine, Andrea went to bed and fell asleep. Sam kissed her forehead, made sure a blanket covered her, and then relaxed on the couch before dozing off.

*   *   *

Sam didn't sleep well. When he woke up the following day, Andrea was still sleeping. Rather than showering and possibly waking Andrea, he decided to prepare breakfast, put on a fresh pot of coffee, and have music playing loud enough to wake Andrea from her sleep.

It took fifteen minutes or more before Andrea wobbled into the living room, looking like she was sleepwalking. She wore a short, tight-fitting robe and greeted Sam with a smile. "Good morning, Sam. I hope you slept well. I went out like a light and didn't move an inch all night." When Andrea sat across from Sam, she purposely opened her robe enough to reveal herself.

Sam couldn't help to notice, and although exhausted, it aroused him. However, he didn't say a word about it. "You looked exhausted last night, Andrea. I'm glad you got a good night's sleep."

Sam thought back to when he and Juli had had fun in bed. He remembered remarking that she was wearing him out, which caused Juli to say, "You're lucky it's me and not Andrea. You'd be down for the count and wouldn't be able to walk for hours."

"Sam, are you out in space somewhere?"

"Sorry, Andrea. I was just thinking of what Juli mentioned to me about you."

"What did she tell you?"

"Oh, no, I'll keep it to myself for now." Sam quickly showered, dressed, kissed Andrea on the cheek, and escaped for Hartford after breakfast.

CHAPTER
45

S am made a quick stop at the Boston ATF office to update his boss
on the state investigation by ten that morning. However, His boss
requested more detail, causing Sam to leave the office later than
anticipated. He then headed to Hartford to testify in the grand jury. He
stopped at his apartment in Manchester to change into a suit before
arriving at the Hartford federal courthouse. Sam first visited the ATF office
to discuss the murder-for-hire case with agents Clarkson, Macheski, and
Ziglar, then met with Brian Murphy to go over his grand jury testimony.
Sam's testimony included a summary of the case against Harrington's son,
followed by a description of the revenge threat Harrington made against
Sam's son. His testimony took just under an hour.

Afterward, he drove back to his apartment rather than join his ATF
colleagues for a drink at a local café. On the way to his apartment, he
stopped at a Walmart to buy Micaela a present he knew she wanted and
then ordered a takeout dinner to eat at his place. After that, he relaxed, had
dinner at his apartment, and began packing a bag for his trip to Boston in
the morning. While packing, he received a call from Andrea.

"Hey, how are you, Andrea? I'm packing for—" Before he could finish,
Andrea, in tears, feverishly stumbled words he could hardly understand.

"Andrea, slow down, please. I can't make out what you're saying."

"They took Micaela, Sam.— I'm, uh, I'm worried sick. I need your help to find her. Please, Sam." She then broke down, weeping excessively.

"Who took Micaela?"

"I dunno who, but it could only be those bastards who killed Juli." Weeping, Andrea had to compose herself before continuing. "A witness, uh, saw a guy grab her—it was a black van," Still sobbing, Andrea tried to get control of herself. "She was waiting for— my sister to pick her up from, uh, school. First Juli, now Micaela. Please, Sam, help me get her back."

"Where are you?"

"Headquarters. We have an APB out on the van."

"I should be there in about an hour. Try to calm down, Andrea. We'll find her."

An hour later, Sam arrived at state police headquarters, where he found Andrea in tears, seated in Major Burke's office with Detectives Bishop and Collins.

When Andrea saw Sam walk in, she leaped out of her chair and rushed to hug him. It surprised Sam she would show such an emotional connection to him in front of her colleagues.

"What do we know other than the description of the van?" asked Sam.

Detective Bishop spoke first. "We know little more other than it was a black van with commercial plates beginning with 51. The van was stolen three days ago in Lawrence. We found the full license number but no luck on the APB. While we debated our options, Andrea got a message on her cell phone. I was the first to see the message." He looked at his notes and read them out loud. "We'll trade the girl for the killers of Al Madari." He looked at Sam. "That's you and Andrea, Sam."

"Well, that message connects the kidnapper to the same terrorist group. Do we know where Abedini and the Imam are yet?"

"We haven't found them yet," answered Burke. "The FBI has heard nothing meaningful off the wiretaps. The DA and the U.S. Attorney have arrest warrants for the remaining suspects. We plan on interviewing Randell and his wife in hopes they could shed some light on this. I've asked for additional detectives and troopers to be here by seven tomorrow morning to help with the search for Micaela."

"I'm not waiting until morning to get started. I'm heading out to find out what I can, now," insisted Sam. "If I have to search all night and kick in some doors, I'm going to find Micaela."

"I'm coming with you," cried out Andrea.

Bishop stood and volunteered. "Ed and I will also go with you." His partner, Ed Collins, said nothing but showed displeasure with Bishop volunteering him.

Burke chimed in with a bit of cautionary advice. "Avoid anything that will hurt our case in court or put the girl in danger."

"Understood, Major, but if I have to bend the law to rescue her, I won't involve the state police," replied Sam.

Burke only nodded, knowing there was something special about Sam's abilities. "Be careful and bring her back to Andrea unharmed."

"If we need help, I have your number," said Sam.

Sam got into Andrea's state car, and they drove off towards Lynn, with Detectives Bishop and Collins following.

"Sam, thank you for not waiting until tomorrow to look for Micaela. I'm glad you are here for me."

"We're going to find her, Andrea, one way or another."

Collins was still annoyed that Bishop had volunteered him to work the rest of the night. "Kevin, why the fuck did you volunteer me to be a part of this? I wanted to go home and have dinner. I worked ten hours already, and I'm tired. Do you think Caviello has a crystal ball and will find the girl tonight?"

"No, I don't, Ed, but there is something about Sam that I haven't figured out yet. I don't know what it is, but he has a nose for finding people. Remember, out of the clear blue, he took us to the mosque, where we found Ganani hiding with his brother-in-law. Besides, if you didn't want to work tonight, you should have said something. I'm not forcing you to work tonight."

Collins was silent but not happy working instead of relaxing at home.

Sam requested Andrea to drive by every location where the suspects lived or operated during the investigation, starting with Akram Ganani's home in Lynn and then the mosque. "I'm fairly sure they wouldn't use Lieutenant Randell's home, but we can do a ride-by to see what activity might be there. From there, we should head to the farmhouse and the Crescent Drive Plaza." Andrea remained quiet while tears rolled down her cheeks. Her thoughts were on finding her daughter. She was perplexed as to why Sam wanted to drive by the locations he'd mentioned, but she knew better than to question his methods. Juli had once told her Sam's investigative skills were unique. When Andrea asked her to explain, Juli said she couldn't tell her, only to trust Sam's abilities.

Their first stop was at Ganani's home in Lynn. "Andrea, drive by slowly. We should look for the van and any unusual vehicles at or near the house." There was no garage, but they both noticed the rear of an SUV sticking out from the back of the house.

"I'll jump out and check it. Be right back," said Sam. Sam held a flashlight to get the plate number and, lighting up the interior of the SUV, saw a child's safety seat on the back seat. After checking the mailbox names, he returned to Andrea's car and asked her to call in a registration check on the SUV. As they drove to the mosque, Andrea received the results of the registration check that came back to a Hispanic female with no record, whose name matched one of the those on the house's mailboxes.

Sam asked Andrea to circle the building at the mosque for suspicious vehicles in the parking lot. Andrea called in the registration check and requested wants and warrants on the registered owners of two cars that turned out to be of no interest to them. Next, they drove by Randell's house on Delaware Drive. Sam asked her to pull over while he checked out the house on foot. There were no lights on in the place. He used his flashlight to shine through the garage windows and saw two cars inside, but no black van. Sam figured no one would hold Andrea's daughter here with Randell still locked up. He returned to Andrea's car and asked her to drive to the farmhouse and then the Crescent Drive Plaza.

On the way to Haverhill, Collins, still upset, questioned what Sam was doing. "Where the fuck is he taking us now? We're doing drive-bys for chrissake. What good is that? Does he have some kind of x-ray vision to see what's happening inside the places we drive by?"

"Relax, Ed, will ya? Let's see what the guy's got up his sleeve first before bitching every few minutes," asserted Bishop.

It was a long ride before reaching the farmhouse where the raid occurred. Sam asked Andrea to drive down the driveway and park by the barn. The farmhouse had nearly burned to the ground. Sam exited the car, circled the barn, and used his flashlight to examine the inside from the open front door before returning to her car.

Collins was angrily bitching again. "Kevin, what the fuck are we doing here? This guy is taking us nowhere fast. I'm tired. I should be home enjoying a couple of beers and a juicy burger."

"Jesus, Ed. I've never heard you bitch so much as you are tonight. What's going on with you?"

Collins shook his head in a huff. "I don't know, Kev. I'm getting too old for this shit, I guess. My wife has been hassling me lately about little projects that need finishing around the house. Plus, my kid quit his job and moved back home with us, and he doesn't do a fucking thing except eat, sleep, and watch TV all day and night."

Once Sam returned to the car, Andrea did a U-turn, exited the farm, took a left on Brewer's Road, and then left on Country Farm Road, heading toward the Crescent Drive Plaza. Sam was disappointed that he hadn't received any sign signaling where the suspects held Michaela.

"Now what?" complained Collins.

"Don't say anything, Ed. Let's play this out. We don't have many other locations for him to check out, and then we can go home. Okay, partner?" asked Bishop.

"If you say so, Kevin."

Andrea drove past the opening in the wall, remembering it was where Juli and the state police SWAT members entered to raid the barn on that fateful morning. She continued driving up the hill where they stationed Trooper Markham blocking the road during the farmhouse raid. As she passed the old white farmhouse where Radir Semnami waited in a white van to pick up the wounded Al Madari, Sam suddenly hollered, "Pull over to the side of the road, Andrea." She didn't hesitate to do as Sam directed.

"Not again! Is he going to circle this fucking house now?" irritably asked Collins.

"I have no idea what he's doing. Let's hope the night is nearly over for us," said Detective Bishop with apprehension about Sam's actions.

The detectives and Andrea had no clue that Sam had experienced one of his sensations, the same phenomenon that Juli couldn't explain to Andrea. Bishop and Collins saw Sam exit Andrea's car and disappear among the high bushes and pine trees. They parked behind Andrea's car thirty yards past the white colonial's driveway. They exited their vehicle and walked over to ask Andrea where Sam was heading.

"He told me to pull over. He was trembling and seemed spaced out for a moment. He then told me to wait here while he checked out the garage in the back of the house we passed."

"I don't know about you, Andrea, but that guy is weird," complained Collins. "What the fuck does he expect to find driving by these places? I don't get it. It's time to go home, and we have nothing to show for our time."

"He's doing all he can to find my daughter, Ed. So lighten up and give him a chance. I trust Sam. So let's wait and see what he says," said Andrea feverishly.

Sam quietly moved across the property toward the back of the garage in the rear of the house. He noticed there were lights on inside the front of the house. First, he walked along one side of the garage, hoping to find a side door to enter, but there was no door. Then, Sam headed back to the rear of the garage to search for windows where there were none. It was an oversized garage that Sam estimated could hold at least four vehicles or three large farm tractors. As he turned the rear corner to the other side of the garage, he observed a dim light from the second-floor left rear window of the house. Sam figured it was a bedroom. He slowly advanced along the side of the garage until he came upon a side door. He tried turning the doorknob but found it locked. It had no windows. He pushed his weight against the door and felt some give on the old door. Sam pushed harder and then, using his right shoulder, shoved the door with all his weight as the door popped open. As it opened, he heard a clang of metal hit the floor. He moved inside, pulled out his tactical flashlight, and glimpsed at a section of pipe that had leaned against the door. Because of the noise he created, he had to examine what vehicles were in the garage quickly. Using his flashlight to light up the interior, Sam saw three vehicles inside. He moved toward the last of the three when, unexpectedly, floodlights lit up the back of the house and shone through the small windows near the top of the garage doors. Sam finished his search, ducked below the windows, and moved back to the side door. He exited the garage, closed the door, and hugged the side of the garage as he made his way around to the back of it. He moved swiftly toward the other corner of the garage when he saw a light beam from a flashlight advancing in his direction.

"What's going on, Ameen?" a female voice said from the back of the house. Hearing the woman's voice, Sam backed away from the corner.

"I thought I heard a noise out here. I'm going to check it out," responded Ameen, holding the flashlight.

Sam hurried to the other back corner of the garage. He peeked around the corner of the structure and saw a guy looking out the second-floor window of the house. Sam had a dilemma. He felt trapped in the back of the garage as adrenaline surged through his body. He couldn't turn the corner and get seen by the guy in the house's upstairs window. On the other hand, staying put meant the guy with the flashlight would likely check the back of the garage and catch him red-handed. *Shit, I'm going to get caught back here*, Sam thought. He surveyed the backyard for a tree or something to hide behind but saw nothing nearby.

He turned to see the flashlight beam looming near the corner of the garage.

I'm cooked, Sam thought.

Unexpectedly, Sam heard a woman's voice shouting out again. "Ameen, we're waiting on you. The pizza guy arrived, and the movie started! Come back in the house!"

"Okay, okay, I'm coming," the man's voice replied.

Sam then saw the flashlight beam disappear. *Phew. Dumb luck,* he thought to himself. He waited a moment to ensure the guy got into the house before gradually maneuvering back to Andrea's car.

Detective Collins was the first to see Caviello heading his way. "Caviello, what in the world are we doing here? It's getting late, and it's dark as hell out here in no man's land with nothing to show for it. So let's all go home and get a fresh start in the morning when we can see what the fuck we're doing."

"We're here to rescue Andrea's daughter, Detective. So why wait until morning when we can do it right now?" answered Sam.

"Now, huh? We've been following you all fucking night, watching you do drive-bys. So we're done for the night, unless, of course, you have x-ray vision and can magically tell us where she is, so we can, woo, go rescue her?" said Collins with his hands swaying in the air, like a ghost scaring them with magical tales.

"Exactly," calmly responded Sam.

"Exactly? What the hell does that mean?" Collins said sarcastically.

Sam wanted to smack Collins but knew it wouldn't do any good. "Just to put your mind at ease, Ed, I don't have x-ray vision, but we are not going home without Micaela. The black van we're looking for is in the garage in the back, and I'm certain Andrea's daughter is held here in that house."

Stunned and looking puzzled, Collins turned to Bishop, unsure how to respond. Bishop said nothing. Then, Collins turned back to Sam, shrugging his shoulders. "You're bullshitting us, right?"

With anticipation, Andrea spoke. "Sam, you really found the van?"

Sam answered her with a stern look on his face, staring straight into Detective Collins' eyes. "Yes, Andrea. The van is in the garage. Now, let's get in that house and bring Micaela home."

CHAPTER

46

Even though Detective Collins was hesitant to take issue with Sam's assertion that the kid was in the house, he certainly didn't feel ready to enter the house with just the three of them.

"What, you want to go storming in the house now? We need backup. First, we don't even know if the girl is in there. Plus, we don't know how many guys with guns are in there to greet us."

Sam knew Collins, for once, said something right but didn't want to give him any credit. Instead, he turned to Detective Bishop.

"Kevin, would you call Major Burke and tell him we found the van in the back of a white colonial farmhouse at 4 Country Farm Road. Tell him I believe Al Madari's associates have Andrea's daughter held inside the house, and we need tactical backup for entry and rescue."

"Got it, Sam." Bishop called Major Burke and repeated what Sam told him but added, "We haven't confirmed the kid or how many occupants are inside."

Bishop listened to Burke's response, answered a few questions, and told Sam the Major wanted to talk to him.

"I bet the major is not in a hurry for us to go inside without some intel," remarked Collins.

Sam took Bishop's phone and walked away for privacy. "This is Sam, Major. What do you need?" He listened to Major Burke request all the necessary information for a judge to approve a telephonic search warrant. Sam then outlined all the particulars he considered sufficient for the warrant.

"Have you verified Micaela is in the house?"

"The van used to kidnap Micaela occurred only hours earlier, and it's here hidden in the garage. They couldn't have had enough time to go elsewhere before coming here. She's in there, Major, I'm sure of it. There are lights on in the house on the first floor. I saw only one light on the second floor that I suspect is a bedroom where she is likely being held. I heard a woman's voice call out to someone called Ameen to come back into the house. Wasn't there an Ameen among the names we had as part of this group?"

Burke said he'd check on the name but wasn't sure they had enough probable cause. In any event, he'd try to obtain a warrant any way he could. He ended the call, telling Sam he'd send a backup team and he'll be with them.

Sam returned the phone to Bishop, saying, "The major is calling in a tactical team and is personally heading up here to join us."

Collins couldn't believe it. The surprised look on his flushed face was telling as he turned away so he wouldn't have to face Sam for being so arrogant. Sam began to pace back and forth beside Andrea's car. Andrea was restless and prayed Sam was right, but she also wondered how he could be so sure Micaela was in the house. She watched Sam pacing, knowing he was impatient and wanted to act quickly. Sam was eager to rescue Micaela but realized he needed backup since it appeared Detective Collins didn't have it in him to confront whoever was inside the house. Consequently, Sam didn't want to put Andrea in any danger, which only left him and Bishop to enter the house. He recognized the need for additional capable backup.

"We have to move away from the house. Some guy just delivered a pizza at the house. We don't know if that guy said anything about us down the road. We don't want one of them to check outside and see us waiting here. So I'll take a position across the road behind the wall in the woods and monitor the house. You guys head to the intersection at Brewer's Road. Stay hidden from traffic in case one of them leaves the house and heads your way. When Burke arrives with backup, have Andrea pick me up, and I'll join you, and we can develop a plan to enter the house," instructed Sam.

On the way to the intersection, Collins was puzzled. "How did Sam know there was a pizza delivery at the house? We saw the delivery, but Sam was checking out the garage in the back. I hope this guy is not making things up as he goes along. If we go in that house and scare an elderly couple enjoying pizza, it will piss me off."

"Settle down, partner. We heard some voices coming from the back of the house. Sam could have heard them say something about the pizza delivery. We'll key on Burke when he gets here. Try to relax, will ya?"

Sam waited in the woods for nearly an hour before Andrea called and said she was on the way to pick him up, saying Burke was five minutes out. Minutes later, Sam was in Burke's car.

"Sam, I haven't received a call back from the judge yet. He's concerned about having enough PC to enter the home. He needs time to research precedent and will get back to me. I had officers search for the property owner's name but only found the name of a property management company, and there was no answer there when we called. So we contacted the town manager at his home. He said the owner died several years ago and left the property to his nephew, who lives in Chicago and rents it out. Unfortunately, we don't have the nephew's last name. So far, we haven't identified the renter."

"It's a stolen van that's hidden in the garage. That's sufficient cause to knock on the door and inquire about the stolen property. If whoever opens the door is suspicious or armed, that's enough for us to conduct a protective search for our safety."

"Yes, but you didn't have a warrant to search the garage. That's a problem for the judge, but he's aware the kid may be in the house and wants to approve the search. Let's give him more time to research the law before deciding on what action we can take on our own."

"What about the name 'Ameen'? Did you find anything about him?"

Burke answered it slipped his mind because he was too busy on the phone with the judge and trying to find out who owned the house.

"While we're waiting, I still have the building director's telephone number. I'll call him on speakerphone and ask if he knows who rented the house," said Sam.

The phone rang several times before Harold Bennett answered the phone. "Mr. Bennett, this is Federal Agent Sam Caviello. You may remember I visited you to view the property plot for the farmhouse on Brewers Road."

"Yes, I remember. That was a terrible thing that happened there, with so many police officers getting killed. The town was in a frenzy over that incident and still hasn't recovered. Anyway, how can I help you? You know it's late, and the office is closed?"

"Yes, I know. There is an old white colonial at the peak of the hill at 4 Country Farm Road. I'm calling to ask if you know who rented that house."

"Hmm. I only heard scuttlebutt. I was surprised to hear Tucker Ferguson, the retired inspector from our office, rented it for his wife's cousin, who needed a temporary place to live. She supposedly works at the Crescent Drive Plaza convenience store. But that's only what I heard."

"Understood. Do you know anything about the cousin?"

"Only that she's a Muslim woman, like Ferguson's wife."

"Thanks for your help, Harold. I'll get it confirmed."

"That's a piece of information the judge will be interested in hearing, so I'll call and let him know," replied Burke. Burke was on the phone with the judge for several minutes. When he ended his conversation, Burke gave a confident nod. "The judge said that connects the dots for an emergency search. So it's a go."

The entry team included three state tactical team members, Detectives Bishop, Collins, Andrea, and Sam. After deciding on a plan, they were ready to execute it. The three tactical team members would be the first to enter, followed by Sam and Bishop. They assigned Collins and Andrea to enter through the back entrance while Burke remained outside as the operational leader covering the front of the house.

Five cars lined up in front of the house and driveway. The last state car had its rear emergency lights on as a cautionary signal to any oncoming vehicles. Once everyone quietly moved into position at the front and back doors, a tactical team member tried the front doorknob and whispered, "It's locked." He knocked on the door shouting, "Police with a warrant!" and waited three seconds before ramming it open as they all entered the house. The two detectives in the back forced open the rear door after hearing the shouts from their colleagues. The tactical members confronted three persons on the couch in the living room. One reached for an assault weapon on the end table, but a tactical officer immediately put him down.

The other two suspects submitted to the officer's command to get on the floor with their hands clasped behind their heads. Sam led Collins up the stairs to the second floor, yelling, "Police." Sam went right, heading toward the room where he suspected they held Micaela. Bishop went left to secure the other rooms. With his gun ready, Sam kicked open the last door on the left. When he entered the room, Sam saw a man holding Micaela in front of him with a pistol to her head. He also saw a woman standing near the guy. Sam recognized the woman, Parnia Semnami, on his right side. Aiming his weapon steady at the guy holding Micaela, Sam yelled, "Police, drop the gun!"

"You drop your gun, or I kill her," Kasra Jahanbani shouted.

Jahanbani, standing over six feet tall, exposed much of himself behind the tiny Micaela. Even though he crouched down, he was open to Sam's aim.

"This is your last warning. Drop your gun and let the girl go," demanded Sam. Sam's hand was steady, but his adrenalin was flowing high. He didn't want to make a wrong decision regarding Micaela's safety. Sam could see the terrified look on her face with tear filled eyes. He could feel his heart beating so hard that it felt like it would burst through his chest.

"No! You drop your weapon. I count to three, then I kill her," retorted Jahanbani with a desperate look on his face.

Sam couldn't chance the guy with desperation written all over him wasn't serious about killing Micaela. He couldn't wait until then. Sam had no viable option but one. He couldn't take the chance the guy would pull the trigger and kill Micaela. Sam, still with a steady arm and careful aim, squeezed the trigger of his gun. The shot was heard throughout the house as the bullet hit Jahanbani right between the eyes, forcing his head to rock back as he fell to the floor along with his pistol. Both Micaela and Parnia screamed. Micaela then ran towards Sam. He grabbed her up into his free arm as he watched Parnia, first cursing at Sam, then attempting to grab the weapon lying on the floor. Sam aimed and shot at the gun as she was about to grab it. The bullet hit her hand, causing her to shift her hand away from the gun, screaming painfully. He moved closer to her and kicked the gun away from her.

Parnia scowled at him. "You killed my husband. You deserve to die."

"Mommy!" yelled out Micaela. Sam took a step back from Parnia and glanced back to see Andrea in the open doorway with her arms open. Andrea's eyes swelled with tears that poured down both cheeks. Sam lowered Micaela to the floor so she could run to her mother. In pain, Parnia swore at him again in her native language as Bishop entered the room, took control, and handcuffed Parnia as she continued cursing.

Andrea placed her hand over her heart while staring at Sam and softly said, "Thank you, Sam. I will never forget you for this." Then, she embraced her daughter, turned, and walked away.

Sam took a deep breath and closed his eyes, feeling relief as the stress diminished inside him, knowing Micaela was now safe. He moved toward the stairs and paused to see Andrea and Micaela still holding on to each other on the first floor. Sam grabbed hold of the railing and slowly walked down the stairs. His legs were still a bit shaky due to the lingering anxiety. Burke saw Sam walking gingerly down the stairs and met him at the bottom with his hand out to shake his.

"You're a hero once again, Sam. After saving Juli's life, she later told me that you have a unique ability. I didn't understand what she meant then, but now I do. I've experienced it firsthand. I'm more than impressed. I don't suppose you would consider working for the state police? I'm pretty sure I could authorize a ranking position for you in the detective's unit."

"That's a flattering offer, Major. Thank you, but I have a great job surrounded by a top-notch crew."

"I'm going to be around for a while. If you ever change your mind, the offer will remain open. I know you will have to return to Connecticut soon, but you'll spend a lot of time in Massachusetts testifying in several cases in Boston."

"You can count on me to be there, Major. These killers need to spend years behind bars, hopefully for life."

As Burke moved back to call and inform the judge, Bishop approached Sam. "I overheard what the major said. I wholeheartedly agree with him. Based on the short time you have worked with us, I have to say, although there's an air of mystery about you, you are one exceptional investigator. I'd work with you anytime. Like a bloodhound, you seem to follow a scent with astonishing results. I don't know what word would best describe it. Maybe, rare or uncommon, but more like miraculous. If I get stuck on a case someday, would it be okay if I called you for advice or help on the case?"

"Enough with the compliments, and of course, you could call me anytime for help. It's been a pleasure working with you, Kevin."

Andrea was near enough to overhear what Burke and Bishop had said to Sam. She moved close to Sam, put Micaela down, and told him that Micaela wanted to say something to him.

Sam knelt in front of Micaela as she placed her arms tightly around his neck. She softly said in his ear, "Thank you for saving me, Sam. I love you."

"I love you too, Micaela, and I have a surprise for you. I'll give you the surprise if you and your mom have dinner with me."

Micaela looked at her mom, who nodded yes. "My mom said yes. We could have dinner with you."

Andrea then whispered, "Major Burke said I should take Micaela home and take some time off. He also directed me to bring you wherever you have to go. So that will be my place, and that's an order."

Later, while driving to Boston, Sam contacted his boss to inform him of the arrest and rescue. The call lasted nearly a half-hour as his boss took notes and had several questions he wanted answered.

"This is big, Sam. I'll send a preliminary fax to headquarters now. I'd like you to prepare a full report as soon as possible. Incidentally, congratulations once again for a job well done."

When the call ended, Andrea recommended stopping for ice cream as a celebration. Micaela agreed. Sam thought it was a great idea. At the restaurant, Sam went inside for the order. He included three small burgers, a large order of fries, and three ice cream sundaes. He was starving. While waiting for the order to be packaged, Sam called Alli Gaynor to inform her of the arrests and rescue on Country Farm Road.

"Alli, if Burke asks, tell him you got a call from a person in the area you had previously interviewed who saw all the police cars in front of the house, and you were trying to find out what it was all about."

"Wow, Sam. You are one busy guy. I'm going to head up there now with my crew. You think we can get together again soon?"

"I heard Forster Harrington and Tony Dellagatti got indicted today. The judge ordered both transported to Hartford for arraignment the day after tomorrow. I'll be there to greet them. Maybe you should too. Anyway, I have to run. I'll talk to you soon."

Sam paid for the food, left the restaurant, and got back into Andrea's car, announcing, "Burgers and three ice cream sundaes coming up, Micaela." She was all smiles, clapping her hands together.

Driving to the apartment, Sam told Andrea about the indictment. "I'll have to go to Hartford when they arrive there. I'll be leaving tomorrow afternoon."

"I'm glad for you that your agents in Hartford prevented anything from happening to your son. I know you worried about him."

"I did, but thank God, it's over now. I'll be back after the arraignment. Maybe instead of dinner out, you can prepare dinner so we can stay in that night?"

"I'd like that. You have a deal, Sam."

Listening to her mom, Micaela said, "I like that too. It's a deal, Sam."

CHAPTER
47

A fter burgers and ice cream, Sam decided to give Micaela the present he had for her. When she unwrapped it, she was ecstatic. It was an iPad Micaela had wanted for some time. She hugged Sam, thanking him with a big hug.

"You are very welcome. I loaded a couple of educational apps, three different game apps, and three stories I think you will enjoy. I can show you how the apps work, and then I could play one of the games with you before it's time for sleep."

Micaela loved the idea, and after Sam showed her how the apps worked, she selected a game they played until it was time for Micaela to sleep. Andrea covered Micaela with a light blanket and joined Sam in the living room.

"I can't thank you enough, Sam, for all you have done. Micaela was so frightened of those creeps. I was afraid she wouldn't get over the fear she had for some time, but you being here with us, the gift you gave her, and playing a game with her lifted her spirits. My little girl put her fears aside, for now anyway, and she seems so happy. I mean what I said earlier, Sam. I will never forget you. I will always love you, and so will Micaela."

*   *   *

The next afternoon, on the way to the Boston ATF office to complete his report on the previous night's incident, Sam couldn't stop thinking of what Andrea had said, that her love for him would never cease. He had never experienced such expressions of love, both physically and in words that he received from Juli, Andrea, and Alli. Sam never felt so much love for more than one woman. But, in doing so, he realized it created an internal dilemma for him with no answer on how to resolve it.

After arriving at the ATF office, Sam met with his boss, who applauded his work for saving the lives of state officers and a young girl.

"The Assistant Director wants to thank you personally and recognize your outstanding accomplishments working with the state police. On behalf of the entire Boston staff, I want to extend our admiration and appreciation for your exceptional work representing our office. In the coming weeks, you will receive commendations from ATF and the state police."

Sam felt humbled and thanked everyone in the office who congratulated him on his way out of the office. He considered stopping at Juli's gravesite on his way to Connecticut but felt it would only stir up his emotions. The loss of Juli caused deep emotional suffering that he needed to get under control. His drive to Connecticut was on auto-pilot. His mind became occupied not only with the feelings he had for Juli but the things these women had told him: 'You can have all of me' from Alli, and, 'I love you and will always have you in my heart,' from Andrea, and of course, the loving words from Juli. He had never experienced so much love from others while simultaneously feeling such emotional heartache. He knew he had to take time off from the job and go on a trip somewhere isolated where he could examine his life, his feelings, and where to go from there.

Once he arrived home, he tried to relax and get his mind off the issues he'd been entangled with while in Boston. Sam decided to watch television and get engrossed in a movie to clear his thoughts. He eventually tired and needed a whole night's sleep. He dove into bed early and hardly moved while sleeping before the alarm went off in the morning.

It felt strange that morning driving toward Hartford instead of Boston. Shortly before nine, he entered the ATF office and saw Agent Clarkson sitting at his desk. She stood up and was about to give him the desk when she saw him enter.

"No, Jennifer, stay where you are. I'll sit in front of the desk. I'm here only to antagonize Harrington when the Marshals bring him in for questioning and witness his arraignment."

"When will you be back full time? I've had enough of acting as the supervisor. We need you—I need you back here. There's no freedom in this job and too much responsibility. You can have it. I'll stick with the fieldwork any day."

"My thoughts exactly. However, you've done a great job, and I'm sure the bosses have noticed.

"Please don't say that. I want to go back to having a low profile."

"My best guess when I'll be back is maybe in about a week or two. After that, I'll have to testify in the grand jury and anticipated court trials against as many as ten defendants in Boston. So that means I'll be spending a lot of time in Boston in the coming months."

Other agents arrived in the office, including Rick Ziglar and Pete Macheski. The agents welcomed Sam back to Hartford and requested coffee together at the café across the street. They all took the elevator to the lobby, and when exiting, Sam saw Alli Gaynor going through the security line at the entrance of the federal building. Being discrete among the agents, Sam greeted Alli by shaking her hand and re-introducing her to the others. Then, Sam invited her to join them for coffee. She accepted, and at the cafe, Sam filled in all of them on the cases he was working with the Mass state police, and the agents filled him in on the case against Harrington, Dellagatti, and Sonny Hooks. When the agents were ready to return to the office, Sam stayed under the guise that he wanted to learn more about Alli's new job in Washington.

"Thanks for the heads up on the arrests and rescue. And, of course, the heads up about the arraignment today," said Alli.

"Just remember it didn't come from me. Anything else I tell you would cause suspicion on how and from whom you got the information."

"I know. I spoke with Major Burke last night at the scene. He, of course, asked how I knew about it. I told him what you suggested, but I'm not sure he bought my story. He agreed to meet with me later today. He gave me enough for an early national broadcast before anyone else. I also called U.S. Attorney Debra Durrell, who was kind enough to give me the scoop on Harrington's plot to have your son killed. I gave a short broadcast shortly afterward."

"I bet your boss must be very pleased with your performance. If I were you, I'd ask for a large multi-year contract with a huge salary increase as part of your recent promotion. You are giving them numerous lead stories on big cases."

Alli replied, "The thanks in big part goes to you. They want me back in DC soon. I'll be sitting down with them regarding my contract. But, more importantly, can we get together again, like maybe tonight, at your apartment?"

"I'd love to, but I'm heading back to Boston after the arraignment. I promised to have a celebration dinner with the Massachusetts detectives I've been working with."

"My boss wants me to continue covering the story since additional arrests are pending in the state case. So, I'll be back in Boston to finish the work on that case you're involved in. Can you tell me who they haven't arrested yet?"

"Off the record, they haven't yet arrested the Imam, the farmhouse owner, his sister, and her husband. The husband was the former building inspector who fudged the inspection reports on the construction of the farm's barn."

"Thanks. Hopefully, Burke will give me the names. Before heading back to the courthouse, I need to ask you something. I hope you know how I feel about you."

"I do. We'll discuss that in-depth when this case is over, and my head is clear. Right now, I'm juggling so many things I can't even think straight."

"I understand. I don't know how you do it, Sam. It's one big incident after another with you. I worry you might get hurt. It seems your job is getting extremely dangerous. Maybe you should think about taking a job at headquarters. That way, you could spend time with me and get your mind off everything that's happened in the past few weeks. I could help with that when you're ready to practice those ulterior motives we talked about."

"That would be nice, Alli. After my work in Boston is through, I plan to take some private time off and travel to a quiet, remote place. Then, when I return, we'll talk, okay?"

"Okay, Sam, but let's stay in touch."

Back in the federal building, Sam met with Brian Murphy to review the procedures when the two prisoners arrived at the courthouse. Murphy, a Yale graduate and a rising star at the U.S. Attorney's Office, was a colleague and friend of Sam's. They often golfed and socialized together. They talked golf for a while before Murphy got down to the business at hand.

"The Marshals will bring in Dellagatti first since he is already in the Marshals' lockup. Then, when Harrington arrives from Allentown, the Marshals will separately bring him to your office, where the agents will process them. Then one of the agents and I will interview him. But, first, we must convince Dellagatti it would be in his best interest to corporate and testify against Harrington."

Murphy called the U.S. Marshals' office at noon, instructing them to bring Dellagatti to the ATF office for processing. Once Dellagatti arrived and was told why they arrested him, he became argumentative and belligerent. However, when Brian Murphy informed him of the evidence against him, he became depressed and somewhat receptive to cooperating.

Sitting across from Dellagatti, Sam spoke first. "We've read you your right to remain silent, but remaining silent will result in maybe an additional twenty years added to your sentence. We know Forster Harrington requested your help in his revenge scheme to kill a federal agent."

"What? No way, man. I got nuttin' to do with killing no federal agent, pal. No fucking way."

"Harrington planned to kill my son. My son is now a federal agent. Killing or attempting to kill a federal agent is an offense calling for long imprisonment. Adding that to the time you already have to serve, they'll be throwing away the key on you. The real culprit and brains behind the murder scheme is Forster Harrington. If you cooperate and testify against him, we could cut you a deal so you can enjoy freedom again in your later years."

"Forster's lawyer will get me a deal for a shorter time in jail, man," Tony said resentfully.

Murphy interrupted. "I'm the prosecutor in this case, and there will be no deal except for those who cooperate. We already have the cooperation of Sonny, who agreed to testify against you. Forster's daughter Rachel, and Gus Walker, also agreed to testify against you and Forster. They are getting a deal. You, however, will not get one unless you cooperate. You won't have to worry about Forster's revenge, as he's going in for life and won't be coming out of prison. Your best shot is with us, not with him. If you don't cooperate, we plan on asking for a similar life sentence for you. You both worked in concert to kill a federal agent. I'll give you five minutes to decide. After that, the deal is off the table."

Dellagatti didn't have to think too long. He figured if Forster's own daughter would testify against him, why shouldn't he? "Okay, I'll cooperate if you agree. I'll get no more than an extra three or four years."

"That will never happen. Your crime calls for twenty years. I can recommend to the court maybe ten. With good behavior, you could be out in seven or eight. That's a lot better than dying in prison. Remember, you won't be serving those extra years in Connecticut, but in a hardcore federal prison where they house all the violent offenders."

Dellagatti didn't know that. That changed his thinking. "You show me the deal, in writing, and I mean a good deal, like maybe eight to ten years to serve in Connecticut, then I'll testify."

With that, Murphy asked Dellagatti to spell out what he knew of Harrington's plan for the revenge murder-for-hire plot. The information Dellagatti gave them was enough to convince Murphy it was enough to sink Harrington. Dellagatti provided a sworn written statement against Harrington before being sent to the Marshals' lockup.

Later, Forster Harrington got transported to the lockup in Hartford. Murphy asked they bring him to the ATF's office. Once processed there, the agents brought him to the interview room. Harrington saw Sam sitting at the interview table as he entered.

"I should have known this was your doing, Caviello."

"Once again, you are wrong, Forster. This is about what you have done. I might add for a supposedly smart business owner, you certainly are an idiot to assume you could get away with murdering a federal agent."

"I don't know what you're talking about. Where's my attorney? I'm not saying a word without him present."

Murphy asked Harrington to have a seat. "I called your attorney, and I understand he will be here momentarily. Sam, step outside the room and send in Agent Clarkson."

Sam would not be a part of the Harrington interview since there was animosity between the two. But, as Sam stood to leave the room, he walked close to Harrington, bent over to whisper in his ear, and said, "You are so fucked. You will spend the rest of your miserable life in prison, not at a country club prison like you're in now, but a hardcore federal penitentiary with violent murderers and sick bastards like you. They'll be watching you, hoping to get you alone."

Sam passed Harrington's attorney at the door as he walked out of the room. His attorney, Darren Rothenburg, was upset that Caviello was in the room questioning his client. Sam entered the adjourning room to watch the theatrics from a one-way mirror.

"What's this all about, Brian, and why is Caviello questioning my client without my presence?"

"Your client has not been questioned. We were waiting for you to arrive. Before we begin, Agent Clarkson will give your client his right to remain silent."

"It's unnecessary. I'm present, and Forster will not be answering any questions," responded Rothenburg.

Murphy began, "We will bring Mr. Harrington before a federal judge at three o'clock. A grand jury indicted him for conspiracy and related charges in a murder-for-hire plot of a federal agent. We will be asking for the maximum sentence of life without parole."

"That's ridiculous. I don't know what the fuck you're talking about. I'm not involved in any plot to murder a federal agent," said Harrington.

"Forster, let me do the talking. Keep quiet," warned his attorney.

"We know a guard allowed you to use his cell phone to call your fixer, Tony Dellagatti, on three occasions. Prison officials record all calls, and we have copies of conversations you had with him and copies of the guard's phone records of calls you made to your daughter right after that."

"So I called a friend and my daughter. That means nothing," argued Harrington.

"Forster, keep your mouth shut. Just listen, and you and I will discuss this later," repeated the attorney.

"We also tapped your private cell phone that Rachel used to communicate with you. We recorded her conversation regarding paying Sonny Hooks after the job got done," advised Murphy.

"That payment was for a small construction job we did for Sonny's friend," insisted Harrington.

"What's with you, Forster? Do you want me here or not? I told you not to say a word. You are just digging yourself into a hole. Everything you say is recorded, and any lies you tell will result in additional charges against you," instructed his attorney.

"Fuck these guys. They have nothing on me. It's all bullshit," claimed Harrington.

"It's no bullshit. We have statements from all those involved in your plan to murder Caviello's son. Every person involved with your scheme has been arrested or indicted and agreed to testify against you. Plus, we have you on record threatening payback to agent Caviello by harming his son during your initial conviction. Finally, I should mention that Caviello's son is now a federal agent."

Surprised, Harrington was dumbfounded and speechless as he looked at his attorney to come to his defense, but his attorney didn't have anything to say to him, only to Murphy. "So, Brian, why are we here? Are you proposing a deal?"

"No fucking deal! They have nothing! Nobody is telling them anything! It's just a ploy to get me to talk!" demanded Harrington.

Murphy countered, "To save the taxpayers loads of money for another trial, I will make a one-time offer that is good only until the close of business today. If Harrington pleads guilty to the charges, we will recommend to the court twenty-five years instead of him being found guilty by a jury with the recommendation of life without parole. Also, if he pleads to the charges, we will recommend no jail time for his daughter Rachel and his foreman, Gus Walker. Otherwise, they both stand to serve up to five years in prison."

"You leave my daughter out of this, you bastard!" screamed Harrington.

"That's up to you, Harrington. You and your attorney have a lot to discuss. See you both in court. Remember, the offer is for today only," informed Murphy.

EPILOGUE

Sam had planned on waiting until Harrington got arraigned but decided to travel to Boston and get the rest of his agenda done before keeping his promised dinner date with Andrea and Micaela.

It was nearly three o'clock, so he stopped at the courtroom before heading back to Boston. He entered the courtroom and sat on the rear bench. He saw Harrington's daughter sitting with her husband, mother, and Gus Walker. Seated in the jury box was Tony Dellagatti with two U.S. Marshals standing guard, and on the opposite end was Sonny Hooks with another Marshal at his side. Brian Murphy arranged this to bolster his claim he had all the witnesses he needed to convict Harrington when he entered the court for his arraignment. Sam smiled while thinking *what a shock Harrington is in for when he sees all those who will testify against him, including his daughter.*

He nodded to Alli, who sat in the courtroom with several other reporters. A few minutes later, the Marshal brought Harrington into the courtroom. Harrington was visibly distraught seeing his daughter and Walker looking the other way as he came in. Sam sensed Harrington knew then the feds had the evidence needed to convict him. Satisfied, seeing the look of defeat on Harrington's face, Sam left the courtroom and headed for Boston. On the way to the state police headquarters in Framingham, Sam called Andrea, letting her know he would stop at Burke's office for a short time before heading to her apartment. He met with the ADA Arnie Carlson, Major Burke, Detectives Bishop, and Collins when he arrived. They discussed procedural strategy, grand jury dates, and expected state and federal charges in coordination with the U.S. Attorney. When the meeting was over, Sam asked for the status of those still at large.

Burke responded, "Randell's not cooperating. He has hired a top-notch law firm to represent him and his wife. Abedini, his sister, her husband, and the Imam are still hiding from authorities. We have arrest warrants for the four of them. The U.S. Attorney hasn't yet indicted Randell's wife and is saving it to pressure him into cooperating. We received info from the FBI that Abedini had connections to the Iranian Ministry of Intelligence, also known as VAJA, Vezarat-e-Ettela'at Jomhuri-ye Eslami-ye Iran. It would have been nice if the FBI had told us this before the raid at the farmhouse. In hindsight, all I can say is you were right, Sam. We should have put off the raid for forty-eight hours to study the property layout and gather sufficient intel before executing the warrants."

When he left the state police office, Sam arrived at Andrea's apartment just before six o'clock. It delighted both Andrea and Micaela to see him. Andrea was starry-eyed, watching Sam's every word during an intense iPad game with Micaela. Andrea loved Sam and believed he would be the perfect father for Micaela and the ideal husband.

After the game, Andrea described what she and Micaela had prepared for dinner. "Micaela and I prepared your favorite, a Hispanic-style halibut and fresh string beans. Micaela even made the mashed potatoes that you like. In addition, I purchased another bottle of that champagne you brought us a couple of days ago. And, for dessert, Micaela is making hot fudge sundaes."

"Mmm, everything sounds delicious. I'm starving too. Thank you, Andrea, and especially you, Micaela. I can't wait to taste your mashed potatoes and the hot fudge sundae."

The three of them enjoyed a fun-filled evening together. They all agreed that the dinner and desserts were outstanding. Andrea savored the time with Sam. Usually, a bit shy, Micaela talked up a storm with Sam, telling him about her new school, teacher, and new friends. She wanted Sam to go to her school to speak about his job. They then watched television for an hour before Andrea reminded Micaela it was bedtime.

"Micaela, go get washed up and ready for bed. Sam will then come in and read to you."

"Okay. I already picked out what story for Sam to read," said Micaela as she rushed into the bedroom. Not long afterward, she called for Sam. She had a story already selected. Sam finished the last chapter when Andrea came into the room and said it was time for sleep. Sam kissed Micaela on the forehead and left Andrea alone with her daughter.

When Andrea returned to Sam, they embraced each other and kissed. It wasn't a passionate kiss, but it was a kiss just the same.

"It's been a hectic several weeks, Andrea. It's so nice to relax and have a wonderful night with you and Micaela. I'm still struggling with everything that has happened, including Juli's death, Micaela's kidnapping, and the fact that I put your life in danger. I'm relieved we got Micaela safely back home to you. Now, she needs you close by to watch over her. I want you and Micaela always to be safe. It would help if you spent as much time with her as possible in the coming weeks. And I should spend more time with my son."

Sam interrupted Andrea as she was about to say something. "Andrea, I think it would be best if you considered requesting a temporary assignment far from the Boston area for a while. Some of the suspects are still out there and will continue to seek revenge. I mentioned my concern for your safety to Burke. I hope you're not mad at me for that. I promise I'll stay in touch and visit, but I need to get away and get my head on straight from all the turmoil and emotional pain that still haunts me. Please understand. I do love you, but the love is more in line with friendship. Tell Micaela I love her too."

They embraced again. Andrea held him tight, not wanting to let go. Her eyes overflowed with tears. Sam squeezed her tightly, then slipped away from her arms. "Be safe. I promise I will stay in touch." He turned away and left the apartment.

When Sam arrived at his son's apartment, he wiped away his own teardrops before greeting Drew.

"Hey, Dad. You look exhausted. Is everything okay?"

"I hope so, son," answered Sam. "After everything that has happened while working with the state police, I will ask for additional time off and take a long trip somewhere remote and serene."

"I think that's great. You've been through a lot and deserve a break."

"Thanks," Sam smiled, but his smile quickly vanished when he thought of the danger still lurking out there for his son and Andrea. "I still worry about Forster Harrington's attempt to get at you. He's probably more determined than ever to try again to get back at me. I'm also worried about Andrea and her daughter. There are several of the suspects still at large who want revenge over the death of Al Madari."

"Dad, try not worrying about everybody. I can take care of myself. Besides, my tour in Boston is only for two years. I'll be applying for an overseas assignment when my tour ends here. The state police have a protection detail around Andrea, her daughter, and her sister's family."

"I know, Drew, but I still worry about those close to me. It's emotionally draining, and I can't seem to put it past me. That's why I need to get away from all that's happened. I need to get my emotions in check." Sam took in a deep breath and exhaled. "The job has changed a lot in the past year or two. It's become much more dangerous. There's too much violence occurring in the country now. I've come too close to death more times than I like." Sam paused, thinking about what needed finishing in the investigation. "I still have work to complete here in Boston when I return. Then, when we find the remaining suspects and the investigation is closed, I plan to step down from my supervisory position and ask for a job with less risk to myself and those closest to me."

"You should do that if that's how you really feel, but I know you, Dad. You thrive on solving challenging investigations, and those always involve an element of danger." Drew reflected for a moment. "Besides, you know you're good at what you do and can handle almost anything, right?"

Sam nodded as a smile found its way to his cheeks. "I guess there's some truth in that, son. I've also heard you're on your way to being good at what you do, too. As long as we have each other and do our job to keep people safe, we'll be just fine. So, let's have a beer and drink to that, and always stay in touch no matter where we are in the world."

ACKNOWLEDGMENTS

I'm grateful to ATF for providing me with a fulfilling and rewarding public service career that also formed a lasting community of friends among thousands of men and women dedicated to serving and protecting the great citizens of the United States.

My thanks to editors Annie Bomke and Laura Apgar, who guided me in developing good characters and dialogue and assessing the strengths and drawbacks that needed further development of the manuscript. Additionally, my gratitude to James Osborne, the proofreader, who revealed and corrected surface errors, ensuring every piece of the book was in its proper place.

Once again, I'm indebted to my friends Dave Campbell and John Tinnirella for their tireless and comprehensive review and input of the initial draft of my book from a reader's viewpoint.

Special thanks go to author and friend Wayne Miller for his continued professional support in providing essential counsel, advice, and needed references in the tedious journey of writing, self-publishing, and establishing readership for new writers.

The publication of my book would not have been possible without the teaching and mentoring by my coach Geoff Affleck, a master at guiding aspiring authors in launching and promoting their books by leading them through the complexity of self-publishing with the goal of optimizing sales and reaching readers. So many thanks to Geoff. I couldn't have done it alone without his expertise and guidance.

My gratitude goes to the book cover designer, placeholder, and book interior designer, Amit Dey. Many thanks to both fantastic book designers.

Again my special thanks and love to my wife Donna, my constant supporter who spent many hours reading draft chapters, circling errors, making suggestions, improving sentence structure, and recommending deletions. Her continuous support and encouragement were the primary incentives I needed to complete my novel. Donna's devotion, love, and encouragement are the inspiration that drives me to write, and I love her for it.

ABOUT THE AUTHOR

Stan Comforti is a thirty-year law enforcement veteran. He was a federal air marshal before becoming a Special Agent with the Bureau of Alcohol, Tobacco, Firearms, and Explosives (ATF). As a field agent, he worked numerous investigations against drug dealers, outlaw motorcycle and street gang members, and felons who possessed, stole, traded, or trafficked firearms, including illegal sawed-off shotguns and fully automatic weapons. Many of his field assignments involved working undercover. Subsequently, as a supervisor in Massachusetts and Connecticut, he directed many high-profile investigations, including a murder-for-hire case where a father paid an undercover agent to kill his daughter by placing an explosive device under the car she drove. ATF arrested the father before any harm came to his daughter. Another investigation involved the unlawful sale and possession of firearms, including a machine gun that involved police officials, one of whom was also engaged in a major police exam-scam operation. Also, for seven years, Mr. Comforti was a leader of Boston ATF's Special Response Team. He led many early morning arrest and search warrant raids against drug dealers and gang members who illegally possessed and used firearms in their illegal operations.

THE SAM CAVIELLO FEDERAL AGENT CRIME MYSTERY SERIES

Book 1: *A Cry for Help*

Book 2: *Chasing Terror*

Book 3: *Finding Ena*

Available at Amazon and other book sellers.

If you enjoyed this novel please leave an Amazon review.

Connect with the author at stancomforti.author@gmail.com, or visit StanComforti.com. You also scan the QR code to reach his website.

Printed in Great Britain
by Amazon

28971901R00158